DEMON'S DREAM

HIGH DEMON SERIES, BOOK SIX

CONNIE SUTTLE

Print Second Edition (2018)
Print ISBN: 1-63478-064-7
Print ISBN-13: 978-1-63478-064-3
eBook ISBN: 1-93975-909-9
eBook ISBN-13: 978-1-93975-909-2

Published by:
SubtleDemon Publishing, LLC
PO Box 95696
Oklahoma City, OK 73143

Cover art by Renee Barratt @ The Cover Counts

To Walter, Joe, Larry, Lee, Dianne, Sarah and Mark.
Thank you.

ACKNOWLEDGMENTS

As always, this book is the result of collaboration. If it weren't for the support of my editor, my cover artist and my beta readers, it would be less than it is. All mistakes, as usual, are mine and no other's.

About the Author:
Connie Suttle lives in Oklahoma with her husband and a conglomerate of cats. They have finally banded together to make their demands, which has proven disconcerting to all humans involved.

You may find Connie in the following ways:
Facebook: Connie Suttle Author
Twitter: @subtledemon
Website and Blog: subtledemon.com

High Demon Series:
Demon Lost
Demon Revealed
Demon's King
Demon's Quest
Demon's Revenge
Demon's Dream

God Wars Series:
Blood Double
Blood Trouble
Blood Revolution
Blood Love
Blood Finale

Saa Thalarr Series:
Hope and Vengeance
Wyvern and Company
Observe and Protect*

First Ordinance Series:
Finder
Keeper
BlackWing
SpellBreaker
WhiteWing

~

R-D Series:

Cloud Dust

Cloud Invasion

Cloud Rebel

~

Latter Day Demons Series:

Hot Demon in the City

A Demon's Work is Never Done

A Demon's Due

~

Seattle Elementals Series:

Your Money's Worth

Worth Your While*

~

BlackWing Pirates Series

MindSighted

MindMage

MindRogue

MindMaster*

~

Black Rose Sorceress Series

The Rose Mark

Rose and Thorn

Black Rose Queen

Queen of Thorns and Roses

Future Wars Series

Buffer Zone

Black Zone*

Other Titles from SubtleDemon Publishing:

Malefactor

Transgressor

Underhanded*

by Joe Scholes

*Forthcoming

CHAPTER 1

"*B*ring everything out that you have taken." Gavril had to be held back by Aurelius; the full force of his compulsion might have torn the woman's mind apart. Her husband stood nearby, restrained by Garde and Jayd.

Reah had been folded away by Nefrigar, and multiple attempts at reaching the Larentii Archivist via mindspeech yielded no results. Lissa, expressing her extreme anger at Gardevik and Kifirin, insisted that they do what they could to retrieve Reah's things. Now, all those who'd gathered at Baetrah's rim stood outside the cottage Reah had occupied for more than twenty years. The new grove supervisor's wife cowered before Gavril in the tiny front yard.

"My wife didn't tell me that she found anything of value in the house," the supervisor denied any part in the theft.

"Lie," Jayd said casually. "Garde, did you even interview these before you hired them?"

"Not nearly long enough," Garde blew smoke. The woman, frightened by Garde and Teeg's anger, rushed inside the cottage and returned quickly with a small, carved box.

"Here's the jewelry, but I sold some of it," the woman's hand trembled as she offered the box to Gavril.

"What is missing?" Aurelius demanded.

"My ring," Gavril muttered angrily, searching swiftly through the box. "You will tell me what you did with it," he snapped.

"This is ridiculous," Lok growled. He'd been silent until then, settling for pacing back and forth and casting black looks at Kifirin.

"It didn't look real, so I sold it for two credits," the woman wept.

"It's Tiralian crystal," Aurelius said, "and worth millions. Where is it?"

"One of the hands bought it for his daughter's wedding."

"Bring them in," Garde snapped. "Bring all the employees in. Now."

"This was hers? I never saw her wear it," a man brought the ring forward with shaking hands.

"Because you don't wear Tiralian crystal to repair the sprinkler system," Gavril said dryly. "Here. As compensation for the ring. There should be ten thousand credits on the chip." He handed a chip bracelet over.

"Thank you. I'll buy a replacement for my daughter," the man nodded respectfully and backed away. "I was hoping Reah would come back. Those two over there are terrible. I only bought the ring because they offered it to me."

"Reah won't be back. We'll try to find someone else who will be better than these," Jayd jerked his head toward the overseer and his wife. "Those two are going back where they came from."

"I know it looked that way to Reah." Jayd paced while Tory sat and watched. His father, Garde, stood off to the side. Tory was angry. With both of them. "Garde said we could give the girls the best of everything here at the palace, so he told Reah that this is where they'd stay."

"So Kifirin waves his fingers and everybody worked together to keep the girls away from Reah, and to keep her poor and in the groves."

"I didn't know how bad it was. I get complaints every day from the disabled, asking where their medications or their socks or their new blankets are," Jayd sighed. "And of course they complain about the food they're being served."

"I thought we were doing what was best for the girls," Garde offered.

"Dad, that's bullshit. Mom said you were pissed at Reah. She said you blamed her for my disappearance. We both know who was responsible for that, now don't we?"

"And we were only listening to what we wanted to hear." Glinda walked into Jayd's study. "We wanted those girls as close as we could get them, so we didn't argue with whatever Garde did to get them here. The truth is that Reah should have been here, too. We left a precious High Demon female out in the groves on the Southern Continent, alone and unguarded. Anything could have happened out there. Admit it."

"Something almost did happen. Today." Tory stood. "What would you do, Dad, if Reah had taken that last step? Would this be your chance to do what you wanted to do all along, and hand all the rights to my girls over to Jayd and Glinda?"

"Son, it isn't quite like that," Garde said.

"Then how is it? How's Mom, Dad? She okay? What if that had been her out there about to kill herself?" Tory skipped away.

"You fucked up," Jayd turned to Garde.

"We all did," Glinda pointed out.

"Again." Lok gestured for Drake to come after him. Drake obliged, both blades flying. Sweat poured off Lok's body, the dragon tattoos glistening in the early twilight. Aurelius stood nearby, watching both Falchani spar. Drew stood next to Aurelius, who wasn't doing very well.

"He's trying to punish himself, isn't he?" Drew said.

"Yes. But not all of us have such a convenient outlet."

"How close was it?" Drew asked. He wanted to gauge how upset Aurelius was.

"A few inches, if that. If the Larentii hadn't come, she'd be gone."

"I heard Kifirin showed up, too."

"He almost drove her to it. Nefrigar stepped between them. The rest of us just stood there, too stunned to move, I think. We're having a meeting later tonight. Everybody mated to Reah will come, except Nefrigar, I think. We still don't know where he took her."

"Would you mind if some of the rest of us come? We know Reah, too."

"I don't mind, but if the others reject outsiders," Aurelius shrugged.

"Then we'll either plead our case or leave," Drew agreed. "I don't believe it was only her mates who were blinded for the past twenty-five years. If we thought about Reah, it's as if the thoughts slipped away and we forgot again. When Kifirin removed the mute, it felt as though we'd been asleep all that time."

"I think that is an apt way to put it," Aurelius agreed. "Farzi and Nenzi turned and went hunting, earlier. I'm not sure anything they came across lived over the encounter. Lendill went off with Norian to question more prisoners. I wouldn't want to be those prisoners, right now."

"Lissa says that those controllers even convinced that young Surnathan's mother to shoot one of those things into his neck and then ordered him to kill all those workers at the electronics plant."

"And then to kill himself," Aurelius nodded. "Dantel Schuul was twisted, as was his daughter. Lendill told me that father and daughter were lovers, likely since she was ten."

"Twisted and sick," Drew sighed.

"What if she doesn't come out of this?" Tory sat on the corner of a low table and stared at Gavril.

"If anyone can do this, it will be the Larentii," Ry said. "Look what they did for you, bro."

"But I just had some anger issues and holes in my memory," Tory pointed out.

"We're here," Lok and Aurelius walked into Lissa's library, where the meeting was to be held. Farzi and Nenzi were among the stacks, gabbling about the books on the shelves.

"Present," Lendill appeared with Norian close behind.

"Erland is managing the palace on Karathia for me," Corolan appeared beside Ry. "If there's an emergency, he'll send mindspeech." Ry knew why Cory had come. He loved Reah still and they'd all gotten the full brunt of the released mute around Reah. Corolan had cursed long and loudly over it.

"We may have extras coming," Aurelius announced, getting everyone's attention.

"What extras?" Gavril looked about, worried that someone unbidden and unwelcome might appear. Farzi and Nenzi had come out of the stacks and settled on a sofa nearby.

"You know, extras," Drake said as he and Drew appeared, closely followed by Lissa, Gavin, Thurlow, Aryn, Winkler, Rigo, Tony, Roff, Connegar and Reemagar. Norian was already there, so only a few of Lissa's mates were missing—most notably, Kifirin and Gardevik. Gavril sighed deeply and nodded with relief at their absence.

"Before we start on anything else, Ildevar has ordered that half the funds confiscated from the pirates go to Reah. And that's turning out to be quite a lot," Norian said. "We've tapped into hidden accounts where the credits were dumped; Dantel Schuul had Matiss Meldrim acting as bookkeeper for Nedrizif and his Greater Demons. Meldrim was quite adept at hiding funds, but thanks to Rigo and Aryn, we got all the information from him before he was, ah, digested."

"Darletta was Dantel's front for a lot of other things, too," Tory said. "He owned Stellar Winds and Starshine through her. Of course, Daddy's little girl got everything she wanted."

"Including Daddy, or so I heard," Drew remarked dryly.

"I was never forced to watch the two of them together," Tory shuddered, his dark eyes filled with remembered pain and confusion. "And she lost interest in me over the last five years or so. She couldn't wait to get rid of me at the end."

"Likely because you wouldn't cooperate all the time," Lissa said. "She didn't count on the fact that you weren't human or mortal."

"Because she never knew," Tory agreed.

"But what are we going to do about Reah, if she comes out of this? Or even if she doesn't? She's still pregnant and it could take a while," Aurelius observed. All were in agreement that there'd been a breakdown of some kind.

"I don't know about you, but I'd like to sit down with her quietly, maybe over dinner or something, and let her know how much I care about her." Corolan wasn't waiting; he wanted everyone to know where he stood.

"I think one on one, or perhaps two won't be so overwhelming," Aurelius said. "As soon as she's up to it. Provided we can get past the Larentii."

"If he hadn't been there today," Lissa shivered. Gavin reached out and lifted her hand, kissing it gently. Gavin was going to be a grandfather for the first time. He wouldn't have been if Reah had taken one more step.

"We would like to give truth," Farzi stood, followed by Nenzi. "The King and his mate, they take Reah's girls. Give them everything. Except they not give. Reah supports Kifirin with gishi fruit. She pay bills and make sure King's palace and King have money. Reah supports those girls. King and his family live off Reah." Nenzi nodded the whole time Farzi spoke. Farzi and Nenzi sat down.

"That's telling it like it is," Drake muttered.

"Nefrigar says to tell all of you that we will be able to visit Reah in five days. She is getting the best of care," Connegar announced.

"Where is she?" Ry asked.

"At first on the Larentii homeworld. After that, she will receive specialized care elsewhere. You may visit her then. He will keep you informed when her location changes."

"Is Reah all right?" Nenzi asked.

"He is keeping her asleep much of the time. She is still suffering from her ordeal on Stellar Winds and Cloudsong. She should have been placed under care when she returned, but she was not. The mute was still in place and nobody thought to do it," Connegar replied.

"I don't know about the rest of you but I am angry with Kifirin." Lok wasn't mincing words.

"Yes, but it sounds dangerous to be angry with a god," Corolan grumbled.

"He said to tell you that you're all entitled to be angry," Lissa said. "And he knows I'm pissed as hell, too."

"We can be angry, we just can't do anything about it," Ry nodded to his mother. "Honestly, if he felt he owed us anything, then he or his parent should help Reah. That would help the rest of us."

"I agree with my brother," Gavril nodded to Ry. "Kifirin put us and Reah into this mess and we almost lost her today. Who knows how long this is going to affect all of us?"

"I'd like to have her back here now," Lok said. "I feel as if I've been absent or asleep for the past twenty-five years." His remark had several nodding and agreeing around the room.

"We'll just have to wait the five days, I suppose," Tory said. "And I have a higher mountain to climb than the rest of you."

"Kevis?" Karzac knocked on his son's open study door.

"Dad! When did you get here?" Kevis looked up from his comp-vid —he was completing notes on a patient. He entered the last bit of information and stood to greet his father.

"Kev, I have a patient I'd like to put in your clinic," Karzac said, walking in to sit beside his son's beautifully polished wood desk. Kevis, a physician for the past thirty years, ran a private clinic for patients with difficult mental problems.

"Dad, surely not one of the Saa Thalarr," Kevis sat down again and hit an electronic key on his deskcomp. Kevis looked very much like his father—nearly six feet tall with light-brown hair and green-gold eyes. He'd opened his private clinic twenty years earlier on Refizan, his father helping financially. Kevis was doing very well for himself.

"No. Not one of those. And I think when we get her, the Larentii will have already made a great deal of progress in her treatment. What we really need for her, I think, is peace and quiet, where there isn't anyone troubling her with something that needs to be done. She hasn't had a vacation in years, has been attacked and made very ill recently and there are other circumstances that have affected her. She almost killed herself three days ago."

"Is there anything unusual about her?" Kevis lifted an eyebrow at his father. He suspected that the prospective patient might not be completely human.

"She's High Demon, son, and hasn't been treated well for a very long time."

"Reah, wake up my love." Nefrigar touched gentle fingers to my forehead. I blinked at him. I'd been difficult to wake lately. And asleep much of the time, too. I was grateful for it, actually. Nefrigar had a way of making me sleep without remembered dreams. That was most welcome. Otherwise, I might have been screaming or crying. I wasn't aware of how many days it had been since I'd thought about taking the dive into Baetrah. It was a few, at least. Nefrigar woke me to eat and bathe, let me sit for a while and if the memories threatened, he'd let me sleep again.

"I am taking you elsewhere, today," he told me. "A private place where you will receive very good care. Visitors will be allowed but if they upset you, they will be asked to leave. I will also visit often, and if you have need of me, send mindspeech. I will come immediately."

"Where am I going?" I asked as Nefrigar lifted me and carried me to the shower. I liked the shower; it was warm against my skin. I felt cold more often than not, although my Larentii warmed the air around me at all times.

"To a private clinic on Refizan, which will allow you to be alone if you want or to interact with others if that is what you desire," my Larentii replied.

"I don't want group therapy. I don't think I'm crazy, Nefrigar. Not that crazy, anyway. I just want the pain to go away."

"I know. We will attempt to deal with that, my love. You will not be locked away or restrained. I ask that you inform me if you wish to leave, however."

"I'll do my best," I said.

"May I have a kiss before we fold away?" Nefrigar smiled at me as he helped me dress.

"Yes." Larentii are always so warm. Like sunlight on a summer day. Nefrigar's mouth was no exception.

"This is Doctor Halivar," Nefrigar set me down inside a quiet, restfully appointed study. Several holographic diplomas were displayed on the back wall, while beautiful artwork adorned the others. The desk was real wood, something that most people didn't get nowadays. A lovely, hand-woven rug was on the stone-tiled floor and everything was tastefully decorated, if a bit austere. I figured it had to do with the type of patients the doctor treated. Doctor Halivar looked familiar, but I didn't think I knew him or had ever met him. I nodded to him when Nefrigar offered one of the chairs in front of the doctor's desk.

"Reah Nilvas?" Doctor Halivar consulted his deskcomp.

"Yes. That is the name I use most often," I said, nodding at the doctor.

"You go by other names?" His left eyebrow rose slightly.

"I have several aliases, through the ASD," I said.

"Ah." Doctor Halivar entered information into his deskcomp. Likely, the deskcomp was also recording the conversation, vid and aud, so he was making notes of some kind. It made me want to get up and see what they were, but I held back. I'm sure he wouldn't appreciate my curiosity in the least.

"I hope these records will be kept private," I said.

"I think sir Larentii there would separate my particles if I didn't," Doctor Halivar smiled. "This is just a preliminary meeting; I have a session scheduled with you later this afternoon. We'll talk more then. A room has been set up and I hope we have all your preferences correct on soap, shampoo and other personal items."

"I'm sure it will be fine, I've learned not to be picky," I said.

"You'll let us know if the bed and the accommodations are acceptable?"

"Of course."

"Good. Welcome to Sea Winds, Ms. Nilvas. Someone will show you to your suite now." Doctor Halivar pressed another button on his deskcomp. A nurse walked in. "Take Ms. Nilvas to the suite on the end, Ceerah," he said.

"Yes, Doctor. Come, Ms. Nilvas." Ceerah's voice was stiff and unrelenting. Somehow, she made me think of Ardalin for a moment. She didn't look like Ardalin, though. Ceerah was prettier than that, with dark hair and green eyes. I watched her closely as she walked down the hall while I followed. I still had my strength and my skipping skills, in addition to being able to turn. If Nurse Ceerah bothered me, she would regret it.

"This is pretty," I said, glancing around the spacious suite. Plexi windows lined one wall and provided a very nice view of the ocean roughly a quarter click away. I was on the second floor of the clinic and it looked more like an exclusive resort than a facility that treated mental patients.

"I will go now," Nefrigar had to duck to get through doorways, and I think that irritated him.

"Thanks, hon," I said, giving him the best smile I could.

"Remember to contact me if there is any difficulty."

"I'll try." Nefrigar disappeared, causing Ceerah to frown. She didn't like non-humanoids, I think.

"You have a limited comp-vid, a vid-screen, access to almost any book and most news programs," Ceerah pointed out the comp in the sofa table and the vid-screen on a wall facing the sofa. The bedroom was close by, with more plexi windows and another pretty view of the ocean. Comfortable chairs were spaced evenly near the windows, allowing occupants to sit and watch the waves if they wanted.

"By limited comp-vid, you mean?" I asked, turning back to Ceerah.

"That some applications are blocked," she huffed.

"Ah. Can't have that," I said.

"Do not get smart with me. This room is normally reserved for our wealthiest patients. You are here as a favor to a friend." The claws were coming out, now.

"Do you treat all your patients this way?" I asked, "Or only the non-wealthy ones?"

"We had other rooms available. This one was requested for you, when we might have filled it with someone who could pay. Enjoy your stay, Ms. Nilvas." Ceerah stalked out of the room.

"You know, I don't have to stay here now," I said. My bags were already inside the room, waiting to be unpacked. I lifted both of them and skipped away.

"You managed to lose her already?" Karzac stared accusingly at his son.

"I asked Ceerah if she said anything. She can be somewhat abrupt at times," Kevis wanted to tug on his hair. The Larentii had been contacted and was now trying to coax Reah back.

"Then don't allow her around Reah again," Karzac said more gruffly than he intended. "Reah is an extremely special case, and I can get the truth out of your nurse if she is unwilling to offer it voluntarily."

"Dad, don't. She's very efficient. I need that at times."

"Reah needs a soft touch and soothing words. Not someone who will get snippy right away."

"I'll see what I can do."

"Good. If you have difficulties with Reah, let me know."

"All right."

~

"Now, Ms. Nilvas, is running away something you do often?" Doctor Halivar appeared shortly after Nefrigar found me and hauled me back to the clinic.

"Whenever I can," I said. "I skip therefore I am."

"Skip?"

"Didn't Nefrigar tell you I was High Demon?"

"He did say that," Doctor Halivar consulted his handheld.

"High Demons skip. We don't fold as the Larentii do. Someone explained it to me as skipping flat stones on water."

"Ah. I don't believe I've met anyone with the talent before."

"I can take you for a short hop," I offered.

"Ms. Nilvas, I assure you that won't be necessary."

"No, you just want to dig around in my head. Ask about my mother. That sort of thing."

"How was she? Your mother?"

"Dead. Shortly after I was born. Next question."

"What did Ceerah say to you?"

"That I was a charity case and this room should have been given to somebody who actually had money."

"Really." He didn't make it a question.

"I try not to lie unless I'm forced to do so," I said. "And I usually speak my mind. Why doesn't this suite have a kitchen?"

"Why do you want a kitchen?"

"I have a Master Cook's license. Do the math. I'm sure the food here is very good. Mine is probably better."

"I'm told you tried to kill yourself recently."

"I did. Almost jumped into a volcano."

"Is that a real volcano or a symbolic one?"

"A real one."

"Why do you think you're here, Ms. Nilvas?"

"A god fucked up my life. Go ahead, record delusional in your comp-vid." I rose to pace. I wasn't really sure what good all this was going to do me, but I promised Nefrigar that I'd give it a couple of weeks when he'd talked me into coming back.

"I try to stay away from that term if I can," he said dryly.

"Lie," I said. Doctor Halivar blinked at me.

"I know when people lie. I knew Ceerah was speaking the truth when she said what she did. You can move me to another room if you want."

"Reah, I'm not moving you. Someone close to me asked for this room specifically for you. Therefore, it is yours. Do not let Ceerah intimidate you."

"She didn't. I skipped away to keep from knocking her through a wall. I'm not in a good mood right now."

"Do you do that often? Knock people through walls?"

"Not recently, but when seventy Greater Demons tried to attack me, my Thifilatha burned them to death. It wasn't pleasant to watch or smell. Burned flesh isn't a nice scent. Did they tell you I'm pregnant?"

"Yes. I have that information. If you need extra food to keep from becoming ill, you only have to tell my staff."

"I've only seen Ceerah so far and I'm not asking her for anything." Doctor Halivar frowned at my admission.

"Now, these Greater Demons, where were they?"

"I'm not at liberty to say. I don't think you have ASD clearance."

"What if I were to get clearance?"

"I'll only believe that if Lendill Schaff or Norian Keef show up and say it's all right," I said. "Unless that happens, you get nothing."

"Would you be more comfortable telling these things to another member of my staff?"

"No. I'm not telling you any ASD business unless the Director or Vice-Director say it's all right." I went to stand beside the plexi windows. The water in the distance was beautiful, with a late summer sun hanging low on the horizon.

"Why were these Greater Demons attacking you?"

"Can't say."

"What's the difference between High Demons and Greater Demons?"

"I can't answer that, because I don't really know. Somebody told me they were Greater Demons after the fact. They can't skip, I know that much. They'd have gotten the hell away from me if they could."

"What makes a High Demon a High Demon?" Doctor Halivar was very curious.

"I don't know. What makes you a male?"

"I was born male."

"I was born High Demon."

"Point taken. What do High Demons do?"

"Most of them do nothing, in my experience," I snorted. "The males turn to full Thifilathi once a month and go stomping around, roaring and beating their chests, mostly."

"And the females?"

"The females don't have to turn. Some of them can't, I don't think. I and one other turn."

"Can you do this for me?"

"I won't, because it burns my clothing away when I turn. I'd be naked when I came back to myself. Won't do that," I shook my head.

"Ah."

"Have you ever seen a High Demon become Thifilathi or Thifilatha?" I asked.

"I'd barely heard they existed, so the answer is no. Are you comfortable talking about the attack?"

"One of the Greater Demons did it during the full moon. They get pissy just like the male High Demons do. I had to allow it to get the information I needed for the case I was working."

"Do you want to talk about it?"

"No."

"About the god who fucked up your life?"

"Kifirin."

"Kifirin." He repeated the word.

"Yes. Stay away from him if at all possible."

"I'll do my best."

"Don't patronize. You seem nice enough. Don't ruin it."

"Tell me about Nefrigar."

"He's the Larentii Archivist. I've only been to the Archives a time or two. I could get lost in one room and not come out for a century or two."

"He has access to the information the Larentii store?"

"He does."

"What if I asked you to request a tour?"

"Ask him yourself. I don't use my position in his life to influence him like that. Nefrigar makes up his own mind. Always."

"What do you have, Ceerah?" Jalan grinned at her supervising nurse. Ceerah and Jalan often pulled recordings of this patient or that and watched the sessions, although they weren't authorized to do so. Ceerah had the codes to get into the recordings, she just didn't have access to the doctors' private notes. Most of the staff lived on the grounds of Sea Winds, in a separate building. Ceerah and Jalan often had dinner together and watched the vids Ceerah pulled.

"The new patient that Doctor Halivar accepted for free," Ceerah grinned. "She's pretty messed up." Ceerah cued the vid and let it play. Both nurses watched and laughed as the female claimed to be High Demon and an operative for the ASD.

"At least she knows the word delusional," Jalan snickered at that point in the vid. "Do you know how much money we could make if we sold this to that reality show?"

"The one that gets the embarrassing moments?" Ceerah smiled.

"Yeah. They call it Temporary Insanity. Only this isn't temporary, is it?" She pointed to the woman in the vid. "And they can cover the faces so nobody knows who it really is."

"Doctor Halivar never watches regular vids anyway. He's always got his head elsewhere," Ceerah smirked. "And since none of the other doctors are seeing this patient," she gave Jalan a conspiratorial grin.

"Come on, let's submit this. This is too good to pass up." Jalan pulled the chip and slipped it into her comp-vid. Jalan transferred the information to the show's site, including information on where to reach both her and Ceerah for payment if the vid was used. "They probably won't use it, but it's worth a try. I've heard of submissions getting ten thousand or more."

"What if we're caught? You know what the laws are on patient confidentiality."

"Come on. We're treating her free of charge. Does she even have any rights?"

"So, Reah, what do you think of the food here?" Doctor Halivar was back after I'd had breakfast and lunch. The food was tolerable.

"It was all right," I said, shrugging.

"Only all right?"

"Some of it barely. The scrambled eggs were runny. I hate that."

"You're very particular about your food."

"I am."

"Tell me about these Greater Demons. What do you know about them?"

"The ones who attacked and raped other women or just the one who attacked me?"

"The last one."

"I can't tell you his name. He figured he was going to have me, one way or the other. He had someone else chain me up and then he bit me and left." I wasn't going to tell Doctor Halivar about a shining woman who'd appeared to prevent Zendeval from raping me. That would constitute a really big section of notes, telling anybody how crazy he thought I was.

"Was it painful? Did he hurt you?"

"Yes."

"How badly?"

"He bit me. Somehow, he gave me an infection. I was sick for days afterward."

"And you knew you were pregnant at the time?"

"No. I found out shortly after."

"And the child is healthy?"

"As far as I know. Nobody says differently. Teeki and Neeki said they were shielding him."

"Teeki and Neeki?"

"Twins. They're Kifirin's assistants."

"Ah."

The patient has been here six days, and still I have trouble getting through to her. Something is there, but I can't get anywhere near it, Kevis wrote in his private notes. Reah speaks readily of the attack and other things, but something is hidden. She displays anger and callousness over the treatment she received from her attacker. Refuses to tell me where it occurred or how she escaped from him. I have never heard of Greater Demons before. I must do research.

Kevis' day had been full and it was very late. He'd not gotten to record his notes on Reah's sessions until now. He was quite surprised when two men appeared in his study, pistols drawn and both growling.

"You came with the highest recommendation," Norian snapped at Kevis Halivar. "Yet I see Reah in a session on a vid program after my agents notified me. Her face isn't even hidden. We have the records of who submitted it; we've spent the last two clicks grilling that stupid fuck producer who aired it. He claims a technical glitch kept her face from being hidden on the program. I want to speak with two of your nurses, now. Where are Ceerah Kade and Jalan Wolk? They couldn't wait to send this in to that stupid program."

"Here they are," two of Norian's agents hauled Ceerah and Jalan into Kevis' private study. Kevis stared angrily at both women.

"Who are you?" Ceerah snapped at Norian, who still held a Ranos pistol in his hand.

"Norian Keef, Director of the ASD," Norian snapped back. "You're both under arrest for violating the patient confidentiality laws."

"There's no way that loony is ASD," Ceerah scoffed.

"Shut up," Norian said pleasantly. "If you don't, I'll allow my Vice-Director here to remove your face."

"What the hell is going on?" Gavril, Tory and Ry appeared all at once, almost causing Jalan to shriek. Ceerah stared. One of the three looked like Teeg San Gerxon, Founder of the Campiaan Alliance.

Gavril was the one who spoke. He was seething and about to let his vampire run free. "We leave her in your care and a few evenings later her face is splashed across the Reth Alliance and she's made a laughing stock? The entire Alliance has seen those vids. They think she's completely crazy. What do you think will happen if Reah sees that? She's been betrayed enough as it is." Gavril was shouting, Tory was blowing smoke and Ry was about to place a spell on someone.

"Ceerah, you managed to get past the private codes, didn't you?" Kevis glared at his head nurse. "How long has this been going on?"

"I won't tell you." She turned her head away. She'd thought at times in the past that perhaps she could convince Kevis to fall for her. That desire had been a vain one.

"Two years," Jalan hung her head. "Only we just sat and watched the funny ones until now. This one; we thought we wouldn't get caught."

"Shut up," Ceerah hissed.

"You broke into the records," Jalan snapped at Ceerah.

"You submitted it to Temporary Insanity," Ceerah shot back.

Norian watched the exchange with interest. No need for questioning if the information was volunteered freely.

"I wish to ask for extradition," Gavril said, anger still in his voice.

"Extradition?" Kevis asked.

"To Campiaa. These two have violated a citizen's rights. I have the right by law to request extradition and place them on trial. Reah didn't give permission for her image to be used while under treatment. In fact, a responsible party should have been approached for permission. Was that done? I understand she only arrived at this facility six days ago."

"Jalan, this is Teeg San Gerxon, from the Campiaan Alliance," Kevis said wearily and sat behind his desk. He felt as if he needed a stiff drink.

"If they aren't extradited, I will certainly lodge a protest with the founding member of the Reth Alliance," Ry said.

"And this is Rylend Morphis, newly crowned King of Karathia," Kevis wasn't even looking up from his desk any longer.

"If I admit I signed off on it, will that keep me here?" Jalan asked. "I couldn't get the vid submitted unless I did. I signed that Nefrigar guy's name."

"You forged documents, after this one broke into private patient records and handed them to you?" Kevis raked a hand through short, light-brown hair.

"You forged a Larentii's signature?" Lendill stared at Jalan.

"A Larentii? They don't exist," Ceerah laughed.

"I altered my appearance only for her when we arrived," Nefrigar appeared, his height crowding the room. He wasn't altering his appearance now.

"Oh, stars save us," Ceerah stared up at Nefrigar in horror.

"Something may have to save you. Reah saw that program and has disappeared again," Nefrigar said.

CHAPTER 2

I'd only been to Avendor once before, skipping there more than twenty-five years earlier to learn how to grow gishi fruit. Now I was back and standing in a line of migratory workers who went from one grove to the next, offering their services to pick, pack, cull or ship the fruit. I was searching for a place that might hold peace, even if it did involve hard work. I'd always found picking fruit to be peaceful work; the trees held no judgment or betrayal. They never withheld information or love, either, with wind whispering through the leaves at times, giving silent thanks for the care they received.

"Name?" The grove supervisor was tired and out of sorts, I think, by the time I arrived in front of his makeshift desk.

"Reah Silver," I said.

"Have you worked the groves before?"

"Yes. In every aspect."

"Good. You'll start picking immediately. Sign here." The comp-vid was shoved across the small table, I used the stylus to sign my name and went to stand with the others who waited for the next bus to come along. I had both bags with me—I hadn't left anything behind on Refizan. If the doctor couldn't control his staff any better than he

20

had, then I had no use for him. Nefrigar had difficulty coaxing me back the first time. I wouldn't go back there again.

The hovertruck pulled to a stop in front of us and we all loaded onto it. "We'll take you by the temporary housing first, so you can unload your belongings. Then you'll get your hoversteps and go to the fields." At least they had hoversteps. Hoversteps were round ladders you could operate with hand or foot controls to raise, lower or navigate around the tree to reach all the fruit. They were a great time saver, if you could afford them. Another crew would likely supply empty crates to replace the ones the pickers filled.

"Select a cube inside, leave your things and come back immediately," the driver dropped us off in front of rows of temporary housing. Long, single-story buildings lined up before us, each with a communal shower, restroom and laundry facilities. My coworkers ran toward the first two buildings. Not wishing to fight with the crowd, I walked toward the third and last of the buildings. Three others came with me.

Dumping my bags in a cubicle at the farthest end of the building, I made my way toward the hovertruck again. Only open seating was available on the back of the truck, with hard benches lined up on both sides to carry the workers. Our feet swung freely over the sides as the hovertruck glided through the groves, taking us toward the designated harvest spot. The trees we passed had already been picked.

"Here's where you start," the driver announced. "And this is supervisor Keedan, who will hand out your assignments."

Supervisor Keedan looked to be nearing two hundred, with nearly-white hair, washed-out blue eyes and wrinkles that spelled character. I imagined that his eyes might crinkle nicely if he smiled. He wasn't smiling now.

"You're our replacement crew," he announced as we gathered around him. "The last crew was fired, every one of them, because they were stealing from the groves. If you think to do that, bear in mind we will prosecute. The last crew is sitting in jail at the moment, awaiting trial for high theft. Gishi fruit is expensive; I'm sure all of you know that. We don't tolerate theft or mistreatment of your fellow workers or harmful practical jokes. You will be assigned a hoverstep, and it will be your responsibility to maintain it and charge it every night. If it breaks down or malfunctions, it is your duty to take it to the repair shop located near your temporary barracks. Food will be supplied for your day meal, but you will prepare the evening meal yourselves. Ingredients for those meals will be provided—within reason. Each barracks has a kitchen and you are obligated to work out a rotating cooking schedule. Fights will not be tolerated and the sharing of duties is expected. Bear in mind that we will terminate your employment immediately if you disrupt the peace of the groves. Follow me."

We followed Keedan until we reached a place where hoversteps waited between seemingly endless rows of gishi fruit trees. Crates were also lined up at regular intervals between trees. "Choose your hoverstep," Keedan instructed. "You will be expected to finish your row by sunset. That is five clicks from now. I will be waiting at the end and checking the fruit that comes from your individual rows. If you can't pick fast enough, you will be released tonight. Go."

We went. Most went scrabbling after the hoversteps closest to us and began clipping fruit from the trees right away. I and the three who'd bunked in the same building went for the outer edge. I took the last row. Hand clips and other supplies were stuffed in pockets around the hoverstep, including a sealed container with plenty of cool water. At least they were prepared. I pulled my crate up, lifted the hand clip and began picking.

Culls were dropped to the ground and the fruit without blemishes went into individual trays inside each crate. The trays were formed to fit gishi fruit and protected the harvested fruit when the next tray was set atop it. I worked as I always did, swiftly and steadily.

With more than twenty turns of experience handpicking gishi fruit on Kifirin, I knew what I was doing. When the trackers learned that I needed more crates than had been left, they stepped up their pace, leaving me as many as necessary to keep up with my picking. I paid no attention to those harvesting around me, humming softly as I settled into the work.

The three who'd gone to the outer edge just as I had, finished shortly after I did. I knew they had experience, whereas some of the others didn't. Gishi fruit harvests generally paid much better than any other type of fruit crop, and good, experienced pickers were often easy to spot. The fruit was much more rare and expensive than nannas, oranges or peaches in any case, and required a certain type of handling as well. You didn't squeeze gishi fruit when you clipped the stem. It would bruise if handled too roughly and cut the price of the fruit by more than half.

My three bunkmates and I were sent to a nearby tent after we finished, where cold water, fruit juice and sliced melon waited. I ate what I could, knowing that soon the pregnancy would progress to the point where I'd become ill if I didn't keep something in my stomach. I'd go looking soon for health bars or something similar that I could carry on my hoverstep.

"Garthe," the first of my bunkmates held out a hand. His hair was nearly blond from the sun, looked to be in his fifties and in his prime, had pitted scars on both cheeks, brown eyes and a nice smile.

"Reah," I took his hand and squeezed his fingers as was appropriate. "You've done this before."

"I have," he agreed, turning to watch as two more joined us beneath the tent. They went right for the food and drinks, just as we had. "I thought to go north to Adrixx and do repair work, but I discovered I didn't like the city all that much."

"I think the trees sometimes sigh with relief when we remove the weight of the fruit," I said.

"I get that, too," Garthe smiled. "Plus, I get to think my own thoughts while I pick fruit. I don't have a customer standing over me, telling me how to fix what he couldn't fix in the first place."

"I know someone who loves to do repairs, but he hates it if someone tries to interfere with his work," I said, smiling and thinking of Nenzi. "He knows exactly what he's doing, so it's a good thing he works with his brothers. They sort of run interference for him."

"Then it's too bad I didn't have brothers," Garthe laughed.

"Yendah," my female bunkmate moved over next to Garthe and

held out her hand. She was much older than Garthe, I could see that, but truly not that old. Perhaps a hundred or so. Still in her prime, she had long brown hair held atop her head with a clip she hid beneath a floppy-brimmed hat. Her brown eyes coolly assessed Garthe. She would learn soon enough he had no interest in women. His eyes had followed our other bunkmate, a man, who had yet to introduce himself.

"Who's going home tonight?" A young man flopped onto the ground near Yendah's feet, a cup of fruit juice in his hand. Sunset was very close and several still hadn't come in. He grinned up at Yendah, who gave a tight smile in return. She didn't like the young ones, I saw that right away. I agreed with her. They tended to be interested in sex and little else.

"I'd say anyone not here in the next ten ticks," my third bunkmate came to join our group. He held a comp-vid in his hand, likely checking the sunset time. Garthe watched him covertly as the newcomer settled beside the young man on the ground at our feet. "Name's Calde," he introduced himself. "Who's cooking tonight? I'm starved." He had black hair, gray eyes, looked to be around forty and was handsome in a rough sort of way. He was staring at the younger male, who offered his hand and said his name was Landor. At least Garthe stood a chance, now. I didn't think Landor was interested at all in Calde.

"I'll cook, if they have something decent to fix," I offered.

"Good. That's settled," Calde grinned.

"Time," Keedan shouted. "Everyone gather round. If you haven't finished your row, someone will take you back to the entrance, you'll collect a chip for today's wages and leave. The rest of you, step forward." All of us rose and made a circle around Keedan.

"Now, I'll identify you first by your hoverstep number," he said. Those had been left at the end of our rows as instructed. "Where is hoverstep three?" Landor held up a hand. "You left good fruit hanging on at least eight trees. Do better tomorrow or you'll be out. Where's number eleven?" A woman held up her hand. "You dumped good fruit on the ground with the culls. You're out as of now. Go to the entrance and collect your pay." The woman turned and left. Keedan went through several others, voicing his concerns about their harvesting skills, bruising of fruit or running their hoverstep into the trunk of a tree. That could damage the tree and leave it open to insect infestation or other diseases. "Do that again," Keedan admonished, "and you'll be fined and asked to leave." The young male hung his head and nodded.

"Now," he said, "who is hoverstep number sixteen?" That one was mine. I raised my hand. "What's your name?" Keedan asked.

"Reah," I said.

"Reah, I couldn't find anything wrong with your work and you finished first, even though you started last. You've done this before."

"Yes," I nodded. "Several years." I wasn't about to tell him how many.

"Good work," Keedan smiled the smile I'd waited all day to see. His eyes did indeed crinkle nicely at the corners. I smiled back at him. "You're dismissed, load your hoversteps on the truck over there and don't forget to charge them tonight. Sleep well; the trucks will be by to pick you up at first light. Be late and you'll be taken to the gate," he grinned.

Hitting the lifter on my hoverstep, I slid it into place on the truck and then climbed onto the seat next to it. We rode back to the barracks that way, many of us leaning our elbows tiredly on our hoversteps as we made the trip.

After getting the hoverstep into my cubicle and hooked up to the power supply, I walked toward the kitchen, where my three bunkmates waited. I'd offered to cook and they were all sitting around the kitchen, waiting. Opening the fridge, I assessed what we'd been left to prepare. We had fowl, so I pulled it out, washed it and went looking for flour, spices and seasonings.

"This may be the best thing I've ever eaten in the fields," Calde said later. I'd served the fowl with a sauce using the meager ingredients I had, plus sautéed vegetables, sliced cheese and fresh fruit for dessert.

"I don't think I've gotten food this good anywhere," Yendah acknowledged.

"I'll cook every night," I offered, "if someone else will do cleanup. Four isn't hard to prepare meals for."

"We'll get sandwiches or something for a noon meal while we're picking," Garthe bit into the cheese. "This goes well with the grapes."

"Yes, it does. I find it surprising that they brought us something that was such good quality."

"People usually melt this cheese over bread or something," Calde pointed out.

"I like it better this way," I said.

"Me, too," he agreed.

Knowing that I had to rise early, I went to bed soon after dinner. At least my cube had a door that I could lock. My days settled into a routine, after that. The harvest was demanding and there were no days off during picking season. Other crews worked the groves, but we seldom saw them. A truck came through each mid-day, handing out a packed meal of some sort. Usually it was sandwiches--those could be finished quickly, allowing us to get back to picking. Keedan showed up at our barracks on the tenth day while I was serving dinner.

"Are you hungry?" I asked, setting food in front of Garthe, who gave me a lovely smile before lifting his fork.

"Of course," Keedan grinned. I'd gotten a comp-vid to order food and supplies, and I'd asked for fish as one of our choices. I was serving it now. Keedan got the extra bit of fish I'd cooked.

"Does she always cook this well?" Keedan asked, stunned after his first bite.

"Every night," Yendah smiled. "We clean up, Reah cooks. Works great for us. I've never eaten this well."

"What about barracks one and two?" Keedan asked, cutting into the fish again.

"I'm not up to cooking for that many," I said. "I'm pregnant and I need as much rest as I can get." If I'd dropped a bomb on the floor, it might have caused less of a stir. Keedan was staring and Yendah was fussing suddenly. Garthe and Calde were staring at one another.

"I've done everything there is to do with gishi fruit while pregnant before," I said. "I'm just not cooking for nearly thirty people after a long day in the groves. Four I can handle. Maybe five or six, but that's it. I won't cook for more than that."

"How far along?" Keedan went back to his food.

"Close to three months. I'll have to see about getting energy bars or something to carry with me soon, so I won't get sick. Besides, the harvest should be done in another six eight-days. I'll find something else after that if you're uncomfortable with an expectant mother working in your groves." I gave Keedan a hard look. I'd picked gishi fruit while eight months pregnant with my middle twins. It certainly hadn't bothered Gardevik Rath that I'd done it. Or Kifirin or any one of my mates.

"Do you have a husband?" Yendah asked.

"I do, but we're not speaking right now. Harvesting gishi fruit gives me a bit of peace and quiet." I dumped the last of the fish sauce on Keedan's plate; he was scraping up the last of it and still had a third of his fish left. Turning back to my dinner, I took a bite of fish and chewed, wondering exactly what it was that Keedan had come to barracks three to say.

"I was hoping you'd work as my assistant," he said, as soon as he'd finished his meal. "You seem to know everything already, although I don't understand how that is. I've never seen you in the groves before, and I've worked with practically everybody, even the ones who work for our two competitors."

"I worked the Kifirini groves," I shrugged. There wasn't any reason to lie about it. "And I have done everything there is to do, including grafting, raising seedlings and pruning."

"Why did you leave Kifirin, then?" Keedan asked.

"New management," I said. "We couldn't seem to agree." That was certainly true. That bitch had stolen my rings and burned my stuff. Teeg could worry about getting his Tiralian crystal ring back—it was worth millions.

"You'll be running errands between me and the big house," Keedan said, leaning back and rubbing his stomach. "And it'll get you quarters closer in. It hurts to lose my best picker, but I think I can depend on you to know what I'm talking about when I send you to the boss. I don't have time to argue with him as much as he wants and still get this harvest in. You start tomorrow; somebody will be here to pick up your things early in the morning. You'll move into your new cottage tomorrow morning, then I'll pick you up and drive you to the big house for breakfast with the boss around nine bells. Got something a little nicer than what you're wearing now?" Keedan perused my jeans and sleeveless shirt.

"I do."

"Don't make it too fancy; we'll go straight to the groves afterward."

"All right."

True to his word, Keedan had someone at the barracks the following morning at dawn. Yendah almost wept when I left, and Garthe and Calde weren't happy either. Yendah hugged me as my bags were loaded onto the small hovertruck by the driver, who gave Yendah more than a cursory glance. He took me straight to a small cottage, from which I could see what Keedan termed "the big house." It was big. Farzi and Nenzi would likely swoon and fashion their next home after it. It rivaled Teeg's palace on Campiaa, with beautiful, curved windows and turrets on every corner. The rest was whitewashed, with blue and silver trim around the windows and doors. Surrounded by the green of gishi fruit groves, it was something out of a myth or legend.

"Ready?" Keedan called after knocking on my front door. My cottage held a small kitchen, a bedroom, private bath and a sitting room. I'd dumped my bags onto the bed but had no time to unpack them before Keedan arrived.

"I'm ready," I said, walking out of the bedroom to greet Keedan.

"Very nice," Keedan took in my outfit. A nicer blouse, black jeans and sandals made up my outfit, and I'd clipped my hair back, letting most of it hang loose instead of braiding it and covering my head with an old straw hat as I usually did. "Come on, the boss and the other three will be waiting." Keedan drove his personal hovercart to the big house, which sat, I discovered, on an artificially created hill so the owner could look over his groves for clicks.

"Is this a competition?" I muttered when Keedan brought me into a private dining room where three other supervisors sat, their assistants sitting beside them. All the assistants were women, and each was quite pretty.

"Maybe, but you're the only one who knows what she's doing, and the prettiest, on top of that," Keedan smiled, his eyes crinkling.

I'd brought a comp-vid with me; in fact it was the one I'd been given as a gift by Pripps Electronics on Surnath. I'd gotten it back from Lendill and kept it with me constantly. Schuul Enterprises had nothing to do with its manufacture, and I preferred it that way.

"And the western grove has arrived with his new assistant," one of the others commented, smiling at me.

"Drennen, of the eastern grove," Keedan introduced the man. "And his assistant, Annita. Crofford of the Southern Grove, and his assistant Retta, plus Phelpas of the Northern Grove, with his assistant Jadis." I was introduced to all the supervisors who ran EastStar Groves on Avendor, the smallest of the four gishi fruit farming concerns on the planet. Word had it that the owner was a recluse, refusing to attend most of the Governor's balls and banquets, as some of the other owners did.

I couldn't blame him; those things were something I'd come to loathe, having been to more than my share on Teeg's arm. President Drix had gotten injured during a meeting on Campiaa not long ago, but word had it that he was recovered and back to work at full efficiency, glad that the pirating problem had been eliminated.

"And this is Reah, my new assistant, who worked in the Kifirini Groves before moving here," Keedan introduced me as we sat down. The seat at the head of the table was empty, but servants were waiting in a wide doorway nearby, hovering in anticipation of their lord and master's arrival so breakfast could be served.

"What did you do for the Kifirini groves?" Drennen of the eastern groves asked.

"Everything," I said.

"Everything?" He lifted an eyebrow skeptically.

"Yes," I said. "I've even been known to lay new water pipes or repair the sprinkler system from time to time, although I don't like digging trenches to lay new lines. We didn't own a trencher for a while and digging by hand always makes my back ache."

"How can they sell their fruit as organic?" Crofford of the southern groves asked. "Surely they use insecticides for pests."

"I can assure you that they don't, they use a natural repellent," I said. Crofford huffed out his disbelief.

"Everyone here? Great." The boss had arrived. I stared at him. He was looking at the others at first, giving them a smile. Until he came to me. His mouth dropped open the moment his eyes rested on my face. He covered the gaffe quickly, however. I had no idea who he was, but my heart was suddenly pounding a click a tick, and that most certainly shouldn't be. He was tall—at least six feet. He had thick, dark-brown hair that curled slightly and bright, hazel eyes that would likely cause any girl to swoon, should those eyes smile in her direction.

Of course, his actual smile with beautiful, even white teeth would make her swoon again. A pale hint of freckles might have been on his face, too, but I was too busy staring at his eyes and smile. I think every female at the table was hoping to wiggle her way into the boss's good graces; I realized that right away.

With the way my heart was racing, I was frightened that I might have joined their ranks. Settling myself with a sigh, I pulled out my comp-vid and made ready to take notes if necessary. Pregnancy notwithstanding, I had too many mates already and none of them had thought to pay attention to me for a very long time. I wasn't prepared to take on another, who very likely would do exactly the same.

"This is Edward Pendley, owner of EastStar Groves," Keedan introduced the boss with a smile. I smiled at the boss as best I could, taking his hand when it was offered and giving him my name. We sat down after that, breakfast was served and we got right to business.

"We're caught up now," Keedan said. "We've hired a really good replacement crew and they've made up lost time after we fired the others." I learned that his previous assistant had been one of the terminated crew. Likely the ringleader, unless I missed my guess. I wasn't about to question Keedan about it. If he wanted me to know, he'd tell me.

"How did you do it so quickly?" Phelpas asked.

"Fired the slowest ones first day and then told the rest they had to keep up with the fastest picker," Keedan grinned. I mentally gulped. That had been me. I hadn't known he'd set me up as the example. I'd have to come out of my own thoughts more often. Plates of food were set in front of us, along with coffee, juice and water.

"Do you have decaf?" Keedan placed a hand over my coffee cup as he looked up at the server.

"We can make it," the young man said.

"Do it. She's pregnant," Keedan said. My cheeks went pink immediately. I was glad when they all started talking business again. I set my comp-vid on record so I could get all the information in case I needed it again. They spoke of how much fertilizer would be needed after the groves were harvested, new groves that had been planted and which ones required grafting to produce sooner. The discussion also turned to how many new employees to keep on the payroll to mulch, prune and spray.

"What did you use to fertilize on Kifirin?" Crofford asked. He seemed unnaturally interested in the Kifirini groves for some reason.

"Cow manure compost," I said, "after the harvests. We composted in between and added that mix when it was time. The Crown owns vast cattle herds, and as you know, the Crown also owns the gishi fruit groves. It was an easy exchange; the only cost was getting the manure to the groves. We worked compost into the soil and the trees thrived on it, with a little natural bean crop mixed in."

"I understand that most of the farms and ranches on Kifirin are owned by the Crown," Edward observed. He'd been quiet for the most part, seemingly content to eat and listen to what his supervisors had to say.

"They are," I nodded, pushing the eggs around on my plate. The food was standard fare—nothing special. "A few people on Kifirin own land and grow their own crops, but most are employed by the Crown in some way or another. The exceptions are the artisans, weavers and such. Kifirin produces very good quality hand-woven cloth and handmade pottery and glass."

"And it's expensive," Keedan agreed. "I saw a bowl in Adrixx priced at five hundred credits. And it wasn't even their top of the line, according to the shop owner."

"You have to forgive the feudal system they have," I said. "It's much better now than it used to be. They're slowly making their way toward the light, I think."

"Sir, I hate to interrupt," a middle-aged man walked into the dining room. "But there's a fire in the southern grove."

Everybody was up and rushing toward the back of the house. A wide deck was there, overlooking the southern portion of EastStar's massive groves. Edward Pendley began to curse—in English. "I'm going down there," he shouted in common and disappeared, just like that.

"Fuck!" Keedan muttered beside me. "Somebody get a hovercar here. We need to be down there, too."

"I can take two," I said, grabbing Keedan and the first one of the others I could reach, (which turned out to be Crofford) and skipped directly to the spot in the groves where the smoke curled toward the sky.

"Get the sprinklers on!" I shouted, dumping Keedan and Crofford before racing toward the manual control. Those were located every quarter click or so within the groves. Turning the wheel as quickly as I could, the sprinklers came to life, spraying water everywhere while the smoke thickened, forcing me to cough in an attempt to get it out of my lungs.

I couldn't imagine what might have started a fire—the groves were moist enough from rain and the sprinklers that came on during the evening hours. Keedan and Crofford had raced in the opposite direction to get the sprinklers on the other side turned on. I had no idea where Edward had gone; he wasn't there when we arrived.

After only a few moments, we were left with a few smoldering trees, smoke that still hung knee-high above the ground and a mystery as to how the fire had started. Edward had finally shown up, looking angry. I understood that look—at least a dozen trees had been destroyed, and each gishi fruit tree was worth around a million credits over its lifetime.

"They were already gone," Edward muttered. He'd gone after the arsonists while we'd hurried to save the trees. We followed him, then, until we found the origin of the fire. Two trees were now reduced to cinders, and they shouldn't have burned that quickly unless they had help.

"Do you have warlocks or sorcerers for enemies?" I asked, crouching down to examine the white, ashy stump that remained of a gishi fruit tree.

"I wasn't aware of any," Edward said dryly, crouching next to me. "At least we got the fire out quickly."

"We?" I turned to look into his hazel eyes.

"All right, Keedan and Crofford." The hazel eyes twinkled with teasing mischief.

"Uh-huh," I muttered, standing up.

"How did you get us here?" Keedan asked while Crofford nodded in agreement.

"It's called skipping," I said.

"I've only heard of a handful of races that might be capable of that," Edward said, curling a hand around the back of his neck and watching me with a puzzled expression.

"I've only heard of one," I replied.

"Which one is that?"

"Mine," I said.

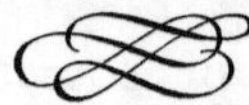

CHAPTER 3

Phelpas, Drennen and all three assistants came along in a hovercar while Keedan, Crofford, Edward and I directed grove employees to dig up the burned trees and haul them away.

"This is the third time in three moon turns," Phelpas pointed out, but stepped back and remained silent when Edward glared at him. The boss didn't need the reminder, it seems.

"How many has he lost so far?" I asked Keedan.

"Nearly a hundred trees the first time. We had a better watch the second time, so we only lost about thirty. This time we cut it to eleven. We worry that they'll attack during the night, but every time it has been in full daylight."

"Round up the employees and we'll ask questions," Edward directed. That's how we spent our afternoon, with Keedan making sure I had something to eat and drink between questioning. Three employees weren't being truthful. Somehow, Edward pulled the same three out and let the others go.

"Now," he said, as all three sat in front of him, "tell me everything you know about this."

I was thankful Edward's office was large enough for plenty of seating to be brought in; we were at the questioning until night fell.

Keedan asked me twice to communicate orders via comp-vid and I did so, telling Garthe to get the employees to do their best and make sure their quotas were filled for the day. He contacted me around sunset, saying that they'd accomplished just that. He also asked about the fire, but I told him we'd have information when we saw him the following day.

It turned out that two detainees had committed theft and the other had damaged a tree without reporting it. None knew anything about the fires. All three were terminated and escorted to the front gate so they could take a bus to Adrixx.

"Let's get something to eat," Edward said. He'd ordered the kitchen crew to go to bed earlier, since we'd been at the questioning for hours on end and now it was very late. We followed him into the kitchens, assistants and all. Edward rummaged through the fridge.

"Let Reah see what she can do," Keedan suggested. Edward's head jerked up and he looked at me. Stepping aside, he gestured grandly toward the open fridge. I went to see what was inside.

"I can't believe this," Phelpas sighed. They'd gotten pasta with chicken and a mushroom sauce that could be put together quickly. I found bread that had been made earlier, sliced it lengthwise, buttered it and sprinkled it with herbs before toasting it and served that with the meal. Then I cut up fresh redberries and served them with sweet cream for dessert.

"You could get your Master Cook's license," Crofford sighed, finishing off his dessert.

"I have one," I said. "Will someone else clean up? I'm tired."

"You have a Master Cook's license, and you're here?" Drennen looked skeptical.

"I do. I own Dee's Restaurant in Targis on Tulgalan. I told Keedan that I'm here because I need peace and quiet."

"What were you doing on Kifirin, working in their groves?" Crofford stared at me. The three assistants were sitting beside their supervisors, waiting for this story to unfold, I'm sure.

"I started those groves," I said. "King Jayd laughed at me when I suggested that we try gishi fruit as a money crop on the Southern Continent. He's not laughing now."

"You're a member of the Royal Family on Kifirin, aren't you?" Edward looked surprised.

"Not that they've noticed, but yes," I agreed. And since nobody else made any move to do so, I began to clean the dishes.

"And she's the wife of the founding member of the Campiaan Alliance," Teeg appeared in Edward's kitchen, making me wince.

"Master San Gerxon," Edward bowed politely to Teeg.

"Don't bow to him. The rat," I said.

"You're calling me a rat?"

"I could call you worse."

"Please don't. Reah, you need to come back with me. Nefrigar says you're still fragile, and we have to think about the baby."

"Oh, now that it's your baby, I'm fragile," I huffed.

"Reah, you know what I'm talking about," Teeg grumbled. He was right; I'd just been able to shove most of that aside for the past three eight-days or so, in favor of picking gishi fruit. The trees got my attention. My thoughts and problems didn't.

"Where's Astralan?" I asked. "I'd like for him to look at a spot where somebody burned gishi fruit trees earlier today."

"Will you come home with me if I call him?" Teeg's nearly-black eyes were begging.

"I'll come," I muttered. "I don't think I can stay here, now, since they know we're married and all."

"Reah, every mate you have is worried to death about you."

"Must be a new experience for them," I snapped.

"How many do you have?" Keedan asked.

"Nine," Teeg answered for me. "Reah is extremely rare. Only seventeen females exist in her race."

"No kidding?" Keedan turned his eyes to me.

"Six of those are my daughters," I blushed and hung my head.

"There's our girl," Astralan appeared at Teeg's elbow. "What do you need, baby?"

"I want you to look at a spot where a fire started in the groves today," I said. "I think a warlock or power holder of some sort started it."

"Then we'll take a look," Astralan smiled. "As long as you come home with us."

"I already said I would," I grumped.

"Good. Let's go."

"I'm coming along," Edward insisted.

"Then we'll all go," Teeg agreed amiably, and Astralan and Teeg folded everyone in the kitchen to the burned trees.

"Definitely a power wielder," Astralan nodded after examining the burned spots. "If I'm correct, not a powerful one. Used the sun as a heat source, just turned it up some to dry out the wood and start the fire."

"Can you locate him or her?" I asked.

"Not a problem," Astralan grinned and disappeared. He came back, hauling Landor with him. Teeg took over then, ordering him with compulsion to explain what happened.

"He's a member of the Dondl family?" Edward stared at Landor. Dondl was one of Edward's rival grove owners. Landor's uncle owned the groves, but the moment he learned that Landor had a bit of power, he'd recruited the boy to his purposes.

"What shall we do with him?" Keedan asked. "I hesitate to turn him over to the authorities; Dondl will retaliate somehow."

"I'll remove his power," Astralan grinned. "And Teeg will remove the memory that I removed it. You'll make a fine employee, won't you?" Astralan pounded Landor on the back. Edward stared in amazement as Astralan did remove Landor's power, and then Teeg placed compulsion, telling Landor that he wouldn't remember. That, of course, resulted in even more compulsion—Teeg didn't want Edward or his supervisors to remember that part, either. I shivered when it was all over.

"Go back to your barracks," Keedan ordered. Landor trotted off obediently.

"Now, we go home. Mr. Pendley, will you be so kind as to send her things to my palace?" Teeg asked.

"I'll have them shipped tomorrow," Edward sighed. "But I have a request."

"Yes?"

"I'd like to visit the palace after the harvest is in."

"Feel free. You've been invited several times. I thought you weren't interested."

"I am, now." Edward stared at me. Teeg gripped my arm and Astralan folded us away.

"No. Absolutely not," I snapped, the moment Kevis Halivar appeared inside my room. I was tired, out of sorts and a little angry. Somehow, Teeg had tracked me down. I was perfectly happy in the gishi fruit groves on Avendor. I'd even gotten a promotion. Now, I was right back in therapy with the one whose nurses had sold me to the Alliance and made me a laughing stock.

"Reah, I've taken a leave of absence from Sea Winds so I can work with you exclusively," Dr. Halivar said.

"Work with me? You want to peel potatoes or something? That kind of working with me?"

"No. You know very well what I mean."

"Where's nurse nasty?" I asked belligerently.

"Ceerah's under house arrest," Lendill appeared. Teeg was still inside the bedroom, and now it was getting crowded. I was feeling dizzy, too.

"She's going down," Kevis Halivar shouted from somewhere far away. Everything went black after that.

"Obviously she feels more comfortable in those surroundings," Kevis pushed his point. "If you take her to the plantation and allow her to work freely among the citrus groves while you visit and I work with her, perhaps it will turn out best for all involved."

"Farzi, is there enough room for us?" Gavril looked to the reptanoid for answers. Farzi and Nenzi were both very much in favor of having Reah come to them. Their plantation was more than large enough, with plenty of room inside the main house and more guesthouses located nearby.

"Yes. More than enough," Farzi nodded.

"Bring Reah soon," Nenzi agreed.

"How is she?" Rylend Morphis appeared, accompanied by Corolan and Erland.

"Sleeping. She overextended today," Kevis sighed. "I've been chewed out by Dad already for not checking her when they brought her in, so don't start."

"Wasn't thinking about it," Ry smiled. "I'm just glad to know where she is and that's she safe."

"We're thinking about moving her to the plantation, since she went straight to Avendor to work in the gishi fruit groves," Gavril said.

"Can I see her?" Tory arrived with Lok and Aurelius. "And we're prepared to move in, bro, so be warned."

"Move into the plantation house, I think we're taking her there," Gavril sighed. "Dee, make arrangements."

"I will." Dee wore a slight smile but said no more on the subject.

Reah, my love? I'm here, sweetheart. Are you all right?

Was I dreaming? I thought I was dreaming. But the voice sounded real. *Huh?* I sent sleepy mindspeech.

No, love, I can feel your weariness. Go back to sleep. Sleep now. You have no idea how long I've searched for you. The words were sent with the gentlest of touches. I wanted to tuck myself against that touch. Let it soothe away what troubled me. Something did trouble me. It frightened me at times and woke me, gasping for breath, on most mornings. *Sleep,* the voice came again. I allowed it to unravel my thoughts and carry them away.

~

"Reah, it's your Auri." I was curled in a ball on a bed somewhere. It was a good bed—a soft bed. A bed that pillowed and fluffed around me, cradling my body like a womb. I didn't want to leave it. Didn't want to wake. Wanted to allow it to hold me a little longer. "Reah, it's time for breakfast. Wake and come with me." I answered by huddling tighter beneath the blankets.

"No, my love." I was lifted from the bed, moaning out my protest. "Shhh," Aurelius carried me easily somewhere. I recalled, still half-asleep, that he'd been vampire and had the strength of that race. He could likely toss my body halfway across the gishi fruit groves on Kifirin.

"She's still asleep," Tory said. I knew that voice. My eyes popped open. Aurelius settled me onto a chair at a table. I blinked, looking around at the informal dining area. Farzi and Nenzi watched me, expressions of hope on their faces. Tory appeared worried. Teeg, too, wore a deep frown. Ry had come with Corolan. What was Cory doing here? I thought he'd gone off with Wylend. Lok studied me with his usual, inscrutable scowl. Lendill rubbed his forehead and sighed. Kevis Halivar was sitting next to Tory, watching all of us, I think. Nefrigar was the only one missing among my mates.

"Reah and the baby are fine this morning," Aurelius sat on the chair next to mine; I was seated between him and Teeg. I knew where I was, now—the reptanoids' plantation. I'd only visited it once before, but the kitchen and dining area hadn't changed much.

"Farzi, Nenzi, your new table is very nice," I touched the wood of the table with a finger. The piece was beautiful and made of solid wood. I figured one of their brothers had shaped the wood; Chazi and Perzi were both good with their hands. Farzi and Nenzi broke into smiles that might have rivaled the sun that morning. I'd spoken to them first.

"Breakfast is coming," Teeg said. "Try not to be too critical."

"I won't," I muttered. I had no desire to destroy the happiness I saw on my reptanoid mates' faces.

"Reah stay with us," Nenzi said. "Can go anywhere on plantation. Help if she wants. We take her wherever she wants to go."

"What's ripening?" I asked as a plate of food was placed in front of me. The woman was middle-aged and smiled at me when she set the plate down. "Thank you," I said. She nodded and set out a plate for Aurelius.

"Oranges," Farzi smiled. "Lemons, too. We try pineapples this year. They come along. Avocados next month."

"I love fresh avocados," I said. I did. I liked to slice them up with a bit of salt and fresh tomatoes and eat that at times. I'd craved it with my last set of twins. Of course, nobody at the table even knew that. They'd all been elsewhere most of that time.

"We want you to rest, too, Reah. You look tired," Ry said. "Laze about. Sleep out by the pool. The weather is nice and warm out."

"If you want anything, or want to go anywhere, all you have to do is ask, baby," Tory said. I blinked at him.

"Sweetheart, your food is getting cold," Teeg called my attention to the food sitting before me.

"This is good," I said, pointing the fork at my plate. Breakfast was ham and eggs, and the eggs weren't over or undercooked, plus the ham was delicious. I wondered where it came from. "Where is the ham from? It's really good," I said, cutting another piece.

"I order it from Fizerali's," the cook was back with more plates and a basket of rolls. She'd named a popular shop in Campiaa City, where they sold cold cuts, smoked meats and specialty cuts of meat. I broke a roll apart and it was flaky and hot. "This looks promising," I said, buttering it generously and tasting it. "Yes. This is very good," I sighed with pleasure. "A little blackberry or redberry jam and this would be incredible."

"I have some," the cook was still smiling and went off to get it. I ate three rolls with redberry jam and a glass of milk.

"That was wonderful," I complimented the woman when I was too full to move. "What is your name?"

"Mathilde," she said. "If you want anything between meals, let me know."

"I will." I liked her already, and I couldn't explain that. She was a little on the plump side and seemed a good-natured soul.

"Let's get you dressed," Aurelius said, pulling me from my seat and herding me down a hall. "This will be your bedroom, unless you want to visit one of us," he added, leading me into the spacious bedroom he'd taken me from earlier. The bed had already been made up and I found clothing inside a closet.

A few things hung there that were appropriate for pregnancy, but I wasn't ready for those things yet. Garwin Wyatt was barely making his presence known. Not sure what to do except allow it, Aurelius helped me dress. Then he knelt and kissed the sensitive tops of my feet before slipping socks and shoes on. He knew what that did to me. I loved having my feet kissed. It was erotic to me. I shivered as his warm lips caressed my skin.

"Kevis says not to push, because of the attack." Aurelius was putting what happened to me in blander terms as his fingers touched my ankles before pulling up my socks. I could still see the pink marks on my shoulder where Zendeval Rjjn had sunk his canines into my skin. Greater Demons. Hah. There wasn't anything great about them.

Kifirin had made them. Just as he'd fashioned High Demons and Lesser Demons. Only everybody said that all the Lesser Demons were gone. Just as well. I hadn't fared well at all at the hands of either of the other two kinds. And Kevis? I knew I shouldn't blame him for what two of his nurses had done, but I held him accountable anyway.

Aurelius offered to carry me to the back of the plantation house where a large, curving pool lay, surrounded by multicolored flagstones that had been fitted carefully together. Lush plants in pots dotted the flagstones, with trees and other greenery surrounding the pool area, giving way to a beautiful, deep-green lawn that employees manicured weekly.

The water was pristine and sparkling in the pool, while an occasional breeze rippled the surface, making it opaque for a few seconds before releasing it to become a clear blue again. I walked, refusing Aurelius' offer. I didn't want or need to be carried everywhere. What I needed was for the holes in my heart to heal and go away. I felt numb most of the time. My mates had left me, for reasons I thought were my fault, only to discover recently that it hadn't been like that.

How many times over the past twenty-five years had I examined every word, conversation or action, trying to determine what it was that I'd done wrong? Now they were hovering, and I didn't know if I had anything left to give any of them. I'd written them off years ago. How was I supposed to pretend it hadn't happened? Maybe their eyes had been opened when Kifirin waved his arm, releasing whatever it was he'd done, but I hadn't been under that spell. There would be no revelation, no opening of eyes for me.

"Reah?" The last person I expected was the one to show up. Wylend Arden, former King of Karathia appeared nearby. Well, I hadn't asked him to abdicate. He'd done that on his own. And I wasn't happy to see him, either. He'd hurt me—hit me when I was at one of the lowest points of my life. And then punched me again while I was down, by telling Tory a half-truth afterward.

"I suppose you're here to tell me that Kifirin influenced your doings too?" I wasn't giving him the best or most polite of welcomes. This wasn't my home, after all. I wondered who'd invited Wylend. And his son, Griffin—the meddler, as I liked to call him—stood right behind his father. They looked very much alike, those two. Tall, brown hair, hazel eyes. Handsome, too, if you didn't despise both of them.

"Reah, I came to offer my apologies. While I realize they won't be accepted, it's something I feel compelled to do." Wylend settled on one of many plump-cushioned chairs scattered about the pool area. Aurelius, standing behind me, moved me toward a seat. Working through the urge to fling his hand away, I sat roughly six feet away from Wylend.

I wanted to tell him that he should have saved himself the trouble. Anger boiled close to the surface with me nowadays. Dangerously close. I swallowed it back as well as I could. "Wylend, there is nothing between us, now. If there ever was."

"Reah, I don't think that's true."

"You are welcome to think as you like." That was an insult, as far as I was concerned. I hadn't been welcome to think as I liked. Wylend had taken my thoughts and words and used them against me. Wyatt, Wylend's heir at the time, wanted to be a healer. Wylend wanted him to step up and be the warlock he desired. My privately voiced opinion had been that Rylend would be the King Karathia deserved. Wylend had written me off and revoked my short-lived Karathian citizenship over it, then went straight to Tory, telling him I'd thought him immature during my first pregnancy—the one that had ended early and in disaster. Apology or not, Wylend had destroyed something fragile between us—trust.

"Reah, I have lived a very long time. I know the intent behind those words. You are correct. You were young and trusting then, and I took full advantage of it, with my age and cynicism. I have paid a heavy price for that." I didn't respond to his words, turning to his son, Griffin, instead.

"Have you found Amara?" I asked.

"No." I hunched my shoulders at his one-word answer.

"I'm sorry," I said. And I was. They'd been together for more than a hundred thousand years. It had taken Wyatt's death to break them up. Then another thought hit me. Did he know that Garwin Wyatt rested in my womb? That Wyatt was returning, as my child? Likely he did. He was the Oracle, after all. "I won't be giving this one up," I stared at him, my anger coming to the fore.

"I know that as well as anyone," Griffin's well-shaped hand went into a pocket of his trousers. "Someone has already come to talk to me about it. I know this doesn't mean anything to you, but I'm grateful."

"For what?" I didn't understand at all.

"That he'll come to someone who will provide love and guidance. Someone I can trust."

I must have gaped at him. I must have. Did I believe him? I couldn't get my truth meter to work on any of the Saa Thalarr.

"I can't lie," he said. "I'm prevented."

"Are you upsetting my patient?" Kevis Halivar came to sit on a chair between Wylend and me.

"I probably am. My timing isn't the best, where Reah is concerned," Wylend murmured.

"Did you ever, even for a moment, really love me?" I asked, standing up. I could still skip away, but that question had bothered me for a very long time. I kept telling myself that he couldn't and didn't. If he had, how could he have done what he did? Shortly after Wylend had dumped me, there followed twenty-five years of being mostly ignored by my other mates, unless they wanted something from me. I brushed off the back of my slacks, although the cushions on my chair were clean. It was a habit, a gesture. Something to do while I waited for an answer, as painful or embarrassing as it might be.

"I did. But I let things interfere. Sabotaged it from beginning to end," Wylend said. "And then allowed something stupid to end it for all time."

"You were looking for an excuse," I said. "Doctor Halivar, your nurses laughed at me when I said I skipped. I'm skipping now." I disappeared, even as he rose and shouted my name.

"Reah, what are you doing?"

"What does it look like?" I was trimming back branches on gishi fruit trees in EastStar's groves. Someone had seen me and apparently reported it immediately to Edward Pendley, the owner.

"You were only taken away from here yesterday by your husband, Teeg San Gerxon." Edward watched as I cut through a branch and tossed it into a neat pile. Cutting back would enable the tree to bear better for the next harvest.

"He's not the only husband I have. Weren't you paying attention?" I looked for other branches that might need pruning.

"It sounds like you're not happy with all of them."

"I'm not."

"Reah, what are you?" Edward's arms were crossed over his chest.

"High Demon."

"Ah."

"You've heard of them?"

"I have."

"Tell me what you are. There's no way a mortal would have disappeared like that, to take care of a fire five clicks away."

"Ah, that." Edward lifted a hand and rubbed the back of his neck uncomfortably. "Have you ever heard of the Elemaiya?" His hazel eyes peered at me through dark lashes.

"Yes." I looked at him in surprise. I knew what happened to them, that was certain. Queen Lissa had removed their power and prevented them from gating between worlds.

"I was brought here," he said. "I'm half. Actually, a little more than half. It's a long story," he tossed up a hand. "I was spending time, gating from world to world, doing this and that, when I got stuck here. The gates wouldn't work any longer. So I put down roots and started planting the groves at someone else's suggestion. Then bought more land and planted more trees. My grove is the second oldest on Avendor. Before, gishi fruit grew on trees in jungles and the locals sold the fruit to passing tourists. Now, things are different." He fingered a dark-green leaf thoughtfully.

"Would you like to meet the person who closed the gates?" I asked. "She did it because the Elemaiya got a little out of hand. Now there's not a lot of them left." I examined his face as he blinked at me in shock.

"You know who closed them?"

"Yeah," I shrugged. "Come on, I'll take you to her. It's not like her sons won't track me down eventually anyway."

"Her sons?"

"Long story. Come on. Maybe I can fix something to eat in her kitchen while she explains all of this to you." I grabbed his arm and skipped both of us to Le-Ath Veronis.

"She'll be here in a minute; the Council meeting is just breaking up," Drew gave me a grin. Lissa had the best Falchani, as far as I was concerned.

"Where are we?" Edward hissed as I led him toward Lissa's kitchen. I didn't even know who worked in it any more.

"You're in the palace in Lissia," I said. "On Le-Ath Veronis."

"The vampire planet?" Edward stopped dead still.

"What are you worried about?" I asked, stopping with him.

"They uh, wanted to turn somebody I know, once upon a time," he muttered. "Someone of my race."

"I think they're past that," I said, throwing out a hand in a dismissive gesture. "Come on, Lissa will pound somebody's head if they look at you wrong."

"You're sure? And her name is Lissa?"

"I am, and yes, her name is Lissa." I gave him an encouraging smile. "Besides, this is keeping me away from a counseling session with the good Doctor Halivar." I couldn't help but feel gleeful over that. "Are you hungry?" I dragged Edward with me until we reached the kitchen.

"This is wonderful," Edward sighed after eating nearly all the crepe I'd served him.

"I have a Master Cook's license," I reminded him.

"You said that. Now I believe it," he said. I heard footsteps and voices approaching and was prepared to make more crepes when several things happened. Lissa drew in a breath when she saw Edward. Flavio, Head of the Vampire Council, stared in shock and Edward stared at the third member of their party before whispering, "Winkler?"

Winkler was grinning like a fool and slapping Edward on the back for some reason, and Lissa was just staring.

"So. I get to explain how we're related and all." She studied Edward for several seconds.

"Can you get him home? He owns EastStar Groves on Avendor. I ought to get back to Campiaa before the herd calls out the dogs." I watched as several emotions crossed Lissa's face. She hadn't expected this, I could tell.

"Reah, you really should let them know where you're going when you leave," Lissa did a little sighing of her own.

"I know. But nowadays they tend to piss me off." I'd borrowed that phrase from her.

"I know this is hard for you." Lissa brushed a stray strand of hair away from my forehead.

"After all these years, I just feel numb. I don't know if I love any of them. I can't feel anything."

"Honey, that will go away. It'll take some time, I know, after what happened to you on Stellar Winds. Don't give up on them. Kifirin was wrong to do what he did."

"Why did he do that? Why?" I was about to break down.

"We'll take her." Teeg, Lok and Aurelius had come. "Come on, sweetheart. Let's go home," Teeg lifted me this time.

"I'll make sure Mr. Pendley gets home," Lissa called out before someone folded me away.

～

Lissa's Journal

"I'm your great-uncle?" Edward Pendley stared at me. He was younger than I, but as immortals, that wasn't surprising.

"And you have family still living. Someday, if you're up to it, I'll make introductions." I was struggling to come to terms with this—Ashe had a half-brother. If I knew Ashe at all (and I didn't know him well—he kept to himself) he probably knew all about this. His—and Edward's—biological mother, my great-grandmother, actually, was still alive, as was my half-Elemaiyan grandmother. I still hadn't told them we were kin. It made me sigh—I wasn't sure I was up to that, even now.

"I see I have a lot of catching up to do," Edward shook his head. Winkler and I sat in Edward's private study at EastStar, talking about how things had gone since Edward had left Earth. My werewolf and I had taken Edward home after he explained that he couldn't be gone for long from EastStar. Edward couldn't believe he had other relatives still living, either. His mostly-human father was still alive, but couldn't pass the boundary of SouthStar. I did (and didn't) want to ask about that. "Tell me about Reah," Edward pleaded. I considered where to begin.

～

I jerked awake with a gasp, just as I normally did nowadays. "Nothing here to hurt you," Kevis Halivar soothed. I wanted to accuse him of lying. Danger was everywhere, including with his nurses, who were now under arrest. He'd attempted to talk with me as soon as Teeg brought me back and dumped me on a chair by the pool next to the good doctor. Instead of answering questions, somehow I'd fallen asleep.

"Zendeval Rjjn appeared benign, too, until he did what he did."

"Reah, you are in a safe place. Nobody is here to harm you."

"I don't know why you're here," I huffed. "Go back to that expensive clinic and treat the rich and famous."

"You don't think you're as important as they are?"

"Most of them are decidedly unimportant," I snapped. "But try telling them and their fame and fortune that."

"While the one who saved them and both Alliances sits here and tells me to go back to them," Kevis murmured softly.

"They all think I'm crazy," I said. "Thanks to your nurses and a not so law-abiding reality show."

"You and I know better."

"Like that's so important and all. I can't even go to the corner store and get ice cream without somebody pointing and either laughing or screaming."

"You think so? Let's test that theory," Kevis said, standing up. "Let's go out for ice cream."

Nenzi drove us with Tory, Lok and Aurelius along for the ride. Nenzi stood very close to me, too, as I walked into a popular ice-cream shop in Campiaa City to order a dish of ice cream. Sure enough, two mothers saw me and moved their children away while the young man behind the counter gulped and stared.

"Point taken," Kevis said as we walked out again, ice cream in hand.

"Teeg will have to get another wife," I said, licking my spoon.

"Reah, he will not stand for that sort of talk," Aurelius chided. "That is his child, you are his wife. That is the end of this discussion."

"You saw those women back there," I said, turning to look at him as we climbed into our vehicle. Nenzi had a very nice hover-limo. I was happy for him; the vehicle was quite luxurious. "They were afraid to let their children get near me," I added.

"Reah, that will die down in time," Kevis said.

"When? Will I be able to take my own child out and not have people shy away?"

"People have short memories," Lok said.

"Oh, and the Falchani speaks," I tossed up a hand.

"Reah, they are angry too, because they were forced to forget you," Kevis said.

"Oh, so you're on board with the whole Kifirin thing now, are you?"

"I've been informed," he said.

Nenzi unloaded us at the front drive to the plantation before pulling away. I felt a sting in my left shoulder and that's the last thing I remembered for a while.

CHAPTER 4

"An ancient weapon." Gavril tossed the bullet onto the table in front of the others.

"I haven't seen one of these for a very long time," Aurelius picked up the piece of copper-encased lead and examined it closely. Norian and Lendill had agents all over the plantation, but there was no sign of the shooter.

"Someone wants to kill Reah," Gavril said flatly.

"Could be anyone. Someone who didn't die or get captured when the pirates, the Schuuls and their cronies went down," Lok said, taking the projectile from Aurelius.

"They were likely aiming for her heart," Tory muttered angrily. "I don't think for a moment they only intended to wound."

"And they were likely following a trail, started by those two women at the clinic," Gavril agreed. "A few well-placed questions and here we are. If I could kill them," his eyes were beginning to turn red.

"Child, calm yourself, you will not do Reah or the baby any good by contemplating the murder of idiots," Dee said.

"The Larentii has placed a shield around the plantation for two clicks in every direction," Lendill and Norian walked into the plantation's kitchen. "How is Reah doing?"

"Karzac, Kevis and Renegar are tending her now. She didn't lose much blood since Nefrigar showed up so quickly. Here's the bullet." Gavril held it out to Lendill.

"I don't think I've seen one of these since I started working for the ASD nearly two hundred years ago," Lendill said, turning the bullet in his fingers.

"We not find anything," Farzi reported. He, Nenzi and their six brothers trooped in. They'd all gone to lion snake and went out looking that way. Norian actually smiled. He figured that if they'd found the culprit, whomever it was would have been bitten quickly.

"Do we keep her here or move her?" Lendill asked.

"I don't like the idea of moving her," Gavril objected. "The Larentii has protected the plantation, and we can place guards here just as easily as anywhere else."

"We'll keep her here, then, but what if she skips away?" Aurelius had already seen her skip earlier.

"We'll have to impress upon her how dangerous that is," Ry appeared with his usual entourage of Corolan and Erland.

"Why don't you do that? I don't think she's as angry with you as the rest of us." Tory was definitely depressed. "I asked Raedah and Tara to come, but the moment their husbands heard that Reah was a target, they refused to consider it."

"Typical," Lok grumbled.

"All is well," Renegar walked in, ducking slightly to get through the kitchen doorway.

"Lands, is that?" Mathilde stared up at him.

"Yes," Renegar smiled, his white teeth a contrast against sky-blue skin.

"I never thought to see one," Mathilde laughed and clapped her hands.

"You have now seen two." Nefrigar appeared at Renegar's side. "My thanks," he nodded to Ren. "I was too angry to tend her properly."

"Understandable," Ren agreed. "I will come again if needed."

Nefrigar nodded gratefully to the other Larentii, who disappeared.

"Can we see her now?" Gavril asked.

"She is sleeping, but yes," Nefrigar said. The kitchen cleared out.

"I've placed a healing sleep and she's come out of it twice, so Renegar placed the last one," Karzac informed everyone who'd walked quietly into Reah's room.

~

A moan woke me. It took several ticks to determine it was my own. A hand stroked my face gently. I didn't want to open my eyes. "Hungry, my little beauty? Thirsty?" The voice wasn't immediately recognizable. "It doesn't matter. We'll get there, someday." The fingers were warm against my skin. "I'll be back," the voice told me softly. I slept again.

"Reah? Love, wake now. You should eat." This time I recognized the voice. Lok. An arm was slipped behind my shoulders and I was lifted into a sitting position while someone else placed pillows behind my back. My eyes finally opened. Lok's black eyes were peering worriedly into mine. "Thank the stars," he sighed. "Love, you need to eat. You've slept the clock through."

"I don't feel good," I lifted my right hand and laid it across my belly.

"Get her head down," Doctor Halivar arrived and handed out orders. My head was bent as low as they could get it. "Breathe, Reah. Deep breaths," Kevis instructed. I did that until the nausea went away. "Better," Kevis said. "We have broth here. Try to drink as much as you can." I felt helpless as Lok held the small bowl up and let me sip from it. Falchani did that all the time—sipping from bowls. Doing so was a great time-saver.

"There," Lok caressed my face after I'd consumed half of what they'd brought to me.

"You look pale," Kevis said. "If you get hungry, or want anything to drink, let us know. The wound is healed, thanks to Renegar, but you'll be weak for a couple of days."

"Ren was here?" I was unconscious and hadn't seen him. I barely remembered Nefrigar coming.

"He was here," Kevis smiled. *Smiled*. The sun might rise in the west, next.

"I love Ren," I sighed, flopping my head back on the pillow.

"He knows," Kevis was still smiling.

"Good. Who shot me, and with what?"

"You should not worry over such things at the moment. Get your strength back and tell Kevis what is wrong." Lok blinked black eyes at me.

"You have such a nice mouth," I said, reaching up with my right hand to touch it. He kissed my fingers.

"Everything about my Reah is perfect," he replied, leaning in to kiss my forehead, too. "Do what the doctor tells you, snowcat. We want you back soon."

"You know, I'm not even going to argue with you about that."

"Good. I love you. I just inconveniently forgot that for a while. Rest, love. Perhaps you will eat dinner with us later." Lok walked out of my bedroom, leaving me alone with Kevis Halivar.

"I was contemplating bringing in a nurse for you, and then had second thoughts," he held up a hand as I started to protest. "Even if it were the best and most trustworthy person in either Alliance, you would still be upset and unduly worried."

"Nobody ever listens to me," I grumped. "I told you after I skipped away from your clinic the first time that your nurse was a problem. Did you listen? Of course not."

"I know now I should have paid more attention. But you have to realize that most of my patients aren't the most lucid or accurate. I hear complaints from them often."

"If any of the complaints had to do with Ceerah, then they were probably valid complaints." I watched as Kevis Halivar settled himself on a chair beside my bed. He wore an expensive, green knit shirt that went well with his eyes, and khaki slacks with carefully placed creases. His shoes, too, would have cost at least a thousand credits. He looked very tailored and likely perfect if he were about to have a session with one of his wealthy clients. I wasn't one of those. As Ceerah had so aptly put it, I was a charity case, dressed in cotton pajama bottoms and a thin-strapped stretchy shirt.

"Now," Kevis said, settling himself and pulling out a comp-vid to take notes, "tell me about your childhood." I laughed. Not because it was humorous, but because it was so typical. My shoulder ached by the time I stopped laughing. "That wasn't quite the reaction I was hoping for," Kevis observed, unruffled by my outburst.

"I think Lendill still has all my old health records," I said. "Get those from him. That should tell you everything you may want to know about my childhood," I said. "All the visits to the hospital emergency service and all the broken bones are listed, likely with a few other notes and observations. He used those notes to help convict Edan and Marzi Desh."

"I understand Marzi is dead now. She was sent to Evensun and died shortly after her second attempt on your life. How does that make you feel?"

"How is it supposed to make me feel? I have no idea what her motives were," I stared at Kevis, taking in the impersonal expression in his green-gold eyes. His mouth might have tightened a little, but I didn't know him well enough to understand what that meant.

"You don't have any guess as to her motives? Or Edan's?"

"No. I don't know why I was beaten when I was young. Marzi may have goaded Edan, but I felt he took pleasure in the abuse. Was Marzi jealous of my mother? She pretty much admitted that. But I was no rival for Addah's affection, and absolutely no threat to Edan, either; he was slated to inherit at the time. Why don't you track him down now and ask? I understand he still holds vague memories of that other Edan."

"But you can't even despise him now for what he did to you, because he isn't the same. You can't work your way to forgiveness, either, because this one has done nothing to forgive."

"No. I can't. Now he gives his work away, helping children who can't afford medical care. He isn't the one who did all those things to me."

"So, the one who abused you will never pay or apologize. Not that you'll see, anyway."

"Kifirin said he spent several lifetimes doing that, but you're right, I'll never see it for myself. Go ahead, put impotent rage in your notes."

"Reah, stop telling me how to proceed with my work."

"Sure. I feel so comfortable, knowing I'm your job. Your only job."

"I made that choice. It was mine to make. If the original Edan were here, what would you say to him?"

"Get out."

"That's it?"

"Get out or I'll throw you out?"

"And would you? Throw him out, that is?"

"Yes. I could throw him out easily. Would throw him out, if he didn't go willingly. He and I have nothing in common, except the abuse."

"When is the last time you saw your father?"

"The current Edan?"

"Yes."

"Probably four moon-turns ago, when he came with my daughters and Karzac, to treat the disabled on Kifirin. They provided care regularly because I couldn't afford a doctor on what the Crown paid."

"Do you talk much with your father?"

"Not usually; there isn't much time for that. I cooked for them when they came, as payment for their work."

"Would you talk to him if he came here? If he walked through the door now, could you have a conversation?"

I had to think about that for a while. "Probably not," I said. "We don't have a lot in common."

"Who do you have something in common with, Reah? Who could sit down with you now and laugh and talk about anything or nothing? Who would make you feel at ease when they walked through the door, knowing that they would support you as a family member, friend or lover should? Who would that be, Reah?"

I sorted through everyone I knew. "Nobody," I said eventually. "I don't trust any of them that way. They all walked away from me, and I spent years trying to determine what I'd done wrong to make that happen. Those doors were closed after a while. Nobody holds my trust, now."

"Even your daughters?"

"My daughters barely know me. They couldn't tell you if you asked what my favorite meal is, or what I like to wear, even. But they'd be able to answer those questions and more about Jayd and Glinda." I stared past Kevis and through the window of my bedroom. A miniature orange tree grew right outside, surrounded by a mulched ring and then flowers around that.

"Do you know what their favorite things are?"

"I made their favorite meals—the ones they asked for, on all their birthdays, including the cakes. Of course I know. And I always got to see the latest thing that Jayd and Glinda bought for them to wear or the music they listened to or the way they wanted their rooms decorated."

"None of that was under your control. Did they ask, ever, what you thought? Jayd and Glinda, or Garde?"

"Very seldom was I asked for input, and then it was only a formality. Decisions were never placed solely in my hands." My fingers were twisting in my lap. "Garde chose the finishing schools for all of them. The most I pushed was to get Raedah and Tara into medical school, because that was what they wanted. Garde argued that when they got husbands, they wouldn't need a profession."

"That sounds somewhat archaic."

"Welcome to Kifirin," smoke curled from my nostrils.

"Does that happen when you're angry?" Kevis noted the smoke and was tapping notes into the comp-vid.

"Yes. More so with the males. I've never seen Glinda blow smoke, but Jayd keeps her placated and happy most of the time."

"Sounds like a common theme with High Demon males in their relationships with High Demon females."

"Except for this one."

"Except for this one." He nodded, repeating my words as he tapped more notes into the comp-vid.

"I think I want to go out for a bit," I said, sliding off the bed.

"I don't recommend it, and our session isn't over."

"It's over," I said, walking toward the door.

~

The workers never said a word as I grabbed a crate and started picking oranges. The fruit was large, the pebbled skin smooth in my hands as I expertly gathered it and set it atop layers of dividers, filling each tray before setting another one inside the crate and repeating the process. Just as with the gishi fruit, filled crates were left at the edge of the row for a hovertruck to gather. I wasn't really dressed to work in the groves and my bare feet might have been a giveaway. Farzi was walking beside me after a while.

"Reah, you get injured yesterday. Why you here today? Let me take you back."

"Honey Snake," I said, "this is better therapy right now than what Doctor Halivar was doing."

"Where your shoes?" He was staring at my feet. Likely at my pajamas, too. I really wasn't dressed to do what I was doing.

"At the house," I said, answering Farzi's question. I'd skipped out to the orange groves without bothering to grab any footwear. Now, my soles were covered in dirt. I didn't have a hoverstep, but it wasn't needed with the oranges.

"Reah," Farzi took my face in his hands. "Something bothers you. We all know this. We want it to leave. We want to lie with you. Hold onto you. Say how we feel. Say how angry we are that we were treated bad. And treated you bad, too."

"Farzi, I don't know how long that will take, or if it's possible, even." I wasn't looking into his eyes any longer. I couldn't. Concern as well as pain lay in those honey-brown depths.

"My beautiful Reah." Farzi pulled me against him and stroked my hair. "So fragile," he murmured, kissing the top of my head. "Let me take you home," he sighed, his breath stirring hair at my temple. "Car close," he whispered, stroking my jaw with a thumb. I allowed him to lift and carry me the distance to his small hovercar. They owned many of those; the vehicles ran between rows of trees easily and didn't interfere with the picking.

"There you are," Tory was waiting with Aurelius when Farzi

parked in front of the large plantation house. The spacious home consisted of two stories, and was built of field stone covered with whitewashed stucco. Many tall windows lined the front and the plantation was beautifully landscaped. The reptanoids certainly had good taste in architecture and landscaped grounds.

"Come, we wash feet," Farzi was herding me, an arm around my waist, toward the house.

"Reah, what the hell were you doing?" Tory blew a cloud of smoke as he crossed his arms tightly over his chest and glared disapprovingly at me. I wondered where the good doctor was; here was a male High Demon venting his anger.

"Picking oranges, but that was before. Now I'm picking a fight with you, apparently." I brushed off Farzi's embrace and stalked past all three of them.

"Don't upset her," I heard Aurelius say as I tiptoed through the house. I didn't want to scatter dirt on expensive area rugs. The reptanoids had employees who cleaned and cooked, but I didn't want to make their jobs harder.

"You should probably wear shoes next time," Kevis said dryly as he found me toweling off my freshly washed feet later.

"Like you wouldn't have tried to stop me from going if I'd waited to find shoes," I snapped.

"I wouldn't have, but I'd have tried to talk you out of it. You're still weak. Tell me; your shoulder hurts now, doesn't it?"

"Yes, it hurts. Don't be an ass about it," I said, dropping the towel onto the edge of an octagonal tub inside my bath.

"You get so defensive," he said.

"Where's your comp-vid?" I asked sarcastically. "Doesn't that need to go in your notes?"

"Already there," he said, smugness in his expression.

"Of course it is," I agreed. "Get out."

"Are you going to throw me out?"

"You're not even worth the effort," I said, skipping away.

I didn't go far; only to the pool. The water was cool and I still felt cold, so I wasn't going in. The spa beckoned, its hot water frothing in the late morning sun, but I was pregnant. Pregnant women shouldn't get into heated water like that. It made me sigh at the injustices in my life. It wouldn't hurt to put my feet in it, though, and that's what I did. Rolling my pants legs up, I dropped to the edge, set my feet into the water and kicked them gently, mesmerized by the water jetting around my legs.

"At least you know not to get in," Kevis settled beside me.

"You don't think I have an active brain cell in my skull, do you?" I glared at him. He muffled a snicker. Leaving my legs in the water, I lay back on the flagstones and stared up at the sky. A few fluffy, white clouds floated by.

"It may rain tonight," Kevis said, lying back beside me.

"Now you're the weather predictor?"

"I have an eighty-seven percent accuracy rating."

"Damn, you are in the wrong business." My words made him laugh out loud.

"Tell me about the ASD," he said when the chuckling stopped.

"What about it?"

"What did you think of working for them?"

"Lendill and Norian?"

"Just in general."

"Did you know that insects and small animals are afraid of High Demons?" I asked, avoiding his question. "I once captured a criminal as he was running through a sewer, trying to get away. The rats were running ahead of me because they were afraid, and they ended up tripping the guy. He was screaming while a thousand rats ran across his back."

"Does it bother you that rats and insects are afraid of you?"

"No. Too bad a few humanoids don't react the same way."

"I hear you were shot a few times while working for the ASD."

"Yeah. And blown up once. Teeg was trying to kill Zellar. I was collateral damage on that one."

"You two have some history."

"You have no idea. Feel free to ask him about that," I said.

"And this is his." Kevis reached out to stroke my belly. Lying down like that, it was almost flat, still. "I hear you won't call him by his given name."

"That person is gone. Teeg is all that's left."

"What happened to the Reah that knew Gavril?"

"Gone, too, I suppose. That Reah trusted him. Trusted other people, too. All that's in the past."

"Pull your feet out of the water, Reah. They've cooked long enough," Kevis said. I lifted my feet out obediently, the flagstones feeling cold beneath them as I settled them there.

"Now, would you like to lie down on a bed or do you want to continue lying on hard stone?" Kevis turned his eyes to mine. He was lying quite close, I'd just ignored him while I examined the sky. I saw that his lashes were long and dark—something that most women would love to have.

"I'm going to ask Farzi if he'll buy a hammock," I said, sitting up. "It's warmer out here."

"Do you feel cold?"

"Yes. A little. It's warmer on Kifirin's Southern Continent. I suppose I'm used to that." I turned back to examining the sky.

"Come along. You're tired and you know it. Let's get you in the bath and then bed. You can sleep after we bring you something to eat." He rose, dusted off his designer slacks and then pulled me up. The doctor had his priorities, after all.

"You want to ask us questions?" Jayd stared at Kevis, who sat inside the King's private study, comp-vid in hand.

"I do. I want to get your perspective on all this, regarding Reah." Kevis had a determined look on his face. At that moment, he looked very much like his father.

"What do you want to know?" Glinda, sitting in a chair near Jayd, asked. Raedah, Tara, Lara and Kara sat on a sofa off to the side. Lara's High Demon husband had grumbled when she'd been asked to come to the palace and speak with the doctor.

"I'd like to direct these first questions to Reah's daughters," Kevis said. He had their immediate attention. "Can any one of you tell me what your mother's favorite food is, or what kind of jewelry she likes?"

All four of them looked at one another. Kevis waited patiently. Glinda frowned, Jayd stared at his hands.

"Perhaps you can tell me what your Aunt Glinda likes to eat, or what kind of jewelry she prefers." The answers were swift in coming.

"Aunt Glinda likes noodles in a sauce that Mom makes, and her jewelry has to be small and tasteful," they all agreed with Raedah's statement. "We just flunked a test, didn't we?" Raedah asked.

"Why wasn't I asked to this meeting?" Garde appeared, angrily blowing smoke.

"I wanted to question you separately, but since you are here now, invited or not," Kevis nodded in Garde's direction.

"He's asking us how well we know Mom," Raedah sighed. "We're not doing that well on the answers."

"What did he ask?" Garde crossed arms over his chest defensively.

"What Mom's favorite foods are, or what kind of jewelry she likes. We didn't know," Tara said. "But we know what Aunt Glinda likes."

"And what Uncle Jayd likes, and what you like, Grampa," Raedah said.

"Now, look at these photographs. Which chin is your mother's," Kevis handed three photographs to Reah's daughters first. There followed a heated discussion over this photograph or that. The results were inconclusive, there was no clear consensus on what Reah's chin looked like. One chin in the photographs had been round, another pointed, a third more square-like.

"Let me see that," Jayd rose to take the photographs. He and Glinda pored over them for a while. "I think either the square or the rounded one," Jayd flipped through the photographs several times.

"But you don't know." Kevis pointed out.

"No," Jayd sighed, tossing the photographs onto his desk. "I don't."

"Was it our fault, or did Kifirin do this?" Lara asked.

"I think it may be a combination of the two."

"And it's too late, isn't it? We should have gone when our father asked us after Mom was hurt. But we didn't." Raedah sounded ashamed.

"I don't know what to say about that," Kevis replied. "Either you care for her or you don't. If you don't, then I ask that you don't hurt her further."

"I don't know if it's possible to take back twenty-five years of neglect," Glinda sighed. "And any move we make might be perceived with suspicion."

"Yes. She is very distrustful."

"She doesn't need any of us." Kevis jerked his head in Gardevik's direction.

"Why do you say that?" Kevis turned green-gold eyes on the eldest of the House of Rath.

"Because it's true. She has skills that will support her anywhere. She doesn't have to rely on us for anything."

"Does that bother you?"

"It does." Garde tossed up a hand in frustration, turning his back on everyone in the room to stare through Jayd's huge window—the one overlooking the city of Veshtul.

"I think she needed love. From all of you. Did you fail her?" Kevis stood and pocketed his comp-vid. "By the way, that delicately pointed chin is hers. You'd have known it if you recognized the beautiful, alabaster skin." Kevis folded away from Kifirin.

"I don't think I've ever seen a photograph of Mom," Kara pulled the pictures to her to take another look.

"Child, I'm afraid I have bad news," Kaldill Schaff glanced worriedly at his youngest son. Lendill, after folding to Gaelar N'Seith, had sat down for a quiet meal with his father, the King of the Elves. Lendill held the title of Prince-Heir now, and had a standing invitation for dinner with his father whenever he wasn't busy with ASD business.

"What's the bad news, Dad?" Lendill seldom used any affectionate term for Kaldill Schaff.

"I'm afraid," Kaldill's green eyes were troubled as he pushed shoulder-length golden hair behind a pointed ear, "that your two oldest brothers are out to cause harm."

"What? I thought they were held inside Gaelar N'Seith."

"I removed Naldill's power so he couldn't go anywhere, but as usual, Reldill, ever willing to come at Naldill's command, has taken his brother out of the confines of the Elven lands. They took the shot at Reah, child. If Reldill had relied on power instead of his skill with the weapon, she might have taken a mortal blow from that stupid thing. It was something from Naldill's collection of archaic weaponry. Now that they know the Larentii has placed a shield around that farm on Campiaa, they have taken themselves off to cause other kinds of harm. They think to get back at us and Reah in this way."

"They blame Reah?" Lendill's dark eyes held worry, which in turn worried his father.

"They do. I should never have mentioned her when I named you Prince-Heir," Kaldill admitted sadly. "She is responsible for removing the spell that Naldill placed upon you. I should have done it myself, but when Reah came along, I knew she would accomplish the same without interference from me. So I allowed it. Now, she is a target. Their target. As are you and anyone else who might get in their way. They know they will never have the Kingship; I have locked them out of it. But they think to have their revenge this way. They never learned this lesson, Lendill. The one where they realize that petty revenge serves no useful purpose. Things come to us that will."

"Father, that petty revenge could have killed Reah. What should we do? Shall I go after them? Haul them back here and lock them away?"

"You are Prince-Heir, Lendill. What would you do if they weren't your brothers?"

"Go after them and press charges. Likely remove Reldill's power so he can't do harm in the future. Send them to Evensun, perhaps."

"Then you must do what you must, according to Alliance law. Perhaps it is time that our people realize that they are citizens of the

Alliance, just as all the other inhabitants are. We were here first, before Ildevar Wyyld ever thought to set foot on the planet and create the Alliance with twenty others of his kind. And since we allowed him to settle here and then watched while he and the others built the Alliance from nothing, we have an obligation now to join with it and uphold its laws. They are generally just, those laws. And I am proud that my son has helped keep those laws in place and weeded out corruption over the years. I am most proud of you, child."

"I didn't think you felt that way for the longest time, Father. I thought you only tolerated me because you loved my mother."

"I did love your mother. Still do, although she is gone from me. But she left you with me, son. The one who always looked for justice. The one who sought the truth, always. Naldill always looked to his comforts, depending upon Reldill to act as his army at times, punishing those he thought offended him. If he had changed his ways at any time, or looked upon the people here as his kin and not his subjects, I might have considered him as my replacement. I waited a very long time for that to happen. I tired of it, as you know. I picked the best of my four sons to take my place. Never doubt my love for you, child. I know I put you through the fire and I apologize for that."

"Father, you don't know how hard it was to deal with that from my end. I can't tell you how many times I thought about cutting myself off from you and Gaelar N'Seith. Whenever Naldill would taunt me about this or that, usually about my lack of power, I considered it."

"I'm glad you stayed the course, child. Perhaps you will forgive me someday for allowing those things to happen."

"It made me more determined that Alliance citizens should be protected, father. There was a benefit, I think, although I suffered through it."

"You have a generous heart, child."

"Father, Reah has the generous heart. She could have skipped away from Kifirin at any time during the past twenty-five years, leaving them to struggle. She paid off a crushing debt to get them on their feet, and they rewarded her by taking her children and dumping more work on her shoulders. I don't even want to talk about my part in all of that. And I begged her, Father, to allow that bastard to attack her so we'd get the information we needed. And then, when all the power went down, we couldn't even get troops in there to help her. She was on her own until the very last, and took them down by herself. They kept attacking her, even when they knew it was useless to do so. Fired rockets at her. Bombarded her. She was pregnant, and they did that."

Lendill surprised himself with the wetness on his cheeks. "She kept all those girls safe, fighting to keep the army Nedrizif controlled from killing all of them. We haven't even paid her for that. How can we compensate for that, Dad? How? What we planned to pay her is paltry and an insult. Ildevar has promised half the confiscated funds from the pirates, but we're still working on getting all that put together."

"I understand that Torevik has promised half of the Schuul's holdings as well. Has he handed that over to her yet?"

"No. She's getting treatment by a doctor since she tried to kill herself. I'm not sure she's cooperating with him at all."

"Son, his nurses betrayed her. What can you expect? I watched that vid and wept. Imagine if you'd been in a session, claiming to be Vice-Director of the ASD and Prince-Heir of the Elves, talking about your torture at the hands of your brothers. Imagine what people might think if they saw it on that foolish program. You'd be ridiculed as well."

"I know." Lendill squared his shoulders uncomfortably, trying to shake off the images of Reah's exposure on Alliance vid programming.

"I am glad I did not witness the near-suicide," it was Kaldill's turn to shiver.

"I don't know what to do for her," Lendill went on. "She could reject all of us. That's the way things are looking right now. She hasn't come to any one of us. Asked us for anything."

"What do you think she might want, Son?"

"Probably for the past twenty-five years to not have happened."

"I need someone who will care for her. Not someone to feel jealousy or treat her badly or with indifference. And I don't know who that is," Kevis held his head in his hands as he sat in his father's study. Karzac sat behind his desk, located in the southeastern corner of the villa where he and his extended family of mates and co-mates lived. Kevis was Karzac's only son, born to Karzac and Grace, one of Karzac's three mates. Kevis wanted to find a nurse and assistant for Reah, but there weren't any candidates.

"What about Franklin?" Lissa appeared in Karzac's study, something she seldom did. "I wish I could get the old Franklin back. She'd trust him, I think, and he wouldn't appear threatening at all."

"I don't think we should mislead her, she's had too much of that," Kevis sighed. "Will Frank even consider it? We don't need someone who is only doing it because they feel sorry for her or obligated to any one of us for any reason. This person has to genuinely care about her and what happens to her. She needs a gentle touch from someone who isn't interested in sex. Someone neutral that she might come to trust."

"Let's take all the healers in while she's asleep, and see if any one of them feels a connection," Karzac suggested. "And if they don't, then we'll look elsewhere."

"Let's gather all of them and let them know what we're dealing with," Kevis agreed.

CHAPTER 5

"Belen has given permission to try this," Karzac announced to all the healers for the Saa Thalarr. "This is a delicate situation, as you might imagine. Reah is pregnant, a recent victim of an attack on Stellar Winds and an attempted suicide not long after that. Kevis is currently treating her, but he needs an assistant. Someone who might feel a bond with Reah in some way. We're going to take you to her while she's sleeping so we won't upset her. If you don't want to be a part of this, then you'll be excused. We want a healer who is willing to walk a few extra miles for someone who more than deserves the time and trouble."

"We'll go," Cleo spoke for all present.

"Then let's go," Karzac said. They folded to Campiaa.

"She's pregnant? She's so frail," Cleo said.

"Has she lost weight? She's very thin," Jeff remarked.

"There's no color in her cheeks," Norton pointed out. Nefrigar had come, making sure Reah was in a healing sleep before allowing any of the healers to touch her. Blankets were lifted back, ankles, feet, hands, heart and the recent bullet wound were examined. Nearly all of them placed their hands on Reah's belly, checking on the child. The child was healthy; Reah's health wasn't nearly as good.

"What problems are you encountering?" Franklin asked Kevis.

"She's defensive and argues with me at times. Not that she doesn't have cause," Kevis held up a hand.

"And she's a cook, too?"

"Probably the best I've ever seen."

"I think I'd like to try," Franklin said. "Anyone else interested?"

"I'd do it if nobody else wanted to," Norton volunteered.

"As would I," Joey said.

"Why don't all three of you move in?" Gavril walked in, finding his mother, Karzac and twelve other healers in Reah's room. "She might not agree to any one of you, so you'll have to be prepared for that."

"We're up to the challenge," Joey grinned. "Besides, maybe we can distract her with video games. I've got something new I'm working on."

"And Norton and I wouldn't mind help with our sauces," Franklin smiled. He and Norton both loved to cook.

"Fine. We'll throw all three of you at her. See how she reacts," Kevis huffed out a breath. "Let's hope this works, everybody."

"It'll be fun, I haven't stayed on Campiaa since Erland owned a casino there," Joey grinned.

"Re-ahhh," the voice was soft and coaxing, almost a whisper. "Re-ahhh, dinner time."

"Go away," I moaned, unwilling to open my eyes.

"But that little baby bump is hungry, too," the voice said.

"Who are you and how would you know?" I cracked an eye open, finding a blond man leaning over my bed, grinning at me. Granted he had a nice smile, but I had no idea who he was. And that was only the beginning. Two other men stood behind him, one dark-haired and quite handsome, who had his hand on the other's shoulder. The last one had brown hair, kind eyes and was also smiling encouragingly.

"I'm Joey Showalter, healer for the Saa Thalarr," the one who woke me said. "And this is Franklin," he pointed to the dark-haired handsome one. "And this is one of my mates, Norton." He slipped an arm around the tall, brown-haired man. Joey was shorter than the other two and he was taking my hand, attempting to pull me off the bed.

"Healers for the Saa Thalarr? Do they have any left?" I quirked an eyebrow at all of them.

"They have a few," the one called Franklin assured me. "And we can always fold away if there's an emergency. Right now, we're here for you."

"That doesn't sound sufficient to warrant three healers," I grumped, sliding off the bed.

"But this is a vacation for us," Norton smiled. "So get that tiny butt of yours into some clothes and we'll go have dinner."

"Do you treat all your patients this way?" I asked, scooting around him to get to the closet.

"Only the ones with tiny butts," he laughed, following right behind me. "No, don't wear that," he pushed the brown blouse away. "This is good," he held up another. It was red. I didn't like wearing red and said so.

"But you'll look beautiful in this. It's a nice contrast to the color of your skin and hair."

"And these are too pale," Joey brushed a thumb over my right cheek. "We have to get some color back in those."

"See, you look great in that," Norton nodded when I came out of the bathroom later, fully dressed in the red blouse and gray slacks. "Shoes or just socks?" he asked.

"Socks are fine," I said, feeling overwhelmed. I couldn't recall being dressed by committee before.

"Come on, let's go see what's for dinner," Franklin grinned. We all trooped down the long hallway lined with bedrooms until we came to the dining area.

"This is an improvement," Teeg, Tory, Aurelius and Lok were there, sitting with all eight reptanoids and Doctor Halivar. Four spaces were left for us. I sat between Joey and Kevis Halivar.

"You don't have a problem with this?" I wiggled a finger at the three healers that had mysteriously shown up.

"Not at all," Kevis' mouth twitched a little, as if he were about to smile and then thought better of it.

"Hmmph," I sighed, looking up as a server set a glass of water and some fruit juice in front of me.

"I love pot roast," Joey smiled as a plate was set before him. I liked it, too, but it generally wasn't something people went to fine restaurants for. I made it for myself when I wasn't worried about cooking for others so much.

"Trade your onions for my carrots," Franklin grinned at me from his seat on Joey's other side.

"I love carrots," I said, passing my plate over. Franklin had the exchange done quickly.

"Call me Frank if you want," he passed my plate back with an extra serving of carrots instead of onions on the side.

"This is great," I smiled at the first bite. The meat was tender, the vegetables cooked just right and the gravy was wonderful. "Tell Mathilde this is amazing," I told the server, who was setting fragile gravy bowls on all four sides of the table. The server, a young man, smiled and nodded.

"See, we don't have to convince her to eat," Norton observed, cutting another bite of pot roast and stuffing it in his mouth.

"I get some time," Aurelius pulled me away from Joey, Frank and Norton right after dinner. Joey wore a disappointed look.

"I was going to show her the new video game I'm working on," he said.

"You can do that later. Reah and I are going to sit down somewhere," Aurelius said, pulling me away. I couldn't decide whether

I wanted to go with Aurelius or with Joey right then, as I was worried over what Aurelius might have to say. I blinked up at him. His shoulders were just as wide as they'd always been, his golden hair falling to brush those shoulders. Brown eyes searched my face before tucking my hand in the crook of his arm and walking me toward the back of the house.

"Farzi had these brought for you," Aurelius said, settling me onto a covered swing. A comfortable-looking hammock swung in the breeze not far away.

"That was nice of him," I said, leaning back against the cushion of the swing. The fabric covering was soft and expensive, I could tell by the feel of it.

"Reah, do you remember when we first met?" Aurelius lifted one of my hands and kissed it. He held onto it, too, when he lowered it again. I stared at his fingers entwined with mine. Of course I remembered when we met. I thought he was someone else at the time. He was posing as Commander Aris on Mandil. He'd been sent there by the Saa Thalarr to eliminate invading Ra'Ak spawn.

"I remember," I sighed, looking away from him. The sun had just gone down over Campiaa, leaving streaks of red, gold and purple on the horizon. I knew that less than fifty clicks to the west of us, the sunset would be burning over the waters of Campiaa Bay.

"The way I felt then is the way I feel now. My love is right in front of me and I can barely touch her because something stands between us. Please don't let us go, Reah. I realize that you've been treated badly for a very long time, and I wish it weren't partly my fault at some level. I should have realized something was wrong and gone to Belen or one of the others about it. I just didn't."

"What would Belen have done?" I'd only heard the light god's name a time or two. They called him a Nameless One, because to name one of his kind was impossible. He seldom made appearances, I think.

"At least he wouldn't have ignored the problem, like the rest of us did."

"Aurelius, stop trying to blame yourself for something that is mostly Kifirin's responsibility. You don't see him here, attempting to apologize, do you?"

"This has robbed all of us." Aurelius leaned down, resting his cheek on my hair.

"When did you see the girls last?" I asked. They called him Daddy. At least they had. Now that Tory was back, I'm sure they were in complete confusion.

"I went to see them this afternoon. I received mindspeech from Raedah; she was a bit upset."

"About what?"

"That neither she nor her sisters could remember what your favorite foods were, or what jewelry you liked."

"It's a little late for that now, don't you think? They're all grown." The rest of my words were unspoken. Not one of them had bothered to come visit after the Baetrah incident. That told me how important I was in their lives.

"Love, I know what you're not saying. They know it, too. We all do."

"And they haven't bothered to even send a message. I'm not their mother. Glinda is their mother." I dropped Auri's hand and stood. "They all got what they wanted, didn't they? More female High Demons, to perpetuate the race. My daughters have a King and Queen as parents; Kifirin arranged that. Where are Jase and Jehrie, Auri? Glinda's daughters? I seldom see them at the palace. Did they think their place was usurped as well?"

"Reah, they visited, you just weren't at the palace at the same time."

"Or at all, at least for the past two years. Since Dara and Sara went to study off-world. Tell Glinda that she can have the children herself, next time." My anger was back and I skipped away without thinking about it.

There I stood, upon Thiskil. I was Queen of a nearly dead planet; Ildevar Wyyld had proclaimed it himself. The planet seemed the same as I—both of us struggling to come back from years of emptiness. As usual, it was mostly weeds and barren ground. Bones of trees and animals littered the forest where I stood. I skipped to the ocean, which still piled its waves on the shore but there were no tiny birds running in the surf, searching for sea creatures as a meal. No kelp or seaweed washed up along those shores, either. Everything had died, including most of the people. The Campiaan Alliance hadn't been conceived when the planet died at the hands and power of Zellar. I'd killed him too swiftly, I think.

"Cloudsong still looks much the same as this." Griffin stood beside me. I wondered how he'd known to find me. Generally, only the Larentii could locate me.

"I know what Cloudsong looks like." I'd been there not long ago, after all. I hadn't thought to go back to it, either. Not since I'd fought off pirates, slave traffickers and Dantel Schuul and company.

"Yes, I know you do." Griffin huffed out a sigh. His breath blew out in a cloud; it was quite cold where we stood, and the sighing of the ocean was the only sound around us. I hadn't realized how much I might miss other sounds until they were conspicuously absent.

"I saw Amara not long ago; she was visiting Lissa," I said.

"I know. I hear things, mostly after the fact. She's avoiding me. Has been for a long while."

"I'm very familiar with that particular experience," I agreed.

"You know Lendill is Prince-Heir of the Elves now?" I looked up at Griffin when he said those words; he was staring out at the ocean.

"I heard." I had. I'd dreamed it and knew it to be true. I also heard in my dream some of the things Kaldill had said to Lendill, just before he'd made his selection and passed over some of the power from the Elven lands. Kaldill said that Lendill had used those under him to achieve the necessary goals.

Oh, he'd put it in more flowery terms than that, but it came out the same in the end. I'd been one of those underlings that Lendill had used. As had Teeg and Norian. But the worst offender of all had been Kifirin, by his own admission. Griffin, too, had used his family without mercy. He'd ultimately paid the price, with the death of his son and the loss of his mate. I rubbed my belly absently and sent a silent *I love you* to Garwin Wyatt.

"Lissa says she found a great-uncle, on her mother's side," I said, when Griffin didn't say anything else.

"I know. I heard that, too. I'm not sure he understands all his connections to the Elemaiya as yet. It gets tricky determining more than half yet less than full. So many Elemaiya donated eggs or sperm to create half-Elemaiya children, which they intended to harvest later to serve as soldiers in their long war. Edward Pendley was one of the few to survive, though."

"He seems like a decent man."

"He is. Much more decent than most, as it turns out. Why are you here, little Demon?" Griffin asked.

"I had to get away," I said. "Now that everybody conveniently remembers that they love me, or so they say, they're all anxious to go right back to what they consider normal. I don't know what normal is or what I feel about them anymore."

"Understandable. Getting ignored for a quarter century and then suddenly they're back, acting as if nothing's happened." Griffin *Pulled* a jacket from nowhere and settled it over my shoulders. I murmured my thanks. The air was very cold around us and I was grateful for the warmth the jacket provided.

"How long do you plan to stay here, little Demon? Rain is coming, and you will become even more chilled than you are already." As if in answer to his prediction, a few drops hit me, pattering on the suede leather of the jacket. "It was Wyatt's. The jacket," Griffin said. "One of his favorites. Keep it."

I nodded, not answering. "I'll go back," I sighed, turning away from Thiskil's northern ocean and skipping away.

"Thank goodness." Joey, Franklin and Norton were waiting inside my bedroom. Joey was the one who spoke. "All your mates are tearing their hair out, I think."

Slipping the jacket off my shoulders and wandering into my closet to hang it up, I thought briefly about telling all my mates that I wanted a separation. From all of them. I couldn't decide if that would improve matters or not, so I left it alone.

"Come along, tiny butt. Let's go face the music," Franklin took my hand and led me from the bedroom.

"Reah!" Nenzi did look as if he had tugged at his hair. He, along with the others, had likely been planning a raid on every place I might possibly have gone. Lendill was there, armed to the teeth, Lok had come with both blades strapped to his back and Aurelius looked as if the claws and fangs might come out at any moment. Teeg had a Ranos pistol strapped to a thigh and my knife—*my Grey House knife*—clipped to his belt.

"That's mine," I went straight to him and jerked the knife from his belt.

"I'm not sure you should keep that within easy reach," Kevis said dryly.

"Really?" I pointed it at him. "I've been looking for this for years. Try taking it from me now."

"All right," Kevis backed up a few steps, his hands up in a form of surrender.

"Don't worry, all of your behinds are safe," I muttered, wondering where I could put my knife so that nobody would take it again.

"I will place it in the Archives, and Reah may have it back anytime she wants," Nefrigar appeared, holding out a hand. Worrying my lip as I gazed up at him, I reluctantly placed the knife in his hand. He sent it straight to the Archives; it disappeared immediately.

"I wish I could do that," I said, studying my toes for a moment.

"Reah," Teeg stepped in front of me. "I want to clear the air a little. Go ahead. Yell at me. Yell at everybody else here. Get it out of your system. I don't know if I can take much more of this disappearing shit."

"Like you didn't disappear? Jerk," I snapped at him. "How many times did you tell Dee to call me because you were too much of a coward to do it yourself? How many times did I get dragged here to play dress up and act stupid for heads of state? *Hello, I'm Reah San Gerxon and I don't have a brain in my head,*" I mimicked, smiling a vapid smile. "I never got to go to college and earn multiple degrees and start an Alliance," I went on. "Addah Desh wouldn't spend a penny on me if he could help it. I never got the choice of whether I wanted to go to school or not, beyond what was required by law. And then the conscription notice came and I became Alliance property. Where was my life in all of that, Teeg San Gerxon? Where? Kifirin saw to it that I was kept pregnant for a while, and Gardevik Rath saw to it that I was trapped on the Southern Continent of Kifirin. I hear my girls don't know a damn thing about me, now, and isn't that a slap in the face?"

"Geez, Reah, I didn't mean to open the floodgates," Teeg rubbed the back of his neck, a deep frown on his face.

"No? Want to hear more?" I asked. "Aurelius and Lok asked for extra spawn hunting duty so they wouldn't have to talk to the old ball and chain. Aurelius came and took my girls out for ice cream many times and didn't bother to stop in to talk to me. Didn't think I knew about that, did you?" I stared hard at Aurelius.

"Lendill had his nose parked on the ASD grindstone, and it was just too much trouble to come see Reah unless he wanted something. Farzi and Nenzi didn't have ready transportation and they were too busy trying to keep Campiaa in fresh fruit and vegetables. Of course Kifirin's little interference didn't help one damn bit in all of that. If you don't count Nefrigar or the past two months with Ry, I think I've had sex four times in the past three years. Doctor Halivar, I hope you got all that. I really don't want to repeat it later." I stomped away from all of them.

"I always thought someone else was taking up the slack," Gavril muttered, a cup of coffee in his hands at the kitchen island. Mathilde had dumped coffee, tea or soft drinks in front of the others, a grim expression on her face. Joey, Franklin and Norton had gone out to the pool area where Reah was sitting, her pants rolled up to her knees and her feet soaking in the hot tub.

"How we get her back? How we make up with her?" Farzi was miserable; it was echoed in his voice. Nenzi was sitting very close to his brother and more miserable than that, if it were possible.

"She's hitting back at all of you for twenty-five years of pain and neglect," Kevis pointed out. "I realize it wasn't intentional for the most part, but that doesn't make any difference to Reah. To her, pain is pain."

"Mom gave me copies of all the messages she and Reah sent to me when the girls were born," Tory sighed. "And the last one said she almost bled out with Dara and Sara. Who was with her, then? Anybody know?"

"I was, as was Renegar," Nefrigar said. He'd altered his height to sit on a barstool at the island with the others. "Three sets of twins in six years were hard on her, and she'd been in the groves working until her labor began. Gardevik Rath has much to answer for."

"Kifirin, too, but good luck on that," Ry folded in to join the conference. Mathilde placed a cup of tea in front of him.

"Is there room for us?" Jayd, Garde and Glinda skipped in. Nefrigar enlarged the island with power, and three more barstools plunked down, manufactured out of air, most likely. The Larentii could command atoms when they wanted.

"Reah wasn't happy that Raedah sent mindspeech to me, upset over the fact that she couldn't remember important things about her mother," Aurelius blew out a frustrated sigh.

"At least they call you Daddy." Tory blew an angry cloud of smoke from his nostrils.

"I have it on good authority that love can't be forced," Jayd said, looking at those gathered about him. "But that doesn't mean it can't be coaxed back to life. Granted, it looks as if those embers may be dying, but we have to find a way to rebuild the fire of it. Kara says that she loved her mother and wanted to hug her while they were together, but the moment Reah was out of sight, it was as if she forgot. Most likely as the rest of you did."

"We should have kept her at the palace. We could have found someone to work with her and tend to emergencies at night. Reah could have skipped to the Southern Continent every morning, and taken a day off at least once a week. I understand that didn't happen," Glinda pointed out.

"Dad, aren't you going to say anything?" Tory looked at Garde, who'd remained silent.

"I fucked this up, son," Garde admitted.

"Yeah? Dad, she has my claiming marks on her neck and she won't let me touch her. You're not the only one."

"Do you ever wear your hair down?" Joey pulled the length of my braid through his hand. Braided, it hung below my waist.

"Once in a while," I said. Ry had asked for it down a time or two. I'd done it for him.

"It's beautiful, even braided," Franklin sat on my other side. I was sandwiched between them, their shoulders rubbing mine. Norton sat on the other side of the rectangular spa, listening to the rest of us. Somehow, they'd cooled the waters, allowing me to sit in it.

"I probably should have it trimmed, but there hasn't been any time," I said.

"We can take you," Franklin offered. "Conner has someone who does her hair and nails. We can set up an appointment."

"That sounds nice," I said. "I've gotten my hair done by those people Teeg hires, but they always look at me like I'm a project, with long hair that has to be piled up on my head in some ridiculous and exotic way."

"Maybe trim it to here?" Joey drew a finger across the small of my back.

"Yeah, that would be a good length, I guess."

"And cut the bangs. Just a little," he grinned, leaning down in front of me. "Oh, shit," he said.

"What?" He, Franklin and Norton were standing in a blink.

"The Saa Thalarr are getting attacked. We have to go."

"I'm coming too," I said, grabbing Joey's arm before he could fold away.

~

"Stay back," Franklin shouted at me. What met my eyes when I was tossed onto the dry grass of a winter field in the middle of nowhere was nothing less than total chaos. Sixteen Ra'Ak and at least a thousand spawn were there, fighting with the Saa Thalarr who were available to come. I saw Lok and Aurelius appear not far away. Their focus was on the spawn—they didn't even see that I'd come. Drake and Drew were already engaging one of the monster Ra'Ak while their father, Dragon, dealt with another. I saw a huge, white Unicorn, a Black Gryphon and a beautiful Snow Leopard.

Over our heads screamed a giant white Eagle with black wingtips. Then, if that wasn't enough, another twenty Ra'Ak came. Aurelius had told me over the years that the Ra'Ak that remained were likely hiding, sending their spawn out to create more of their kind. Now, many had chosen to appear at once. Dragon was attempting to fend off four of the creatures and Drake and Drew had more to deal with as well. The Eagle overhead was popping heads off spawn, but the moment she came close to one of the Ra'Ak it leapt at her, snapping its poisonous teeth.

"No!" Joey screamed as a Ra'Ak scraped its teeth against the side of the Unicorn. Dragon, too, roared in pain and frustration as he was nicked by one of the four he fought. There wasn't much time. I was High Demon. I and my race had been created for this. King Lendevik had conveniently forgotten that, but I hadn't. Turning quickly to my larger Thifilatha and pulling energy from the stars over our heads as I ran, I raced to take on the Ra'Ak.

My gold scales were shining like a yellow sun by the time I arrived, and the Ra'Ak attempted to get away when they realized I was among them, but I wasn't having it. I was filled with energy from the stars, glowing with it, pulsing with it. They had no ability to escape me in my present state; I made sure of it. No power worked while I was such. Even the Saa Thalarr were backing away; their folding skills wouldn't work until they got quite far away, actually.

With the precision of a laser pistol, I pointed fingers and released what I'd gathered. Ra'Ak exploded before me, barely able to shriek before they died. Did the spawn think to attack me? They fizzled out of existence upon coming into contact with my scales. Like tiny, flying predators that burn against an insect lantern, they winked into sparks and blew away.

Only three Ra'Ak remained and I killed them leisurely, almost, screaming at them. "Did you think to escape me?" I cried out, scalding tears dripping down my scaled cheeks. Had I realized I was crying? Not until then. "You will never harm again, I promise it," I wept and killed the last two before dropping to the ground and curling in upon myself.

"Reah, we have to go! Dragon and Kiarra have poison in their systems!" Norton shouted up at me. I barely heard him over the sounds of my sobs.

"No," I moaned. Dragon was lying on his side, still in dragon form, but the Unicorn had become someone I recognized—Kiarra of the Saa Thalarr. Her head lay in Joey's lap and he was trying to help her, but the rake she'd received was a severe one. I knew the Ra'Ak poison was running through both of them. Using the short fangs I had while Thifilatha, I bit into my own hand, opening a wound on the palm. High Demons were immune to every poison, including that of the Ra'Ak.

Skipping to Dragon's side, I slapped my hand over his wound, allowing my blood to mingle with his. I knew when the poison was neutralized; it didn't take long. "He's all right now," I said, before going to the woman.

"Here," I became humanoid and knelt, completely naked in a winter field, shivering and placing a bleeding hand over Kiarra's wounds. I smeared my blood from one end of the wounds to the other, going by feel again until I knew the poison was neutralized.

Joey stared at me when I finished. "You should be able to work your mojo now," I said. "I got rid of all the star power."

"Is that what it was?" Joey blinked at me in confusion.

"Yeah. It's cold here, did you know?"

"Here." Kevis wrapped a blanket around me and lifted me from the ground. My feet were completely frozen, I think, and it wouldn't take much to snap them off. "I'll meet you back at the house; Dad's about to have a fit." I stared at Kevis Halivar as he folded—yes folded—me somewhere.

Karzac was waiting as Kevis settled me on a stone floor inside a beautiful kitchen, and when I saw Kevis and Karzac next to one another, I knew exactly what was going on. "I ought to punch you," I poked a finger in Kevis' chest. He was Karzac's son. I saw the resemblance with them so close together. "No wonder I never saw you in the same room together." A sandy-blond man that looked very much like Adam Chessman snickered behind Kevis.

"Reah, you're naked," Kevis pointed out. My blanket had dropped to the floor.

"Yeah? I thought you were a doctor. Surely you've seen this before," I snapped, poking him in the chest again.

"Reah, it's a little undignified, arguing naked in my mother's kitchen," Kevis sounded embarrassed.

"You were the one who brought me here," I reminded him, lifting the blanket and wrapping it around me. "I'll go home now." I started to skip away.

"No!" Karzac and Kevis shouted in unison.

"Young one, you most certainly will not skip away until we have examined you and determined that what you just did harmed the child in no way. And your hand is bleeding," Karzac grumped.

"I had to bite it to neutralize the poison in the others," I huffed.

"And Dragon is very grateful. Kiarra is still in shock, I think."

"Is she all right? They didn't hurt her too badly, did they?" Now I was worried.

"She is fine, she just had no idea who you were at the moment; she was in too much pain. She also had no idea where you came from or why you were naked and smearing blood all over her stomach. I had to send someone to explain." Karzac was almost tapping his foot with impatience.

"Why don't you go help her?" I turned back to Kevis. "It sounds as if she's scarred for life, now." The sandy-haired man laughed out loud when I said that.

"Come along, you," Kevis lifted me off the floor and hauled me down a lengthy hallway. Karzac, trailing behind us, slapped the door shut when at least three other people attempted to get inside. I didn't recognize any of them, although the sandy-haired man was one of the three.

"Now, Reah, you will sit there while I examine you and the child. Honestly, what kind of stunt was that anyway?" Karzac was muttering his displeasure as he placed his fingers on my hand first, healing up the wound. Kevis found a cloth and wet it in a small sink in the corner of the room to wash off the blood. Looking around me, I decided the room was a doctor's office. Supplies and equipment were stored inside—not that any of it was needed—except for the cloth Kevis used to clean blood from my hand. Karzac placed a hand over my bare chest. "Does anything hurt?" he asked quietly, acting as if he were listening to my heartbeat.

"My feet are freezing," I said. "And I'd really like to make sure my toes won't snap off when I kick Kevis' ass."

"Reah, I get that you're the toughest woman on the block and all that," Kevis said. "Hush now, Dad and I are checking on the baby." I rolled my eyes as two sets of hands went to my belly.

"Must not be anything like the Saa Thalarr. The baby's fine," Karzac sighed, straightening up.

"What does that mean?" I asked. "I changed the whole time I was pregnant before. I had to in order to get the insects out of the groves."

"Reah, you should probably stop talking now before Dad has a stroke." Kevis gave me a level look with the gold-green eyes he'd inherited from his father.

"Karzac, don't have a stroke," I mumbled, ducking my head and suddenly feeling ashamed.

"Little one," Karzac lifted my face, "I will not have a stroke. But it was a very close thing this time," he gave me a small smile. "I know not how you did what you did, but I had visions of a miscarriage. I am most happy to see that will not be the case."

"Where is she?" The door banged open and Dragon, with Norton and Franklin almost hanging off him, strode into the room.

"Don't tell me you're having a stroke, too?"

"I may have worse. Is she all right? Is the child well?" Dragon demanded.

"Everything is fine; it seems she's done this sort of thing throughout all her pregnancies," Karzac released a long-suffering sigh.

"To clear insects out of the groves," Kevis added, almost in an identical tone to his father's.

"It keeps everything organic," I huffed, crossing arms angrily over my chest. What were they so upset about? I shook my head in confusion.

"Reah, you reached your fourth month of pregnancy two days ago. Saa Thalarr women cannot change or use their power after four months or they will miscarry," Karzac said.

"Obviously I'm not one of them," I pointed out while nobody in particular paid any mind at all.

"How is she otherwise?" Dragon asked.

"Fine, except for the," Kevis tapped his head with a finger.

"You know, I think my feet are warmed up enough now," I threatened. "Is this how you handle all your crazy patients?"

"No, just the short ones who can turn to something with scales, wings and stands around fifteen feet tall afterward," Kevis grinned.

"You—I have no words," I said, sliding off the table I'd been dumped on. Tugging my blanket tighter around me, I marched out of the room with as much dignity as I could muster before skipping away.

~

"Dad, do you think all that scar tissue on her womb will affect the baby?" Kevis asked after Reah skipped away.

"I hope it won't, but I worry that it may not stretch as normal tissue might," Karzac shook his head. "I don't want to mention it, in case it doesn't turn into a problem—she has enough to worry about as it is and so far the baby is fine. Just keep examining her often, and tell the others not to alarm her over this. It may be nothing, after all."

"All right. I need to go after her, anyway." Kevis sighed and folded to Campiaa.

"Where have you been?" Teeg was close to shouting when I arrived on Farzi's patio. He and Nenzi were peering around Teeg, worry in their eyes.

"I just went with Joey, Norton and Franklin," I said. "Some Ra'Ak showed up. They're all dead now."

"And you killed them." Teeg tossed up a hand in frustration.

"Most of them," I nodded. "I zapped them. Like a zap oven." I walked behind Teeg and put my arms around Nenzi's neck. "Nenzi, I'm tired. Can I go to bed with you and Farzi?"

Nenzi didn't say anything, he merely hauled me off the ground and walked as fast as he could toward the house.

CHAPTER 6

*N*enzi was snuggled against my back as lion snake when I woke. I was lying with my head on Farzi's shoulder. They'd never been able to have sex in a conventional manner—those who'd manipulated their births neutered them when they were young. If Nefrigar and I had energy sex, they could be included in that backwash of pleasure. Normally, though, Farzi, Nenzi and I settled for snuggling together in bed. The snuggling was nice, actually.

Nenzi poked his head over my shoulder, his tongue tickling my skin. Sleepily I reached up to stroke his triangular head. He blinked at me, telling me he liked it. It's strange—most snakes can't blink. Only lion snakes have eyelids and blink often. If one knew what to look for, one might know they stared at a lion snake—shortly before they died, I'm sure.

"Come here, sweet man." I pulled his head toward me and kissed the top of it. Nenzi snuggled beneath my chin. I stroked his scales.

"We miss this," Farzi nuzzled my ear.

"I missed it too," I sighed.

"Are we getting up?" Kevis walked into the room as if he belonged there.

"I was thinking about it. Nenzi, honey, can I get up? I'm beginning to feel a little queasy."

"Head down," Kevis' hands were on the back of my neck and Farzi and Nenzi, who'd changed back, were helping. I was breathing slow, deep breaths until I thought I could make it out of the bed without heaving.

I got help with my bath from Farzi and Nenzi while Kevis waited (not so patiently) outside. I was dressed, hauled off to the dining room and found Joey, Norton and Franklin eating breakfast as if nothing had happened the day before.

"So," Kevis said later as I swung lazily in the hammock outside, "Tell me about your grandfather."

"Which one?" I asked.

"Either one," Kevis shrugged.

"I think Denevik is still trying to make his wife Breszca pregnant. I have no idea how that's going. She's my grandmother, and we've never spoken."

"You haven't spoken to her? What about him?"

"Her, never. Denevik—not for two years or more."

"How do you feel about that?"

"Is that your favorite question? And how do you feel about my asking you that?"

"Reah, this is your session. Not mine." Kevis was the professional today. I didn't point that out to him.

"I don't know how I feel about that. We really don't know that much about one another."

"If you could see anyone you wanted right now, who would it be?"

"I'd like to see my mother," I said. "Since we never got to meet."

"Does that bother you?"

"Of course it does. Wouldn't it bother you? And bother you even more if you learned that somebody killed her? Yes it bothers me. Fills me with some of the impotent rage you've already recorded."

"I see. Who would you like to see that is actually alive?"

"Let's see," I searched my mind for an answer. "Edward," I said. "He seems like such a good person. I think I'd like to sit down and have tea with him. I'd say a drink, but that's out of the question right now. We could talk about his gishi fruit harvest. How that went. How Keedan is doing, and his other supervisors."

"So, you found someone who has common interests."

"I guess."

"What would you like from any one of your mates at the moment?"

"I think I'd like for one of them to come and lie down beside me, without any expectations, and rub my belly and tell me everything was going to be fine."

"Even Tory?"

"I'm not sure Tory has that in him," I replied. "I'm not really sure any of them have it in them, except for Aurelius, maybe." I suddenly felt like crying, and knew it was likely because of the pregnancy. The fourth month always turned into an emotional one for me. I told Kevis that. "This is likely the pregnancy speaking. I always get emotional around this time. The last time, I recall that Garde showed up on a bad day and he just threw his hands up and walked off. I think I skipped to the house and cried my eyes out after that."

"Some men don't know how to handle things like that. I understand that a surrogate birthed his son, so there wasn't any way he might have dealt with that issue with his own mate."

"Yeah, I get that about him."

"Tell me about the claiming marks on your neck."

"I really don't want to," I said. "Everybody else got anesthetic and physicians immediately afterward. I didn't."

"I've heard that the male apologizes to the female, continuously, afterward."

"Tory tried, I'll give him that. But it all came out of nowhere and happened so fast. And I'd just gotten shot in the shoulder when he turned and skipped me away. I was unconscious there at the end because it was too much."

"Is anything ever easy with you?" Kevis asked in a resigned voice.

"You didn't know I was the worst project you could ever take on, now did you? I bet you're pissed at your dad because of it."

"Reah, I wouldn't have accepted the case if I didn't want it. And I don't discuss my notes with anyone."

"No, your nurses just break into the records and then sell them," I snorted. Kevis winced at my accusation. Our session ended shortly after that, so I went to the groves, Joey, Franklin and Norton right behind me.

"So, this is how it's done," Franklin, his hands encased in gloves, placed the lemons he'd picked into the dividers inside a crate.

"Yes. This is how it's done. Don't they smell wonderful?" I held a lemon to my nose and sniffed it.

"If you say so. I prefer to get my lemons at the market, I think." He grinned mischievously.

"You think they just sprout at the store?"

"Don't they?"

"Stop playing hopeless, I know you're not," I said.

"Reah, the doctor says you've been out long enough. You should come back, eat something and have a nap before dinner." Tory, driving one of the larger carts, stopped beside me. The cart would hold all of us if we scooted tightly together. We finished filling our crate, left it in the proper place and squeezed onto the cart.

"You know, as tall as you are, you wouldn't need a hoverstep to harvest most of the fruit," I told Tory, who blinked at me in surprise, most likely because I'd spoken to him voluntarily.

"I'll keep that in mind," he said, winding his way through the groves toward the plantation, the hovercart making its quiet whine as he drove.

"Don't plan anything for tomorrow." Kifirin appeared in the kitchen while Teeg discussed an upcoming meeting with Dee. Tory, Lok, Aurelius and Kevis were seated at the table, having coffee while Reah slept.

"Why not?" Kevis didn't appreciate Kifirin's appearance and apparent command.

"Because we're taking a trip." Belen appeared beside Kifirin. "My Dark brother and I are going on a fact-finding mission, I believe you'd call it. We'll bring others along as well. Meet us here directly after breakfast. Reah could use some time alone, I think."

"I'll have Astralan stay with her," Gavril frowned.

"Very good. Bring the warlock. He will watch over her quite well, I think," Belen's smile almost blinded Gavril before the Nameless One disappeared.

"What's that all about?" Tory grumbled.

"Don't ask questions, young Demon. Just show up." Kifirin disappeared as well.

"A fact-finding mission? With gods? That doesn't bode well," Kevis sighed.

"There is business to take care of, so Astralan will provide protection," Teeg informed me after breakfast. "Kevis also has things to attend to. You will be here with the three healers and Astralan. Try not to skip away from them?" Teeg begged.

"Fine. There shouldn't be any reason to worry. If I want to go somewhere, I'll ask Astralan to take me."

"Good enough," Teeg said and walked away, leaving me swinging in the hammock near the pool.

"That looks comfy," Astralan grinned as he settled on a chair nearby.

"You should try it sometime," I smiled at him. Besides Ry, whom I hadn't seen for days, Astralan might be my favorite warlock. If I asked him questions, even personal or sensitive ones, he always answered them patiently.

"What are we doing today?" Joey, Norton and Franklin all appeared and sat near Astralan.

"I think I want to visit Avendor," I grinned. Astralan lifted an eyebrow speculatively before grinning back.

~

Gavril was shocked. Kifirin transported him, Kevis, Aurelius, Tory, Lok, Farzi and Nenzi to Le-Ath Veronis, where they were met by Lendill, Norian, Ry, Garde, Jayd, Glinda and Lissa. Two others were there, seemingly against their will. Radolf and Ilvan stood together, and both appeared quite sullen.

"We will be traveling the timeline today," Belen announced, drawing everybody's attention. He stood next to Lissa and rubbed her back absently while he spoke. Kifirin blew a bit of smoke but didn't say anything.

"I don't like this," Garde muttered.

"But you will come," Kifirin snapped.

"Ready?" Belen asked. When nobody spoke, he transported everyone through time.

"You will not be seen or heard," Belen said as they all stood in the gishi fruit groves on Kifirin. Reah, eight months pregnant with a black eye and swollen face, attempted to loosen a bolt on a hovertruck's solar collector. The bolt was rusted in place and she was having difficulty with it. Lissa drew a sharp breath at the state of Reah's face.

"What happened to her?" Gavril growled while Reah continued to jerk the wrench on the bolt, trying to loosen it. A replacement collector sat in packaging nearby, waiting to be installed. Reah was doing the repairs herself.

"One of the disabled that Gardevik sent to her was mentally damaged. Without medication, he would turn violent at times. He hit Reah," Belen said.

"When is this?" Jayd asked. He was unable to gauge the proper time.

"A little more than twenty years ago. Reah is pregnant with her last set of twins, Dara and Sara." Belen watched as Reah continued to work on the bolt.

"No," Nenzi moaned. Reah had positioned herself so that her weight might be used to work the bolt loose. Doing so was dangerous in the extreme; if the bolt came loose suddenly, she could fall.

"You may not approach," Kifirin held Nenzi back. Reah jerked the wrench, the bolt came loose and she fell with a cry, flat on her back in the dirt between rows of gishi fruit trees. That's where the truck had broken down and she'd had no good way to move it.

They all watched in horror as Reah rolled over to rise stiffly before raising a hand to her head. Every breath she took after that was a bone-shaking sob. That went on for several minutes before she moved, pulled the broken solar collector off and replaced it with the new one, wiping tears the entire time.

"Now, we go," Belen moved them. They stood in Garde's study inside the palace.

"Garde, she needs the procedure or her baby will die," Reah was pleading someone's case in front of Gardevik Rath.

"Reah, we can't hand out money every time one of your workers needs something," Garde blew a curl of disgruntled smoke.

"But the baby will die," Reah was nearly in tears.

"Babies die all the time, Reah. You're not responsible for them and neither is the Crown." Garde was done with the conversation. Reah skipped away. Belen followed her. Reah stood inside her bedroom at the tiny house in the groves. Carefully, she lifted a carved wooden box from a bottom bureau drawer. Lifting the lid, she drew out a necklace of diamonds and rubies. Touching the stones gently before shoving the expensive jewelry in her pocket, Reah wiped her cheeks, checked her appearance in the mirror and skipped away. Belen followed her.

They'd landed in a secondhand jeweler's shop. Rows of jewelry were displayed in plexi cases beneath the counter. Reah waited while a woman and her husband bought rings before approaching the desk.

"What might I sell you today?" The proprietor asked. Nearly bald, he only had the leavings of thin hair over his ears. His eyes were a washed-away blue and the wrinkles around his mouth traced a constant frown.

"I don't want to buy, I came to sell." Reah drew the necklace from her pocket.

"Ah. This looks quite expensive," the man held the jewelry up to appraise it. "Might I ask if it was acquired, ah, legally?"

"It was a gift," Reah said stiffly.

"I might be willing to offer top credit," the man said, turning his eyes on Reah, "If you'll agree to spend the afternoon in my bed." Aurelius growled at the proprietor's words. The necklace was snatched away from the man so quickly he hardly realized it had left his hand.

"I'll go elsewhere," Reah's voice expressed her anger and frustration. "And I'll make a stop at the magistrate's office afterward," she snapped.

"No! No, no," the man was pleading, holding out a hand. "It was in jest, I assure you. I will pay what the necklace is worth. Secondhand, of course."

"Of course. Give me your best price or I will leave and will still visit the magistrate," Reah warned.

"I will," the man whined and named his price. Reah almost walked away. He upped it, and then upped it again. When the right amount was spoken, Reah nodded her head. She also pulled a comp-vid from her pocket to check the credit chip before leaving the store.

"Where did that necklace come from?" Tory asked.

"I gave it to her," Aurelius grumbled.

"We will go," Belen said.

Their next visit was to a hospital, where Reah spoke to a doctor.

"The baby will live now," the physician said. "If she had waited any longer, that would not be the case."

"Good," Reah sighed. She was dressed very poorly, Gavril noted. Lissa glared accusingly at Kifirin, who merely looked grim.

"Didn't she have better clothing than this?" Glinda asked, horrified that Reah would appear in public this way.

"Shall we check her closet?" Ry gave the Queen of Kifirin a nasty smile.

"No. I know what we'll find. No," Glinda held up a hand.

"And this is surely while you were stealing from her," Lissa glared at Radolf and Ilvan. "If she'd had the funds from the restaurant at least, she wouldn't be selling off her jewelry to pay for something that

Gardevik should have at least looked into." Garde was the next one to receive Lissa's angry stare.

"We go," Belen said and they were gone again. This time, they appeared in the rotunda of the High Demon palace. Reah had skipped in, dressed as well as she could be under the circumstances.

"Ah, lady Reah," a servant walked over and nodded to Reah. He was tall, thin and dressed much better than Reah was.

"Randik?" Reah turned to the humanoid servant.

"If you're looking for your daughters, they are not here," Randik sighed patiently. "Master Aurelius came and took them for ice cream. They have not returned as yet." Reah's shoulders sagged at Randik's words.

"Did he say anything about coming to visit the groves afterward?" Reah asked.

"No, lady. I believe he told Princess Raedah that he had to get back after their trip for ice cream."

"Oh. Well, thank you, Randik. Tell them I'll be here tomorrow evening." Reah skipped away. Belen followed her. Reah was wiping her eyes as she prepared a meager dinner afterward and washed clothing by hand after that.

"She didn't even have a washer?" Glinda kicked Garde.

"I didn't know she needed one," Garde muttered angrily.

"I guess she was out of jewelry and her profits from the restaurant were going elsewhere," Lok shot angry looks at Ilvan and Radolf.

"Remember, we are giving a broad cross-section only. This is by no means inclusive of everyday trials," Belen said. "We will visit one other place." He transported all of them away.

"I'll give you half the profits if you'll consider this," I said. Edward sat beside me in the western grove. The fruit was halfway harvested, to the best of my estimation. Joey, Norton and Franklin were examining the harvested trees while I sat on a narrow bench between Astralan and Edward.

"Reah, I'd give you all the profits if you'd marry me." Edward rubbed my back gently. I stared up at him, shocked by his proposal. Yes, I'd felt a connection to him the moment I'd met him, but I had too much baggage dragging behind me. He didn't need to be exposed to that.

"I'll settle for half to start," I said. I'd made gishi fruit ice cream for him inside his massive kitchen and watched while a slow smile spread across his face when he tasted it. Astralan and the three healers had gotten a dish of ice cream, too, and they were just as excited. Edward and I were now discussing a gishi fruit ice-cream plant to be placed on part of EastStar's property, using the slightly blemished fruit that couldn't be shipped with the rest of the crop. Edward either sold it to local vendors or used it for seed for future plantings. I was offering an alternative for the blemished fruit.

"How quickly do you think we might get started?" Edward asked. "I have contacts in exclusive shops everywhere. They already carry my gishi fruit. It won't be a stretch for them to carry the ice cream."

"I think we can be up and operating on a limited level in four eight-days," I said. "We can set up in one of your empty buildings near the barns while we build another facility. We can clean up, install the ice-cream machines and get the inspectors out. As soon as they pass us, then we can begin making ice cream. We'll see how well it sells."

"How much do you think we can charge for this?" Edward hugged my shoulders. Astralan surprised me by taking the hand closest to him and squeezing my fingers simultaneously.

"I think we can get one hundred credits for a tink, wholesale," I said. "I believe your vendors can sell it for one-seventy-five, retail." A tink was close to a half-gallon, in Aurelius' measurements.

"And since it's frozen, it'll keep a lot longer than gishi fruit," Edward chuckled. "Let's try this. I'll get a crew on one of those buildings this afternoon. I'll send a message when everything is clean, whitewashed and ready to go. Then we'll go looking for ice-cream machines and set up an inspection. I'll make arrangements with a dairy for the milk and you can look for suppliers for the other ingredients. I want this to work, Reah. That ice cream was incredible."

"I think we can turn a good profit on it," I agreed. Edward leaned down to kiss me. Did I wonder where the magic had gone? Edward wasn't fooling around, I could tell. I blinked up at him. He was wealthy, had everything he might ever want and more, yet he'd asked me to marry him. And there I was, pregnant with Teeg's child. I didn't know what to do.

"Don't worry, I'll settle for a date first, if you're willing," Edward smiled. "Just don't forget about me, all right?"

"All right. You have my comp-vid code. Let me know what's happening on your end, and I'll go looking for spice and sugar suppliers."

"I will. And you can visit anytime. If I'm in a meeting, those people should be prepared to get thrown out."

"How about we get together in a couple of days and make a few tinks of ice cream for your vendors to sample? We'll whet their appetite a little," I smiled at Edward.

"That sounds perfect. I'll get some packaging put together and we'll look good when we take it to them," Edward agreed.

"Wonderful. I'll be back in two days," I said. Astralan and I gathered the healers and folded to Campiaa.

"Boss, you're not going to let that little girl get away, are you?" Keedan gave Edward a shrewd look moments later.

"I have no intention of doing so. I just have to convince her that adding me to that stable of men she has is a good idea." Edward was grinning wider than Keedan had ever seen.

"I've missed this," Astralan sighed, swallowing his first bite of fish. Mathilde had offered to cook lunch, but I told her to sit down and take a break while I did it.

"Oh, my, this is wonderful," Mathilde sighed. "If I ask, will you help me work out a few glitches in recipes once in a while?"

"I'd be happy to. Your pot roast is the best I've ever had," I added. "The cooks have to stick together."

"And we will," she assured me, cutting into the fish again.

"This is incredible," Franklin piled sauce onto a bit of fish with his knife. "And that gishi fruit ice cream? Best ever," he stuffed the bite of food into his mouth.

"We could get Reah to do the dessert for your mother's birthday," Norton said, staring at Franklin.

"Your mother?" I lifted an eyebrow at Frank.

"The Unicorn. Kiarra is my mother," Franklin grinned.

"Oh, gosh. And I smeared blood all over her," I sighed, my cheeks burning.

"And we didn't have to do a darn thing to neutralize poison," Joey pointed out. "Usually, if one of them gets hit, we can neutralize most of it, but it takes longer and they're weak for several days, at least. This was an instant fix," Joey tossed up his hands.

"I'm glad, even if I did traumatize her," I said. "I'll be happy to make dessert for your mother's birthday. Just let me know when."

"It's next week," Franklin grinned.

"How many will be there?" I asked.

"Probably forty or fifty," Joey laughed.

"I can do that, I'll just have to ask Edward for gishi fruit."

"I think he'll give you anything you want," Norton observed dryly.

"Teeg back yet?" Dee folded in with Stellan, Galaxsan and Celestan.

"Not yet," Astralan shook his head.

"Who do we have here?" Celestan and Galaxsan were staring at Joey, Norton and Frank.

"Joey, Norton and Frank," I pointed out the proper healer at the proper time. "Healers," I added.

"For the Saa Thalarr," Joey was grinning again. I think I expected to see sparks any moment between the healers, Celestan and Galaxsan. The two warlocks were in a female cycle, according to Astralan.

"You boys want to go to the mountain and snowboard this afternoon?" I asked innocently.

"There's snowboarding?" Joey was already standing.

"We'll show you, if Dee can do without us," Galaxsan grinned.

"I can make do with Stellan," Dee agreed.

"Come on, we'll rent the equipment," Celestan offered before they all disappeared.

"Ask Teeg to contact me as soon as he gets in," Dee said. "Reah, I think you need that nap."

"Yeah, I was going to go back to the hammock as soon as the kitchen's cleaned up."

"I'll take care of that, go get some sleep," Mathilde smiled.

"Come on, shortness," Astralan pulled me off the barstool I'd perched on.

"There's something you should consider before you marry that man," Astralan said as we walked toward the hammock.

"What's that?" I stopped and looked up at him. He and his brothers all had dark-brown hair and dark eyes. Enough to turn many a head, I knew. Franklin and the others had certainly been taken by Galaxsan and Celestan.

"That I saw you first," Astralan replied. I got a kiss from Teeg's number-one bodyguard warlock, who went one better, using power to settle both of us in the hammock. "Comfy?" Astralan's arm pulled me close so my cheek rested against his shoulder.

"I'm getting that way," I sighed and closed my eyes.

"Oh, no." Ilvan knew what was coming if the rest of them didn't. They'd landed inside Edan Desh's office at Desh's number two on Tulgalan. Edan's anger radiated off him as he flipped through record after record on a comp-vid.

"Reah's father, whom she still believes to be her brother, has gotten notice that Addah Desh, his father, may have discovered that he is siphoning funds away from the business. He is moving credits around to cover the missing amounts," Belen offered information, giving Ilvan a hard look. Ilvan quailed before those eyes, filled with stars as they were. Edan came to some sort of decision, slapped the comp-vid into a desk drawer and rose, trailing past his invisible audience and slamming the door behind him. Belen led the crowd out of the office behind Edan as he stalked through the busy kitchen, snatching up a heavy steel ladle as he walked.

Gavril drew back and stopped but Kifirin, who brought up the rear, forced him forward. Reah was there, her back turned to Edan Desh as she rolled out pastry at a table. Too short to reach the top comfortably at age ten, she stood on a short step stool to work. Her clothing didn't fit and hung loose about her, likely hand-me-downs from an older brother, her hair hung in a long braid down her back and she was completely focused on her work, using the wood pin to roll out a flaky crust.

The first hard blow from Edan's ladle hit her between the shoulders and she cried out, falling from the stool. He then proceeded to hit any part of her he could. Face, hands, back, ribs, legs. When she fell in the floor and curled up in a ball, the blows still rained down.

"I think she's dead," one of the kitchen helpers, never thinking to intervene, finally said.

"Really?" Edan snarled. Tossing the ladle into the nearby sink, Edan lifted a foot and stomped down on Reah's ankle, crushing it.

Kevis wanted to weep, kill Edan Desh and then weep again. Lissa was staring in horror at what she'd seen. Belen was rubbing her back again. This was very similar to the treatment Lissa had received at the hands of her stepfather. A younger Ilvan had stood on the other side of the table, watching Edan deal out his anger against a helpless child. "Call an ambulance," Ilvan said to one of the assistants.

Gavril watched, his anger seething as Reah was loaded onto a gurney and hauled to the nearest emergency facility. Belen got his company there as well. Edan showed up shortly after Reah arrived, pulling the head of surgery and the hospital administrator aside.

"Six months of free meals at Desh's, if you say this is an accident," he offered. Lissa cursed under her breath when both hospital employees agreed. Reah was treated for broken bones, her crushed ankle was reassembled using a surgery robot and then taken to a room while still unconscious. Bruises were everywhere, cracked and broken ribs were bandaged and casts were on the ankle and a wrist.

"She's only ten," Belen pointed out. "If you hadn't ordered an ambulance, Reah would have died." He looked again at Ilvan, who lowered his head before the god. "But before we leave, we'll go forward two days." Belen flashed them to the appropriate time. Reah's small body still lay on the hospital bed, unconscious. Two nurses walked in. Kevis drew in a breath. He knew one of them. Quite well, in fact.

"Who'll know?" she hissed. "Do you know how much we can get for natural hair this color? Do you?" A young Ceerah Kade pulled scissors from her pocket and proceeded to cut through Reah's long braid, right at the nape. Stuffing it inside a medical waste bag, Ceerah and her fellow conspirator walked out of Reah's room.

"Edan wouldn't pay for a haircut afterward," Ilvan's hands shook and he wouldn't look at anyone. "The hospital staff claimed her hair was cut so they could treat the head wound. It was crooked of course, and Reah was teased and mocked by her schoolmates and the kitchen staff before it grew out again."

"I want to kill you," Lok had a knife at Ilvan's throat. "And go back and kill that evil that was your brother. Do you see this?" Lok hauled Ilvan toward Reah's bed. "She's ten, for fuck's sake. And you stood there and let Edan beat her. Except you didn't turn out much different, did you? He stole from your father; you stole from her. Addah might not have missed the money. Reah did."

"I'm sorry," Ilvan whined. "I thought all of you were taking care of her. She had that house in Targis and everything."

"The house you helped yourself to?" Gavril was as angry as Lok, his eyes red, fangs out.

"She asked us not to harm you," Lissa said, standing before Ilvan and Radolf suddenly. "Radolf, how could you do this to her? How?"

"The spell Wylend placed wore off," Radolf sighed. "And I thought the same as Ilvan. That someone else was taking care of her. I wanted revenge against Wylend, but what can you do to the King of Karathia? I took my anger out on Reah. I see now that was a mistake. What are you going to do with us?" Radolf looked at Belen.

"I won't do anything," Belen replied. "But when you leave this life, you will choose your own form of punishment in the next one."

"That one," Kifirin pointed at Ceerah, who was back, checking the machines monitoring Reah's heartbeat and respiration, "that one will certainly suffer in her next life."

"I intend to see that she suffers in this one," Lendill hissed.

"And Reah can't even despise her father now," Kevis sighed helplessly. "She can't work through the anger, ever, because she can't be angry with a man who is no longer the one who fathered her. He wears the same likeness and she is powerless against that."

"It was a failed experiment," Kifirin admitted quietly. "I thought to give her a parent. That wasn't the one she needed. I also wasn't the one she needed."

"It's too late to take him back now. He's an important member of Karzac's team," Lissa pointed out.

"I know this," Kifirin said. "But his life will not be extended, as I thought to do at first. He will have to understand that."

Kevis left them all standing there, discussing the current Edan Desh. Approaching Reah's bed, he held out a hand. "Pretty girl," he whispered, touching her face, feeding her the slightest bit of healing power and repairing the damage a steel ladle had done to a small head.

"Not too much, just enough," Belen whispered at Kevis' side. Kevis nodded and went to the ankle after treating what could have been permanent brain injury. Bits of bone in the ankle fused together, reforming until there was only a clean break left. "Very good," Belen said, pulling Kevis away.

"We will go now," Belen announced, landing them inside Lissa's palace library. "Perhaps you should serve refreshments?" Belen told Lissa before folding away.

"Garde, you're not welcome here," Lissa snapped at him.

"Oh, he has sliced his own hand," Kifirin said. "Don't tell him to leave, avilepha. Or me, either. We will both bear the weight of our treatment of Reah."

"I'm going to a jewelry store," Aurelius moved away. "I'll get something to eat while I'm out."

"I'm coming with you," Gavril said. Lok, too, came along. Farzi and Nenzi, who'd mostly remained silent and troubled during the entire ordeal, nodded and slipped behind Gavril. Tory, Lendill and Ry, not to be left behind, joined the group.

CHAPTER 7

"Too gaudy." Lok shook his head at the huge diamond ring presented to him. "The cost isn't an issue," he assured the sales assistant, a bright young man who was hoping for his largest commission ever. Eight men stood inside the jewelry store, all determined to buy something.

"Something smaller and more tasteful," Ry agreed. "Reah won't wear anything that huge. She'll just use it the next time somebody needs medical treatment."

"At least she had something to use. I don't mind that a child's life was saved through the sale of a necklace," Aurelius said. "But I want to get a replacement. Today."

"This," Farzi and Nenzi were in total agreement. The gold and platinum had been etched in a snake scale pattern on the bracelet and necklace. It wasn't too thick, either, and both knew the set would be striking on Reah.

"Where are our rings?" Lendill asked Gavril.

"I have them at the palace," Gavril replied. "In her jewelry box. I was waiting to make sure she wanted them before returning them."

"Gav, she could have sold your ring by itself and had any life she wanted. You know the first things she asked that thieving woman about were her rings." Rylend referred to the woman Garde had hired to take Reah's place in the groves. The woman, with her husband, had taken Reah's things and burned what they thought to be trash. Those things had been important to Reah, else she wouldn't have kept them.

"You're right," Gavril pinched the space between eyebrows. He had all of Reah's rings inside her jewelry box at the palace in Campiaa City. "And she needs clothing and shoes and anything else she wants. We should take her to one of those places that sells cooking knives and utensils. That woman on Kifirin took those, too."

"She won't go out in public. Not after that fucking nurse screwed her. Twice. I can't believe it's the same woman who cut her hair and then sold that recording to a reality show. That one should have been locked away long ago."

"Norian is going back through her employment records, to see if any other incidents happened around her. We'll get to the bottom of this," Lendill said. "What do you think of this?" He held up an emerald necklace. It looked like delicate filigree, with an emerald drop.

"Perfect for her eyes," Gavril said. "Are there earrings to match?" He and Ry went to look.

"I don't believe this." Gavril stood, stunned at the sight of Reah sleeping peacefully against Astralan on the hammock. Astralan grinned cheekily at Gavril before placing a kiss against Reah's forehead, waking her.

"Huh?" I looked up at Astralan, who gave me a gentle smile.

"Time to wake, I imagine, your mates are here."

"Oh." I turned to blink at Teeg, Lendill, Ry, Lok, Tory, Aurelius, Farzi and Nenzi.

"Have a nice nap?" I shrank away from Teeg; he didn't look happy.

"Baby, don't." Teeg held out a hand. "I should have seen it coming a long time ago. Astralan, don't make me shorten your name by mistreating Reah."

"As if I would. And you'll have other competition, too, I think. Edward Pendley asked her to marry him this afternoon. I think she's settled for a date first."

"What were you doing with Edward Pendley?"

"Working on my future, I hope," I said.

"Gishi fruit ice cream," Astralan grinned and then employed power to get both of us out of the hammock. "She's going back in two days to look at what he's done with a temporary building and make some samples to take to vendors. They'll buy, no matter how much it costs. That's the best thing I've ever eaten."

"Reah, come here, sweetheart," Teeg pulled one of my hands to his lips and placed a gentle kiss there. "We picked up a few things while we were out. You need to come see."

The kitchen island was covered in jewelry. I stood, shocked, staring at all of it.

"This for you, love of our hearts," Farzi smiled.

"Farzi," I sniffled, wrapping my arms around his neck.

"What are you doing?" Karzac stood in the doorway to the bedroom Kevis kept at the villa.

"Righting a wrong, I hope," Kevis replied, tossing a few things into a bag. "I'll be back tomorrow if everything goes well."

"You're not getting into trouble, are you?" Karzac lifted an eyebrow.

"Trouble? Me?" Kevis folded away.

"These cartons are nice," I held one up. The container was gold on the outside, with black and silver lettering. The cartons would have to be nice to convince a customer to spend at least one hundred seventy-five credits on it.

"I have an office in Adrixx, complete with an advertising account," Edward said. "Apparently when I say jump, they don't even bother asking how high. They just jump as high as they can and see if that's good enough." We were ready to fill the cartons with ice cream to take to Edward's vendors. It was a gift of sorts; an attempt to get them to buy.

"The inspectors are coming in three days," Edward added. "When are we going on our date?"

"Edward, we need to have a talk," I said. "You see how I'm crazy and all, according to my mates and the doctor. And a nurse in the Reth Alliance sold some sensitive vid to that stupid reality show, Temporary Insanity. The whole Reth Alliance and at least half the Campiaan Alliance thinks I'm crazy. Some think I'm dangerous, too. You should have seen those mothers pulling their babies away from me when I went out in public."

"Those people are fools," Edward huffed. "Reah, if you think we can't go out somewhere on a date, then we'll stay in. I have a pool and a game room and a vid room and a lot of other rooms I probably don't realize I have."

"Then we can stay in, as long as I get to cook."

"You don't have to do that."

"But I want to. You can help if you want."

"Sweetheart, I can scramble eggs. That's about it."

"I like an honest man," I smiled up at him.

"You have something for me?" Dandril Wond asked. Dandril was Edward's gishi fruit distributor throughout the Campiaan Alliance. Edward set a tink carton of gishi fruit ice cream in front of Dandril and offered him a wrapped plastic spoon.

"A new product that's about to go into production," Edward smiled. "I wanted to give you first crack at it."

"What is it?" Dandril lifted the top off the carton and gazed at the contents.

"Gishi fruit ice cream," Edward's smile widened. "Go ahead, try it." Dandril dipped the spoon in and lifted ice cream to his lips. And then lifted another, larger spoonful. "I want everything you produce," Dandril declared, dipping out more ice cream.

"I was hoping you'd say that," Edward laughed. "Dandril, this is going to make us three times as wealthy as we are. Production starts in an eight-day, and we have an ad campaign to plan."

Kevis had been gone for three days and my healers came out of bedrooms every morning with wide smiles. In fact, two of Franklin's mates, Shane and Tomas, had come, met with Celestan and Galaxsan and that was that—they were hooked. We went up the mountain with them one afternoon and watched, Astralan and I, while they snowboarded down. "Reah, I don't think I've ever been this happy," Astralan sighed, leaning over to give me a kiss.

"Hon, don't say that yet. I don't know when I'll feel like sex again."

"You will. Kevis will get you back to us. Besides, I've waited this long. I can wait a while longer. Tell me you care for me, Reah, that's all I need."

"I do," I said. "I can't say how much right now, because I'm still numb from Cloudsong. You're going to need that patience, honey."

"Teeg just hunches his shoulders around me, now. He doesn't know how this will fit into our working relationship," Astralan said. "I don't mind, as long as it doesn't interfere with us. Come over here. You look tired. How's that baby?" Astralan rubbed my belly soothingly as I watched Franklin fly down the slope, just ahead of Galaxsan. We'd gotten a private room with a balcony so I wouldn't be subjected to the scrutiny of the other guests. Ceerah had ruined the possibility of my going out in public and remaining anonymous. She'd likely gotten me shot by whoever had a vendetta against me.

"You have good hands," I said, tracing the veins on the back of the hand that wasn't rubbing my belly.

"Those hands want to touch a lot of things," Astralan breathed against my ear. "Don't tempt me, Reah. I'm patient if you don't dangle that in front of me."

"I can't touch you?" I turned to look up at him.

"Reah, you set my blood on fire. You have to be careful, my heart."

"All right. Go back to the belly rub," I sighed.

~

"Reah is coming to make dessert for Mom's birthday," Franklin grinned at his father. Merrill, the former King Vampire, was now a member of the Saa Thalarr's elite corps of Enforcers.

"I hear you're going to introduce a couple of new mates as well," Merrill smiled. He had a very dry sense of humor, when he employed it.

"Reah is responsible for that," Frank was still grinning. "They fit right in, Dad. Joey, Norton and Bearcat aren't the only ones who have a warlock mate. We have two."

"I didn't realize it was a contest."

"Dad, I love you," Franklin gave Merrill a hug.

"I love you, too, son. Always have. Do you know what Reah is making for us?"

"I don't want to spoil it, but word has it that it's the most expensive dessert you'll ever eat."

"Then I'll look forward to it. How is Reah, by the way?"

"I think she has three people panting after her, and only knows about two of them," Franklin's dimple appeared.

"Besides what she already has?"

"Well, yeah. That Edward Pendley guy asked her to marry him already."

"He's at least half Elemaiya. Was born on Earth, did you know that?" Merrill smiled.

"And now he grows gishi fruit."

"And now he does. Perhaps you should invite all of Reah's mates and prospective mates to the party. I wouldn't mind talking to Mr. Pendley, son."

~

"Reah, can you make twice as much ice cream as we originally thought?" Frank moved the hair off my neck and fanned it gently—it was hot out by the pool. "Those are claiming marks?" He examined the four punctures on my neck.

"Yes, those are claiming marks," I said. "And I can make three times the original amount, if you want it."

"Let's do that, then," Frank grinned before hugging me. "I think I love you as much as any gay man can love a woman."

"Hey, now," I turned to poke him in the ribs. "Those eyes are way too tempting. You should watch out," I hugged him back.

"Got those from my dad," he laughed.

"On your birthday, right?"

"First one."

"I'll bet your dad is something," I said.

"He is. Mom is, too. She says she's not freaked out or scarred for life, she was just shocked that a naked nymph was drawing designs on her belly."

"No designs, I promise," I said. "I know nothing about the naked nymph thing."

"It's hot. Let's get in the pool," Franklin lifted me up, and just like that, every stitch of clothing I wore disappeared. As did his. We were floating around in the pool in no time. The water was nice, actually. Farzi, Nenzi and their six brothers showed up and dropped into the pool as lion snakes.

"Honey Snake," I reached out to stroke Farzi's head.

"You can tell them apart?" Franklin didn't know what to think about eight snakes swimming around him.

"By the patterns," I nodded. "They're all different. See, this is Nenzi," he lifted his head and I kissed him between the eyes. "And here's Chazi," I pointed out the slight differences in his pattern. "Bekzi, Hirzi, Yanzi, Perzi and Darzi," I pointed all of them out. Nenzi curled around my neck. "Sweet man," I stroked his scales.

"A party?" Teeg walked out, immediately dropped his clothing and slipped into the water.

"Damn." Joey and Norton came out of the house, drinks in hand. They were impressed by the snakes and the males in the pool.

"Holy shit." Kevis chose that moment to come back.

"Aw, come on. I'm in here," Frank said.

"Baby," Teeg moved Nenzi aside and hugged me against him. "Put your arms around my neck. Come on." I worried my lower lip while staring into his dark eyes. "Come on," he coaxed softly. "Yeah, that's right," my arms went around his neck. "How's our baby doing?" A hand slipped between us, stroking my belly. And then he pulled my head against his shoulder.

"There's nothing to worry about, unless you attack one of them or Reah," Astralan slapped Kevis on the back and shucked his clothing too. Astralan didn't have a thing to be ashamed of, sliding into the water easily. "Just right," he sighed with pleasure.

"I will join you." Nefrigar, whom I hadn't seen for days, appeared in the water and sat in a corner. His head was far above the water in the four-foot depth on one end.

"Kiss me, baby. Tell me you still care about me," Teeg murmured against my ear.

"Teeg," I hugged him tighter.

"That's good, sweetheart," he sighed. I was glad the reptanoids had built a huge pool after a while. Everybody was in the water. Mathilde came out with trays of drinks, didn't even blink and went back for more.

"Bro, can I get a turn?" Tory was behind us, tapping Teeg on the back.

"This looks like fun," Ry, Erland and Corolan appeared. Was I prepared to see Erland naked? I guess. Ry got every bit of his good looks from his father.

"Come on, baby, come to your High Demon," Tory sighed, sliding me away from Teeg. Except for Nefrigar, Tory was the tallest one there. Tory held me, but I had difficulty meeting his gaze. He tilted my head up. "Do you know how sorry I am?" Tory said softly. "I can't believe what kind of fool I was." He tilted his head and kissed me.

I should have remembered about the linking. I should have. I hadn't had a High Demon lover for twenty-five years and I'd forgotten that until the moment we came into contact. His desire linked right into mine. It didn't matter whether I wanted him to start with. Tory's rush of fire heated my blood. What he wanted, I wanted. And he wanted everything. Right away. "Don't be scared, don't be scared," he whispered against my mouth. Was he going to do this, right in front of everybody? He skipped us away at the last possible moment, landing us in a bed, somewhere.

"Won't hurt, I promise," his body pushed against mine. I only had a moment to be frightened before we were one. It didn't hurt. Didn't burn or sting. His body was treating mine gently, with careful strokes. Instead of bites, I received kisses. Whatever he could reach was kissed and teased and caressed. "Love you, Reah. Love you. Love you. *Love you.*"

"It's the linking," Gavril blew out a sigh. "All he has to do is touch her and it activates."

"Linking? Have I heard this before?" Kevis asked. He'd finally gotten into the pool with everyone else. Dee had come and was now coaxing Mathilde into the water.

"Once a High Demon puts his teeth in a High Demon female's neck, the next time forms the linking. His desire is hers and vice versa. Hard to stop, once it's started."

"Your brother told you this?"

"Uh, not exactly. I was a curious child," Gavril admitted.

"Uh-huh. Care to talk about that?" Kevis asked.

"I'm not having a session with a naked man," Gavril groused.

"Point taken," Kevis sipped his drink and grinned.

"I'm much older, guaranteed," Dee pulled Mathilde along, her nicely plump form an enticement to the old vampire.

Gavril grinned. "Time to get out," he said quietly. Kevis agreed. Everyone slipped out and quietly made an exit.

~

"That is a fool's errand," Maldak, the Copper Ra'Ak Prince glared at the ones standing before him. Both claimed to be Elvish Princes. "We have no power against one of that kind," Maldak continued. "I will not even consider it."

"But we will pay very well. Offer sacrifices, if you want."

"Faugh. You think to tempt me with that?" Maldak snorted. "We can get our own. We do not need such brought to us. Leave now and you keep your lives."

"Come, Naldill," Reldill grasped his brother's arm. "We'll find another way." Maldak's eyes narrowed as he watched the two elves disappear. He'd known about the rogue attack upon the Saa Thalarr. Had it on good authority that a High Demon had come and destroyed all thirty-six rogue Copper Ra'Ak. Just as well. It saved Maldak the trouble of killing them himself.

~

"Reah, baby, are you hungry?" Tory traced a finger down my cheek. I huddled farther into his warmth. Why were the men always so warm? Unless there was a heat wave, I felt cold most of the time.

"Cold, avilepha?" I was gathered closer. I still hadn't opened my eyes. Tory was practically reading my mind. "Do you feel all right? How's the baby?" A hand, warm, splayed on my belly. "Come on; let's get you fed before you feel nauseous." I was lifted off the bed, carried into the shower and finally forced to open my eyes when the spray of warm water hit my skin.

"See, those pretty eyes can open," Tory smiled at me.

"Where are we?" Tory grabbed the soap and began working over my body, not answering my question for a moment.

"The palace in Lissia," he finally said. "My suite." It must have been updated since I'd visited last, but that had been more than twenty-five years earlier. Of course it had been updated since then.

"Great. Now your mom and everybody else will know." I pushed wet hair back from my face. I hoped at that point that I could get it trimmed soon. The length was almost too long for me to handle.

"Know what?"

"That we—you know."

"Is that a crime? Reah, we're mated."

"Since when?" I turned away from him.

"Don't go back on me now," Tory turned me around and blinked concerned, dark eyes into mine.

"Tory, we were mated long ago. I don't know what we are now. You never married me, if you'll recall."

"I know. Baby, that was long ago and I've learned my lesson at least ten times since then. Can't we let it go? We were good last night. You wanted it as much as I did."

"I don't know what I want anymore. Not as far as we're concerned."

"You have to sort this out with Kevis. I know that. Whatever it is. He'll help you."

"And then what? I can just forget about the last twenty-five years?"

"Look, I know that's not possible. I was hoping we could set that aside and go on from here." He raked wet hands through his dark hair in frustration.

"Tory," I dropped my face in my hands. Here he was still not offering to marry me. Not taking responsibility. What did he want from me? Confessions of undying love? I wasn't sure I was capable of that. Not in my present state.

"Can we agree to a truce, at least? Until we figure this out? Tell me you didn't enjoy what happened between us. I wish I hadn't been so thickheaded about all that. Darletta couldn't even come close to what we have."

"You had to bring her into it, didn't you?" I skipped angrily away.

"Don't ask." I walked furiously past Kevis, naked, wet and angry. Turning on the taps in the shower, I stepped inside, intent upon finishing what I'd started on Le-Ath Veronis.

"What happened?" Kevis was inside the bathroom, asking questions while I was cleaning up. Well, he'd seen all of me before, why would this be any different? Why didn't I just walk around naked all the time? I slapped the soap onto the shelf and scrubbed my skin.

"Torevik Rath, that's what," I muttered. "He proceeded to tell me that the sex he had with me was better than the sex he had with Darletta. Like I wanted to hear that."

"Perhaps he thought to pay you a compliment."

"Bringing up sex with the woman you married to the one you didn't isn't a good idea in my book," I grabbed the shampoo bottle and squeezed out a generous portion. "I don't care how good he thinks the compliment is. Want to go into the outside world with me while I get my hair trimmed today?" I snapped.

"Reah, I will go anywhere with you, but we'll look for a place where you won't be harassed."

"Good luck on finding that," I huffed.

"We'll find something, I promise."

Mathilde was smiling and humming as she placed breakfast in front of us. Teeg had an eyebrow lifted but didn't say anything when I sat between him and Kevis at the table. Farzi and Nenzi were watching too, but remained silent. Joey, Norton, Franklin, Celestan and Galaxsan ate quietly. Astralan stole a look in my direction occasionally but didn't interrupt my meal. Lok and Aurelius weren't there. I wondered where they were but didn't send mindspeech or ask the three healers.

"We're going to get our hair trimmed," Kevis announced when I finished eating.

"Huh?" I turned to him. He'd said *we*.

"We're going," he repeated. "As many as want to go." He made a circle with a finger, indicating everybody at the table.

"Ah. Mathilde, would you like to come? Get your hair washed or something?" I looked at our cook.

"If the bosses say it's all right," she smiled.

"It all right," Farzi nodded.

"Then I'll come."

"Let me brush my teeth. Where are you taking me again?"

"Reah, this is Conner." I was introduced to a beautiful woman with long, blonde hair. Not as long as mine, but most women didn't have hair that long.

"Honey, we're going to take you to my favorite salon. You and Mathilde both." She had a slower way of speaking and a lovely accent. "We'll get your fingers and toes done, too." We were folded to an exclusive salon, with private rooms and such. Mathilde and I were allowed inside the same one. We were given manicures and pedicures first, then the hairdressers arrived.

"Is this your natural color?" The young man stared at me in surprise.

"Everything about her is natural," Connor observed dryly. "We just want a bit of a trim. About eight inches, I think," she added.

"To the middle of the back?" he asked, drawing a finger across the designated spot. "My name is Todd," he introduced himself.

"Maybe a little longer than that," I said. Someone named Mari worked on Mathilde while Todd walked around me. I sat in a hydraulic chair that Todd raised quite high. My hair hung over the back of it.

"Let's trim those bangs and taper them. We'll make the hair softer around the face," Todd said, chin in fingers as he decided what to do. "You must have had beautiful parents; you got great genes from somewhere," he said as he worked on my hair after wetting it down for the cut.

"Ixnay on the arents-pay," Conner said. I didn't understand what she said at all. And I didn't want to go into my troubles with a hairdresser, so I remained silent.

"See, you can still pull it back, but it'll be feathered around the face and not so severe if you do pull it into a braid," Todd showed me later, holding the length in his hands. "But look at this." He turned the chair around and gave me a mirror to examine the back. My hair was cut to the right length, the heavy weight curling under slightly. "Honey, that is movie star hair. No doubt about that. I know women who would kill to get it."

"They'd have a fight on their hands," I handed the mirror back to him. "I like your work," I added.

"Thanks," he smiled. Mathilde was finished shortly after I was. She'd gotten her shoulder-length, reddish-brown hair colored and layered. She looked quite nice. Dee would be impressed, I think.

Conner insisted on paying, and all my men rose from their seats in the waiting area when we walked out.

"Beautiful," Teeg walked around, examining the cut. "Very, very nice," he moved hair aside and ran a finger down my cheek. "Here." He tossed a wad of paper currency to Todd as a tip. My hairdresser caught it with a smile.

"Will you come to the house for tea?" Conner asked.

"We will," Kevis answered. We ended up at a manor house. The architecture was archaic. Certainly not modern, but well-kept for all that.

"This is where we live," Franklin informed me. "Shane, Tomas and I. We'll bring Celestan and Galaxsan here soon. Conner wants to meet them."

"That's wonderful," I said. "They've been looking for you for a while, I think."

"We know about the hundred year thing," Franklin said. "But they say it won't matter."

"I've heard that it doesn't with your true mates." Ry had told me about it.

"That's what they say," Frank grinned. "I'm afraid we don't want to give them up. Come along, let's have tea and cake."

"These are very good," I said. The tiny cakes were lightly frosted and melted in the mouth.

"I love petit fours," Conner laughed.

"You ready for tomorrow?" Joey asked.

"Nearly. I need to pick up a couple of things and get the fresh gishi fruit from Edward, but that's it."

"We can take you when we leave here," he offered.

"That sounds good. I need to talk to Edward anyway."

"Here it is, and the inspectors passed the temporary facility. We're laying the foundation for the other one tomorrow. It'll go up quickly after that." Edward smiled and led me to a barn where crates of gishi fruit waited.

"Here are the sugar and spice suppliers," I handed my comp-vid to Edward, who tapped his codes in to transfer the data.

"Are you available to come tomorrow?" Franklin asked Edward. Frank, Norton and Joey had come with me; the others had gone back to Campiaa.

"I would be happy to go if Reah is going," Edward grinned.

"Then please do. We'll come pick you up," Franklin smiled.

"I'm surprised you love cooking so much, when working in the kitchens when you were a child was so traumatic for you," Kevis said, watching me pull dark chocolate cakes from the oven. The cakes had to cool before I set them inside boxes for transport. Franklin had gone to get Edward, who'd agreed to come with us. The gishi fruit ice cream was prepared already and packed in cartons inside the large freezer in the reptanoids' kitchen. Edible gold flakes were stored inside shakers, the fresh oxberries and redberries were already washed and ready to use.

"There you are," Edward appeared with Franklin inside the kitchen.

"Want something to drink?" I asked.

"Of course I do," he grinned. He was such a wonderful man, and not difficult to look at, either.

"Kevis?" I raised the pitcher. I was about to make the rum and fruit drink that everyone seemed to like so much.

"Sure." He nodded at me while pulling a stool out for Edward.

"This is very good," Kevis sighed, sucking the last of his drink through a straw.

"You only get one, unless you want to attend the party a little sloshed," I said.

"All right, but I may want to be sloshed later," he smiled.

"Good enough. Let me know when you want the sloshing to commence," I said. "Just make it before my bedtime."

"Okay, boss," Kevis laughed.

"You've had too much already," I pulled the glass away from him.

"Are we ready?" Franklin asked later, after I'd gotten cakes settled into boxes. Everything else, including the ice cream, was sitting on the huge island, waiting to be transported.

"I'm ready." I'd changed clothes, although I still wasn't dressed for a party. I wasn't an invitee, just one of the cooks, after all. Garwin Wyatt had finally made his presence known, too. I couldn't fasten the waistband on any of my pants, so I'd worn a pair of black jeans with the stretchy front, coupling them with a jeweled blue top gathered slightly between my breasts. The outfit was comfortable and looked nice enough. Low, black heels finished everything out, and I'd elected to wear the jewelry that Farzi and Nenzi had purchased for me.

"This nice," Farzi grinned when he saw the jewelry. All my mates had been invited, in addition to Edward and Astralan. I just shrugged and allowed Franklin, Joey and Norton to fold us to the party.

∾

"This is my mother," Franklin introduced me to Kiarra, who refused to tell us how old she was.

"We've met," I nodded at Kiarra, who smiled graciously at me.

"I should have known," Frank laughed. "Mom gets around, and half the time she forgets to tell me. This is my father, Merrill," Franklin added. Frank looked very much like his father, who also had black hair and piercing blue eyes.

"We'll place everything in stasis, so it won't melt or spoil," Merrill informed me when we settled everything on another huge island. "Dinner is about to start. We'll let you know when it's time for dessert."

I nodded to him; he smiled and then went immediately to Edward. "You don't know me," Merrill held out his hand, "but I know of you."

"How's that?" Edward asked, clasping Merrill's hand.

"I used to be vampire," he said. "I know about the half-Elemaiyan children. What I wanted to talk to you about is gishi fruit. Adam and I would like to either buy into one of the groves, or purchase it outright."

"EastStar isn't for sale, and I know the owner of SouthStar very well. He won't sell, either. You might be able to approach WestStar and NorthStar. I don't get along with them; they're always looking for ways to sabotage my groves," Edward huffed. "They think I'm cutting into their business, and they're terrified of SouthStar's owner and his manager. They don't try anything with them, but they love to dig at me whenever they can. The feud has gained local notoriety," Edward admitted with a wry smile.

"You're famous?" I smiled up at Edward.

"Not really. I'm just the guy who grows gishi fruit. Those other two fail to realize that there's a ready market for everything we produce, collectively."

"Growing gishi fruit works for me," I said. "Can I have your autograph?"

"I offered you my name. You haven't said yes, yet." He laughed.

"We haven't had our date yet."

"True enough. We'll do that soon. Don't forget, we start making ice cream in four days."

"I have shipments of supplies coming your way," I said. "I sent that information to you."

"And I received it. We'll make this work, just wait and see."

They should have asked you to do the cooking, Teeg sent to me. The food was good, but Teeg obviously thought I might do better. It didn't matter, dessert had tired me out. At least seventy people had come, so I was glad we had enough dessert for around a hundred.

Many of the dishes were vegetarian, too. Franklin's mother didn't eat meat, like several others, there. I'd met Kevis' mother, Grace, as well as Karzac's third mate, Devin. They were very polite; I learned both were vegetarian and they kindly asked about the baby.

"Now, let's have some of that dessert," Franklin said when everyone had retired to what he called the ballroom. The cooking staff would supply coffee and other drinks; it was my job to get the dessert ready for the guests.

"Just tell them what you want them to do," Franklin led me into the kitchen, where a line of temporary employees waited for instructions.

"Cut the cake thin, like this," I sliced a piece that was little more than an inch at the widest part. "This cake is very rich, so we don't want it to overpower the ice cream and fresh berries. Now, scatter a good mix of berries around the top, like this," I demonstrated what I wanted. "Then, add a sprig of mint, dip a generous scoop of ice cream and drop it at the bottom of the cake, and sprinkle the entire thing with gold flakes."

"That looks pretty, how does it taste?" the cook demanded. I think he'd been insulted that someone else was inside his kitchen.

"Taste it, this one is yours," I handed it to him. He dipped up a bit of the cake with a little of the ice cream and tasted it.

"Holy shit," he sighed and dipped up more. "What kind of ice cream is this?"

"The most expensive you'll ever eat," Franklin said, patting my shoulder. "Come on, let's get it onto plates and serve the guests." We put an assembly line together and trays filled with dessert went out quickly.

"You're telling me this fruit only grows on two planets?" The cook, who said his name was Rio, asked.

"It's true. It harvests two or three times a year on or near the equator, in a particular volcanic soil. They've tried to grow it elsewhere, but the trees just die or the fruit is bitter."

"Amazing," Rio said. "I think I could ask any amount if I could get it here."

"There's barely enough to satisfy the demand as it is," I informed him. "I used to manage the groves on one of the planets. It turned into a very lucrative business."

"So you decided to make ice cream with it?"

"I did. I took the slightly blemished fruit that we couldn't sell and made ice cream for the employees. They loved it."

"Sounds like a nice bonus for them," Rio said.

"They deserved it."

"Reah, this is Glendes Grey, of Grey House," Joey introduced a dark-haired man to me. He took my hand and kissed it.

"I'd pay whatever you asked, I think, if you'd come and make this dessert for a special occasion sometime," he smiled at me.

"Your house made my favorite knife," I said. "I'd do it, just for that."

"Reah, are you frightening Rio?" Franklin asked.

"I hope not," I said. "We were just having a great conversation with the Eldest of Grey House, here."

"Rio, you won't be able to repeat a single word of this outside this house," Franklin said, "and I'm sorry for that. Knowledge of our race protects its own."

"I won't be able to tell my brother?"

"Not unless he's here now."

"He isn't."

"Sorry. Reah, it probably isn't a good idea to tell him anything else. It may frustrate him when he finds he can't pass the information along."

"But am I included in that?" I asked. "I'm not one of you."

"The Larentii are taking care of you and the others tonight. It will all be the same."

"Rio, ask any question you want, and I'll answer it," I said. "But as Franklin says, the information will remain with you afterward."

"I don't mind, I've seen and heard a lot that makes me hopeful tonight," he said. "What is your race, Reah? Which one do you belong to?"

"At times, just the mention of my race conjures up the wrong image," I said. "Just bear in mind that some of us, not all, but some of us have gotten an erroneous reputation. I'll show you what I am." I turned to my smaller Thifilatha and Rio, poor soul, fell over in a faint.

CHAPTER 8

"*R*eah, sweetheart, he asked, you answered." I was wrapped in Edward's shirt inside Kiarra's kitchen, shaking a little while others revived Rio. "I'm so sorry," I said, reaching toward him when he opened his eyes.

"Uh, what did you turn into?" He asked while Franklin and Joey helped him up and offered him a glass of brandy.

"They call her kind High Demons," Teeg supplied the information. "And while the term demon on this world has a very negative connotation, where Reah is from, it is quite different. They don't come from the underworld," he added, grinning.

"Can I see it again? I wasn't expecting something like that," Rio rubbed his forehead in fading astonishment.

"I don't want to burn your shirt," I looked up at Edward.

"Then stand behind me, take it off and then turn," Edward suggested. "It won't hurt the baby to turn again that quickly, will it?"

"She's pregnant?" Rio's voice went up an octave.

"With my son," Teeg replied. "Go ahead, baby. Show him again."

I did as Edward suggested, going behind him, removing the shirt and handing it to him before I turned.

"Everything is gold, except the eyes and hair," Rio breathed. "Is it safe to touch?"

"It is now," I said. If I willed it, my skin wouldn't burn. I'd taken Teeg for a ride several times in the past, when he needed my larger Thifilatha to accomplish a task.

"Don't ever touch unless she says it's safe," Teeg warned. Rio came forward and with a shaking hand, touched my arm and then a wing.

"Gosh, her skin is so warm," Rio said in wonder.

"Reah is the only gold demon. The males are black when they turn, Queen Glinda is all white," Tory came in to explain. I still wasn't speaking to him, so I let him talk.

"You're a demon, too?" Rio asked Teeg.

"No. Tory, here, is High Demon," Teeg corrected.

"I don't recommend asking him to change," I said.

"Why not?" Tory sounded offended.

"Tory, you're scary," I muttered, hanging my head.

"Baby? You're afraid of me?" Tory held out a hand.

"Now may not be the time," Kevis intervened. "Perhaps we should go elsewhere and discuss this."

"Reah, are you ready to go?" Edward turned to me.

"Yeah. I think so," I said. "Rio, it was a pleasure cooking with you," I held my hand out to him. He surprised me by taking it and kissing it.

"Now, let's go to Campiaa and sort some of this out, I hope," Kevis sighed. Somebody folded us to the plantation.

"Will somebody please tell me what's going on?" Tory blew a cloud of smoke-filled frustration.

"Torevik, Reah was attacked recently. That included a vicious bite. Tell me how you claimed her the first time?"

Tory cursed. We were in the reptanoids' large family room, where there was enough comfortable seating for everyone. I still wore Edward's shirt and now sat squeezed between him and Teeg. I was cold and humanoid again. Edward gripped the fingers of my right hand in his, while Teeg held the left.

"She should know I wouldn't hurt her. Not like that," Tory fumed, pacing about the room. Everybody was there, including

Farzi, Nenzi, Lok, Aurelius, Lendill, Nefrigar and Ry. Astralan had also come.

"She may know that logically, but not emotionally," Kevis said. "After all, you walked away from her when she needed you. How is that not harm? I realize you have your own trauma to deal with, and she knows that as well unless I badly miss my guess. The question comes down to this—do you still love one another? And if you do, what kind of commitment are you willing to make?"

"Dad always said she was just a quarter," Tory sat down hard next to Aurelius. "He always said he wasn't sure how our children would turn out since I was half."

I was standing and infuriated in seconds. I wanted to weep. I wanted to hit Torevik Rath. And then hit his father. They were looking down on me because I was only a quarter High Demon? I held every one of a High Demon's gifts and abilities, including some that none of the others possessed. Yet Gardevik wanted to split hairs.

"That's what this is about, isn't it?" I shouted. "The race isn't pure any longer. Fuck you, Torevik Rath. And fuck your father, for handing prejudice to his son. We're done. Get out. I never want to see you again. Get out!" When he didn't move, I was the one who skipped away.

"Nice work, bro." Ry stared at Tory. "And why haven't we heard any of this before? Is your father crazy? Reah keeps the race from dying, and he lets his prejudice show? Nefrigar, do you know where Reah is?"

"I do. She is fine but very upset at the moment," Nefrigar admitted.

Kifirin appeared with a sigh and a slight curling of smoke from his nostrils. "This is why I told Lendevik that his daughter must go to Jaydevik, Pendevik Rath's third son, instead of Gardevik, his firstborn." Kifirin stated. "Jayd had tolerance, while Garde had very little. I hoped that Garde would develop something of what he needed when he recognized Lissa as his mate, but that did not help Reah, did it?"

"You mean Dad might have been King, instead of Uncle Jayd?" Tory gave Kifirin a confused look.

"Yes. Your father would have been King if he'd been flexible and empathetic. He is neither. How long were you going to hold that secret inside? Reah was troubled from the beginning when you claimed her as you did and then never offered to make the marriage vows. Yet you couldn't wait to rush away and marry a full humanoid, at the first hint of an imaginary slight. I will give Reah time to come to a decision, but if she asks after that, I will remove your claiming marks."

"Why couldn't I keep my mouth shut? Why?" Tory buried his face in his hands.

"How much of a chance will your son have of getting a High Demon mate if Reah turns him away?" Lissa fumed. "There are no other High Demon women available. That aren't his daughters, that is. And they're already promised to others. You and your brother saw to that," the Queen of Le-Ath Veronis went on. "Garde, I never thought you to be so prejudiced. Are you that narrow-minded? Or is it just Reah that you're targeting? If so, I'd sure as hell like to know why."

Garde knew Lissa was furious, and his relationship with her was likely hanging by a thread. "I always wondered why Lendevik chose Jayd over me," he sighed. "Now I know."

"I send a gift to you and your race and you belittle it," the one who'd identified himself as Kifirin's parent appeared in a burst of light. "You stand to cheat your son out of the High Demon female meant for him. What else will you do to destroy your kind, Gardevik Rath?" The god disappeared quickly.

"Is that what you've done, Garde? Worked to destroy the High Demons?" Lissa folded away.

"Brother, I must resign my position. It seems I have to take time and examine my priorities," Garde appeared in Jayd's study.

"Why is that?" Jayd frowned at his oldest brother.

"My son repeated my words to Reah, and she no longer wants him for a mate," Garde sighed. "And he did not misrepresent or misinterpret anything. I belittled Reah for being only a quarter High Demon. Worried over how their children might turn out, since my son is only half-blood. I was just chastised by Kifirin's father, for misusing the gift he gave to us."

"What gift?" Jayd was worried.

"Reah, apparently. And when it looked as if my granddaughters would be all right and suitable for High Demon mates, I gathered them away as quickly as I could."

"And handed them to Glinda and me," Jayd nodded. "I should have known something was off, but we failed to question. We thought the gift had been given to us."

"The gift was given to you, and you snatched it away, never thinking to share. I hope you will recognize that sort of thing in the future, King Jayd." Kifirin appeared from nowhere.

"I have learned my lesson, High Lord," Jayd bowed respectfully.

"At least some still know to bow to me," Kifirin said and disappeared.

"I do not accept your resignation, brother," Jayd said. "Although I will accept the fact that you need to reflect upon your views of our race. Come to terms with this. I hope Reah does not turn your child away. All her children with him are females. I still hold hope that we will have more."

"I will go check the gishi fruit groves, then," Garde sighed. "I hear things are not going well."

"They need more money to operate, or so they say, and the new manager says we have to spray for insects. He does not know how Reah managed to keep them away."

"I will look into it," Garde nodded before skipping away.

～

Reah, where are you? This is scaring me. The mindspeech came from Edward. I was on Thiskil (again) when he contacted me. On the Southern Continent, this time, where a warmer ocean washed up on the beaches. Bits of old shells still littered the sands, but no new ones had come ashore for a very long time. Everything had died when Zellar drained the core.

"Did you mean to kill everything you touched, Zellar?" I asked the wind. *Edward,* I sent to him, *I am safe for the moment. I will come back soon.*

"I am being punished," Zellar's ghost stood before me. I blinked in surprise and took a step backward. I recognized him, however; his face was disfigured as it should have been, before he'd traded bodies in the many transferences he'd performed.

"How?" I asked.

"I will have no rest until all the worlds I killed or damaged are whole again. That will take a very long while, they tell me."

"They?"

"The ones who see to such things. I am not allowed to name them. They take me from one empty world to the next, so I can wander there, alone and lost. They call you the Lifegiver," he went on. "I beg you to bring life back to these worlds so I can move on to the next level of my recompense. Had I known what my actions would ultimately cost, I would have settled for a quiet life of charitable deeds."

"Hindsight," I muttered. Did Tory have that, too? It no longer mattered. I wasn't good enough to be his wife. He would have to look for another, now.

"Yes. Certainly that," Zellar agreed. "I should kneel at your feet and thank you for cutting my punishment in half on this level. You saved so many of the worlds I destroyed."

"I killed you," I pointed out.

"And if you hadn't, imagine what this would be if I'd continued on my destructive path. The ones who watch me now say I would have killed nearly everything in the end. One tile falling into another, until all had fallen. I was foolish. I know better now, since I am in a place where those things are visible to me. I see how one thing affects another, like ripples in water." Zellar came to sit beside me on the sand. "You glow, like some who watch me," he added. "Do you know what it's like to see others and crave their touch, and not be able to feel it? Their hands slide right through me. This is the most horrible of things, Lady Demon, and I understand I have a very long time to suffer through this."

"Did you take pity upon any that you killed?" I watched his face, scars and all.

"I didn't. Thought them beneath me. Now, I am the smallest of the small. You are the only one I've found who could hear me in my present state."

"I'm not sure how or why that is," I told him. "Shall I weep for you now, as I wept for those you killed? Somehow, it is in me to be troubled by any that suffer. That does not alter my opinion that your actions were reprehensible and caused terrible pain and suffering."

"I know. They tell me that kind hearts feel this. I never had a kind heart."

"It sounds as if you have lessons with these beings."

"I do. At times, their lessons are very difficult to learn."

"How long will you be here, on Thiskil?" I asked, unsure whether I wanted to be greeted by a ghost if I visited again.

"Is that where I am? Thiskil? How many died here?"

"Millions," I said, feeling sadness over that fact. "The Reth Alliance managed to move some away, but many died anyway. At the last, only those with a great deal of money were able to escape."

"All my fault," Zellar looked as if he were weeping, silvery traces of tears flowing down ghostly cheeks.

"At least you accept responsibility," I said.

"That was my first lesson," he wept.

"I understand responsibility all too well now," I said, rising. "I must go. Are you a danger to anyone in your present state?"

"No. I have no power, including showing myself to anyone. Except you, it seems. I thank you for speaking with me."

"Good-bye," I said. I wasn't going to give him any sort of

absolution. I figured that someone else would have to do that. Zellar sobbed when I skipped away.

"Reah, where have you been?" Kevis was waiting for me, as were Teeg and Edward. The others were gone. Farzi and Nenzi were likely in the groves, checking on the harvest. It didn't matter where Tory was. I knew how he felt about me now.

"I won't tell you where I went; it's a sort of sanctuary for me when I need some time," I replied.

"What were you doing? At least answer that," Teeg grumbled angrily.

"Talking to Zellar's ghost," I replied. Let him make of that what he would. "If you'll give me a moment, I'll get your shirt back to you," I told Edward. He was still wandering around bare-chested while I wore his shirt.

"Reah, you can do whatever you want with that shirt," Edward said. "I'm just glad you came back."

"That's a nice answer," I said. "You see how Teeg is just angry. He never says he's glad to see me." I removed Edward's shirt and handed it to him, standing naked inside the family room. "I'm going to get a shower. I feel tired and a little hungry." I walked past all three of them, down the long hallway and into my bedroom.

"How is it that every move I make is wrong?" Gavril paced in an agitated manner.

"It was the way things happened between you, don't you think?" Kevis asked. "When was the last time you told her that you loved her? That you were glad to see her, or acted interested in what she was doing?"

"I don't remember."

"Try."

"I can't."

"You can't try, or you can't remember?"

"I can't remember, all right? I thought you were treating her, not me."

"The more I see of things, the more I think she's not the only one who needs help," Kevis pointed out. "How much do you hate Kifirin for doing what he did to you? How much do you blame Reah for being the cause of what Kifirin did to you? I realize you asked for what you got, but she was the reason you asked, was she not?"

Gavril stared at Kevis. "Is that what this is?" He blinked in confusion. Edward, who'd listened to the exchange, remained silent.

"I think it's possible that you blame her on some level. Admit it—nearly everything she does makes you angry."

"It does." Gavril raked fingers through dark hair. "What am I supposed to do? It isn't something I can turn on and off, I think."

"Either learn how to deal with it and let it go, or let Reah go. It's as simple as that. You can't keep torturing her for something you requested."

"You think I'm torturing her?"

"What do you think?"

"I think I'm afraid I'll lose her."

"What are you doing to keep her, then? Besides getting angry?"

"Not a damn thing, I guess," Gavril admitted reluctantly. "I tend to upset her most of the time."

"She carries your child. I'd think you'd be trying to keep her calm and happy," Edward observed. "If you'd noticed what I did when you first showed up to take her away from my home, you might worry a bit more about what's going on with her. She was pale to begin with, but she blanched when you appeared. Is that any way for a wife to react when the father of her child appears? Is there someone who can take me home, now?"

"I will take you, and Reah will come with you." Nefrigar appeared inside the room, a sleeping Reah in his arms. "I placed a healing sleep; I ask that you feed her after we arrive. I will shield your home and surrounding area, just as I have done with this one. My love does not need more violence," the Larentii added.

"Wait!" Kevis and Gavril both shouted as Nefrigar folded Edward and Reah away.

~

"Reah?" Fingers stroked my jaw when I woke. A view of gishi fruit groves, stretching for clicks met my gaze when my eyes opened. Now I knew the voice in my head—it had been Edward, all along. I wasn't sure he knew how much I was coming to love him.

"Where am I?" I asked, shoving my thoughts aside.

"You're on the balcony outside my suite of rooms," Edward answered from above. I discovered that my head was in his lap and we sat on a swing of sorts that had a canopy stretched overhead. It looked to be late afternoon.

"How did I get here?" I asked, sighing with pleasure as Edward's fingers continued to stroke my face.

"Your Larentii brought both of us," Edward replied. "Are you hungry? Comfortable? Tell me what you want, sweetheart."

"Avocados and tomatoes," I sighed. "But I'm too comfortable to get up."

"Reah, I wish I could keep this moment forever," Edward said. "I'm happy."

"This is the perfect view," I said. "And you get to wake up and see it every morning."

"And you could wake and see it every morning, too. If you want. Come on, let's go find avocados and tomatoes."

"It's a pregnant thing," I salted the sliced avocado and tomato on my plate. "This is so good," I sighed, taking my first bite.

"Do I get a bite?" Edward grinned. I fed him some of each. "I like this stuff, too, I just don't eat it together all that often."

"Are we ready to make ice cream?" I asked.

"We sure are. And the ice-cream makers are programmed to add the right amount of everything, so only you and the comp will know the recipes. And word has it that the patent might be rushed through the screening process," he grinned at me. I might be able to watch that grin for a long time.

"Edward," I said, setting my plate of food aside.

"What, sweetheart?"

"Will you kiss me?"

He didn't reply, he just did. And very nicely, I might add. And I got a ride on Edward's back after I finished eating; he carried me through his house that way until we reached the media room.

"These are old vids from when I was young," he loaded them into the vid system. I saw a much younger Edward, along with others. He did have freckles splashed across his face and was completely adorable.

"These are two of my friends, Salidar and Ashe," Edward pointed out a boy with dark hair and eyes, laughing with a taller boy, who had light-brown hair and blue eyes. "Salidar is a werewolf," Edward added. "Ashe, well, he's something different, too. That's Ashe's mother, Adele," he went on. I stared at the woman. She had dark-blonde hair, brown eyes and she was laughing at something Edward's friend Salidar had said. "That's Sali's dad, Marcus, and his mother, Denise." I nodded as he introduced each one to me.

"You loved them, didn't you?" I hugged his arm as he sat beside me.

"I did. They were the first real friends I ever had. Some of them are dead, now."

"I'm sorry, honey," I said, leaning my cheek against his shoulder.

"I've been told that people are reborn, but it's never the same," he said.

"I talked to Zellar's ghost," I agreed. "For real. That isn't the crazy talking. He said he's being punished. Do you know who Zellar is?"

"No," Edward shook his head. The corner of his mouth twitched slightly, though. I wanted him to kiss me again. He did without being asked.

"Ask Ry or Teeg or Lendill about Zellar," I said. "They can give you as much information as you want." I wondered if Zellar's corporeal head still rested inside the treasury on Karathia.

~

"This suite connects to mine through that door," Edward indicated the door between our rooms later, as I stood inside my new bedroom. "It'll stay closed unless you want it open."

"All right," I nodded.

"Ah, just in time," Kevis folded in. "We have time for a short talk before bed," he announced as if he belonged there.

"Do you need a room as well?" Edward lifted an eyebrow at the doctor.

"Probably. And I had an argument with several others, who all wanted to barge in, too."

"There's plenty of room, but I don't want them to upset Reah," Edward said.

"Will they upset you?" Kevis looked at me.

"I don't know," I sighed. "Farzi and Nenzi won't, but they're in the middle of a harvest."

"Reah, they have six brothers. I'd feel sorry for them if they couldn't be gone for a while," Kevis pointed out. "And Astralan is about to wear a hole in the floor, pacing."

"Fine. If Edward doesn't mind," I grumbled. Kevis grinned. All of them, including Tory, showed up in ticks.

"I'm going to bed," I told all of them.

"But I get a little time," Kevis said.

"Fine," I snapped again. He followed me as I wandered into a closet that had somehow been stocked with clothing. Had Edward done that for me? How was he so good? How? Kevis watched as I dressed for bed, brushed my teeth and washed my face.

"Now, you never did answer my question about the ASD," he reminded me as I settled into the huge bed. Plump pillows at my back, I wriggled in the comfort of it. "How did you feel about working for the ASD?"

"I didn't like it most of the time," I answered honestly. "I learned a lot, but felt I was used. By Norian, Lendill, everybody."

"You had special talents, Reah. Were they utilizing what they had?"

"Yes. It bordered on abuse at times. I was nineteen when I was shoved into Arvil San Gerxon's camp. I was barely out of RAA training, and since Norian and Lendill wanted all the information on him that they could get, I was placed in some terrible situations. I watched one of my kitchen helpers get shot in the head right in front of me, and then Arvil's mistress died the same way, because Arvil was angry after they'd slept together. I watched other people die, too. None of them in a nice way."

"Did Arvil ever mistreat you?"

"Not in a physical sense. When his brother and cousins died, he made Teeg and me his heirs. After Arvil was killed in an ASD raid, Teeg took over, told me he was taking my half of Arvil's fortune because I'd violated the contract Arvil had us sign and disappeared with Farzi, Nenzi and their brothers. He betrayed me, then. I thought I loved him up to that point."

"And he hasn't offered you anything since then? Since creating the Campiaan Alliance?"

"No." I hugged myself. These were bad memories for me. "And when I was injured in the explosion years later, when Lendill sent me after Zellar, Teeg grabbed me, tied me to a bed, blindfolded me and had Jes treat me when he should have sent me home so Karzac could take care of me."

"How do you feel about my father?" Kevis asked.

"I love your father. He's like the father I would have wanted. Tough when he needs to be. Protective when that's needed. He was good to me from the start. I hope you get along with him," I added.

"I do," Kevis smiled slightly. "I never doubted his love, or my mother's."

"You were lucky," I said, leaning back and closing my eyes.

"Why do you think your mother married Addah Desh?"

"I don't know," I opened my eyes to stare at Kevis. "I can't imagine that he had a romantic bone in his body, so I can't answer that. I've gotten very little information on my mother. Even Fes didn't know much about her, and there weren't any photographs left after she died. Marzi probably destroyed them."

"It's too bad you didn't run into Addah's ghost, then, instead of Zellar's."

"Addah didn't destroy worlds. He just destroyed his children," I said. "Perhaps his father or mother mistreated him—he never talked about them."

"You think he might have treated others the way he was treated?"

"Maybe. But that's really not an excuse. If you know something is wrong that way, it's up to you to change it."

"You never hit your daughters, did you?"

"Are you kidding? And put them through that? No," I shook my head violently.

"I don't want to upset you, Reah, so let's back away from that for now," Kevis said gently. "Do you need someone to spend the night with you? I imagine any one of your mates would be willing."

"I don't want sex right now," I mumbled, feeling embarrassed.

"Reah, they know that. Torevik should have remembered before pushing it as he did. And his admission later was most unfortunate. I think he doesn't believe as his father does, but he loves his father. That bit of prejudice his father holds has influenced Tory. He's working to overcome it."

"Maybe that'll come in handy with his next mate," I muttered sarcastically.

"Reah, the question still stands. Do you want company for the night? Just to provide a warm shoulder?"

"I wouldn't mind a warm shoulder, or even a warm back," I said.

"Then I'll ask and see who volunteers," Kevis stood and stretched.

"Not Tory," I said, lowering my head.

"I understood that," Kevis said. "Someone will be in shortly."

"Deah-mul," Lendill slipped into bed beside me. I'd already turned out the light; it took more than the short time Kevis had estimated when he left. "My father has threatened to remove my libido for months if I do anything except keep you warm," Lendill murmured against my ear. "Go to sleep, breah-mul. I will try to do the same."

Zendeval Rjjn and Perdil the Liffelithi dwarf had made their way steadily southward, searching for warmer temperatures. Cold weather had set in where they'd been dropped on Nrath weeks earlier. Zen had done all the hunting; Perdil had no skills or experience in that area. Thankfully, Zen held both.

Most nights they were able to start a fire to cook what Zendeval had trapped or caught in a stream, but on rainy nights, they'd eaten something raw if they didn't have cooked meat left from the previous day. Zen had no weapons to go after larger game, so smaller creatures such as rabbits, squirrels and fish were their main diet. That meant little left over for the next day, rainy or not. The sun was now high over their heads, the weather most certainly warmer and Perdil was sniffing the air.

"Zen, I smell bread baking," Perdil turned wide eyes on Zendeval. Zen, lost in his own thoughts, blinked at Perdil in surprise.

"Dwarf, I believe your mind is tricking you," Zen sighed. He'd dreamed about bread, too. Among other things. Mostly, though, he dreamed of Reah. He woke with clenched hands and shortened breaths, most mornings, dreaming he still held her small body close against his. He knew now just how thin she was. How weak from the illness. But he'd been controlled. If Perdil had been the one to shoot that foul and cursed thing into his neck, the dwarf would be dead already. Instead, his cousin Nedrizif had done it himself. Zen sighed, and then drew in a breath. Perdil's arm was grasped in Zen's fist quickly. "Dwarf, perhaps your mind isn't playing tricks after all."

"I don't want to go forward with this unless we're sure we have the right woman," Andelis of Roorthi complained.

"You've seen her, the image is exact," Tevan of Shillverr pointed out. The image was indeed displayed on a very large vid-screen inside Cynthin of Xordthe's private office. Cynthin, smiling and examining her freshly manicured nails, had drawn these two in. If it could be proved that this insane woman, whose face was plastered on vid-screens across both Alliances, was Teeg San Gerxon's wife, it would only be a matter of time before Teeg San Gerxon's power was undermined and someone else could step in and take over the Campiaan Alliance.

Teeg presided over the Council of Campiaan Alliance Worlds, but Cynthin had designs on that seat. Oh, she'd promise Tevan and Andelis a sharing of power, but it would be hers when push came to shove. All they had to do was contact the media, which was still running vids depicting all the crazy and outrageous things Teeg San Gerxon's wife believed about herself.

"I think we should contact San Gerxon first, and give him the opportunity to step aside quietly, without this being made public," Andelis suggested.

"And miss all the fun and the publicity we'll get out of this?" Cynthin snorted delicately. She fully intended to make as much of this as she could, since her position within the Campiaan Alliance was relatively weak. Xordthe wasn't at the forefront of industrialization, had nothing that stood out as an export and had been under the influence of unsavory characters before the Campiaan Alliance offered membership.

Cynthin had stepped on a few heads and even more toes to get to the presidency, which she'd held for three years of a five-year term. Things might not go so well for her during the next election, so she was looking to move herself into an even better position. During her tenure in office, the economy hadn't improved and relations with most of their planetary neighbors had deteriorated. The President of Shillverr and the Crown Prince of Roorthi were her last remaining friends, and that only because she'd taken both of them as lovers.

"Then where do you intend to take this? Which media outlet?"

"Oh, I'm going to the network that produces that Temporary

Insanity show. I know they're fighting a legal battle with the Reth Alliance over patient rights violations, but we'll just take the information given and make our own complaints. They'll run it, simply to get back at the ASD."

"You're sure this will work? San Gerxon has a lot of firepower at his back." Tevan shivered. Teeg San Gerxon had four very powerful Karathian warlocks working as security, as well as others rumored to be employed as his personal protection. Tevan hadn't been there personally when the initial votes had been cast to form the Campiaan Alliance, but word had it that the founder had something incredible at his disposal if needed. One of the other members who'd been at the signing described it as a tall, golden creature with wings who'd fought off the Strands and their allies. Tevan's source said that if the creature hadn't been there, the Campiaan Alliance would have died in infancy.

"Can he use that firepower against us?" Cynthin smiled slyly. "If the media is watching his every move, how can he?"

"But none of us were there when the Alliance was born. There are plenty of others who might make a case for replacing San Gerxon," Andelis argued. "I've only held this position since Father handed the responsibility to me. Tevan has held his presidency for two years and you for three," he nodded to Cynthin.

"Don't worry your handsome head about it," Cynthin crooned. "We'll use the media. This will work, have no doubt. I'm placing the call this afternoon, and I'll forward the images we have to them if they bite. Never fear, this will be all over both Alliances in two days."

CHAPTER 9

"How is everything going?" Edward walked into our temporary ice-cream plant. I smiled at him. He smiled back.

"Everything is great and the new freezers you got are amazing," I said. "The ice cream is kept at the perfect temperature."

"I have transport coming tomorrow morning to take it to my distributor," Edward said. "The ad campaign is scheduled to start tomorrow, too. I hope people will ask for it before it even gets to the stores."

"You amaze me," I said. He did. I'd never seen follow-through like this before. Everything Edward promised, he delivered. And then some. I'd seen the vid-ads. They were great.

"Then I'm ahead of the game," he leaned down to kiss me. I had three assistants working with me, mostly to monitor the equipment, load the containers of ice cream into the freezers and clean the equipment when we were done for the day. Edward and Kevis refused to allow me to work more than four clicks per day. Edward had hired my assistants, and they were very good and quite dedicated. "And our new facility is coming along. Want to come see?" He took my hand and led me out the door.

140

The new building was going to be four times the size of the temporary one, with more equipment and more employees when it was finished. "I can't wait for this to be ready," I said, looking at storage areas and stainless prep tables covered in heavy, plastic sheeting.

"You're going to be wealthy, Reah. Are you prepared for that?" Edward put an arm around my shoulders as we looked over the half-finished building.

"I've never been that," I sighed. "I don't know what to say."

"Say we'll have our date soon. I'm looking forward to it."

"We'll do it soon," I leaned back to gaze at him.

"Good." I got another kiss.

"Mr. Marolla, I hope we're close to finishing this project," Lendill stood inside the investigative journalist's office. "I've had word from an insider that the network that ran that piece of shit in the beginning has allied with three from the Campiaan Alliance who seem bent on replacing Teeg San Gerxon. Now, I don't know if you're familiar with the Campiaan Alliance, but my sources are convinced that it will die and go back to what it was, a collection of lawless worlds, if Teeg doesn't keep a firm hand on it. I'm not willing to go back to fighting criminals from those worlds. We need to release this two days after those three and the network have had plenty of time to spew their lies. Then we'll present our information and see what happens," Lendill said.

Hild Marolla, respected investigative journalist, smiled at Lendill Schaff. "Vice-Director, we're editing the last interview now. The information provided by Dr. Kevis Halivar has been most helpful in building this story. I can certainly release this piece two days after the others have managed to hang themselves. I must admit, I've never seen anything like this. Please express my gratitude to Dr. Halivar and Deonus Wyyld for their cooperation."

"There's something else for you to add," Teeg San Gerxon

appeared, Astralan and Stellan at his side. Teeg held a comp-vid containing information and images in his hand. "It's all there," he said. "And what you see may shock you even more than you have been already, but it's the truth. I think it's time that a few eyes were opened."

"What did you bring?" Lendill asked. Teeg turned the comp-vid so Lendill could see. A single image graced the screen. "Ah," Lendill sighed.

~

"Nedrizif was Bandelif's son," Yidrizin pointed to the hand-copied records. Zendeval stared at the huge book that bore names of Greater Demons going back hundreds of thousands of years. Yidrizin, acting Prime Minister for Nrath (what was left of it, anyway), showed Zen and Perdil through the royal archives.

"I don't remember this place," Zen looked around him in awe. The treasury was there, the crown and crown jewels were also there inside the archives.

"You wouldn't, you were only a child when you were hauled away by those foul creatures," Yidrizin grumbled. "They convinced your father, the King, that greater things awaited him if he'd just follow them off-world. A foolish mistake, as it turned out. No disrespect meant, of course."

"None taken, I realize fully what kind of mistake it was." Zen had seen a handful of women inside the castle when the guards had brought him and Perdil in for an audience with Yidrizin. "Tell me about the females," he said.

"All we have are inside these walls and mated," Yidrizin stated sadly. "Six we have, and all have grown weary of childbearing."

"I was told that we were the only remaining Greater Demons," Zen sighed. "And now I learn this is not true."

"No, it was true when you heard it," Yidi replied. "I was visited by the god shortly after you were dropped here. This is in your past, Zendeval Rjjn. Twenty-five thousand years into your past. Kifirin said that you had much to atone for, and that twenty-five thousand years might do that. He also said that you would give the race hope, where there was none before. Likely the reason we died off before," Yidi remarked thoughtfully. "Now, Kifirin has promised a new day, if you work with us and tell us of the outside world as you knew it. Perhaps it will bring that hope to us."

"What I would most like to know is how you handle the moonrush when it comes," Zen said. It had cost him Reah. He realized that.

"Moonrush? That is an archaic concept," Yidi snorted in derision. "Here, follow me. I will show you how that should be handled. There is no need to terrify the women or cause them pain." Zen, with a wide-eyed and puzzled Perdil following close behind, walked with Yidrizin to the palace kitchens.

"This," Yidi held up a flask, "is moonwine. It is taken the day before a full moon. It eliminates the blood change that occurs in Greater Demons, forcing the moonrush, as you call it. Early in our history, females died because of it. The god came and gave this to us. The wine is formed from the darkberries grown here, with a few other herbs added. It is barbaric to subject the females to moonrush, and we cannot afford to lose any of them. They are too precious. The code says it and we know it to be true. The only purpose moonrush might serve is to fight off enemies. None come here, now. We are an abandoned world."

"How will I get my Reah back now?" Zen moaned to Perdil.

"Reah?" Yidi was curious.

"One taken during moonrush," Perdil jerked his head at Zendeval. "She became ill afterward. That is a very long tale."

"If she became ill, then she could bear your children," Yidi said.

"Out of his reach," Perdil shrugged as Zen moaned again. "By twenty-five thousand years, as you say." Perdil bowed to Yidi. "And the god called her High Demon."

"Stars and the god save us," Yidrizin dropped to his knees.

~

"Reah, this will only last for a day or two," Kevis assured me as I was led into the media room at Edward's manor. "I promise," he added, settling me on a comfortable sofa before the huge vid-screen. He, Lendill, Teeg and Astralan had come to get me from the ice-cream plant.

Edward had gone to the southern grove earlier in the day to check on the harvest there. He walked in now, looking angry. Something was up; I was just waiting to see what it was. I was settled on the sofa between Edward and Teeg, both of whom held one of my hands as Lendill touched the remote control, bringing the vid-screen to life.

"This was recorded earlier," Teeg muttered beside me. I didn't recognize the woman speaking, or the two men behind her. It didn't take long to determine what they were attempting to do, however.

"This woman," Cynthin Gerg, President of Xordthe, said, pointing to two photographs of me, side by side, "is married to Teeg San Gerxon. Now, I don't know how you feel about this, but she is clearly delusional, making these outrageous claims." One of the photographs showed me on Teeg's arm at some ball or other, unnecessary event for the Campiaan Alliance. The other was an unedited photograph from that foul reality program to which Ceerah and Jalan had sold my private records.

"While I have sympathy for any patient whose rights have been violated," Cynthin went on with fake emotion, "I cannot ignore how dangerous or distracting this might be to the founding Alliance member. It is, in my opinion, in all our best interests if he steps aside for now until this matter is resolved."

The program then went back to a journalist that not only called for Teeg to step aside but to leave Campiaan government altogether, due to the severity of my condition. The more I watched, the angrier I became. Everything I'd said to Kevis Halivar had been true. Ceerah and her fellow conspirator had done this—not only to me but to Teeg as well.

"Divorce me," I said to Teeg the moment the recording ended. "That will get them off your back and things will be normal for you." I tried to rise, but Edward and Teeg wouldn't release my hands.

"Let me go," I said as calmly as I could. At that moment, I'd have given anything to be anywhere else and anyone else. This was as bad as the attack and intended rape. Perhaps worse. Before, I'd been violated by a single man. Now I was being violated by every member of two Alliances. Had I ever had hopes of walking freely in daylight without people pointing or shying away? The last remnant of that hope skittered beyond my reach.

"Reah, don't run away from this. We're preparing a response; it will take two days to put it up," Teeg said.

"And what are you going to tell them?" I turned to Teeg. "Liar, liar, pants on fire?" The words were voiced in English, an old phrase that I'd learned from Gavril, long ago. Gavril. Just the thought of him, seventeen and still innocent when he'd been taken by Kifirin, made me want to weep. "Kifirin screwed both of us, didn't he?" I wept as I looked at Teeg.

"Baby, don't," Teeg pulled my head against his shoulder. "We'll get through this, I promise."

"I don't know how you can. Divorce me publicly, Teeg. It's the only way they won't tear you down. The Campiaan Alliance needs your hand on it to survive. As much as we have our differences, I know that. It'll die if you walk away. Divorce me now and be done with it. I should never have healed the core on Xordthe. Look what it's gotten me." I finally pulled my hand away from Teeg's grip and tossed it helplessly, still weeping.

"Baby, I haven't come this far, against such impossible odds, to let you go," Teeg said. "We'll have a response in two days. They'll bluster again tomorrow, and then it'll be over. Just hold on. Do it for me and for the others. If things don't turn out the way you want, then I'll listen after that. It won't stop me from loving you, though. Or Garwin Wyatt."

"Reah, come here, sweetheart." Edward stood and pulled me against him. "Those people can go fuck themselves," he muttered against my hair. "Come on; let's go check the trees in the western grove."

~

We walked on soft, black soil between rows of harvested trees, a breeze rustling through dark-green leaves. Edward had an arm around me while I wiped tears. When he wasn't looking at me, he had a grim expression on his face. Eventually, we were joined by Lok, Aurelius, Farzi and Nenzi.

"Honey Snake," I wrapped my arms around Farzi's neck while Nenzi crowded close against my back.

"They come close, they not live," Nenzi muttered. I was hugging both of them after that.

Did I think the first version of the venom against Teeg and me was terrible? That was nothing compared to what came on the second day. Other news agencies picked up the story and I was called everything from crackpot to dangerously insane. Many political pundits asked outright for Teeg's resignation. Of course, Cynthin Gerg was calling for the Council of Campiaan Alliance Worlds to step in and remove Teeg in favor of someone more reliable. And all because he had a crazy wife who made delusional claims about not being humanoid and belonging to the ASD.

I felt numb. What else could they do to me? I refused to talk to Kevis. He and nurse nasty had ruined my life. I think he knew how little I wanted to speak to him and blessedly stayed out of my sight. Edward coaxed me to eat. I didn't want to, but when I dry-heaved after a while, he convinced me to eat yogurt and toast. Farzi and Nenzi, so upset they couldn't handle being human, turned to lion snake and patrolled Edward's manor. The servants had been warned and stepped out of their way. Lion snakes weren't native to Avendor, so most of the staff didn't understand how dangerous they were.

"Come with me, baby," Teeg appeared at nearly eight bells. He led me toward Edward's media room, where a real crowd had gathered this time. Lissa had come with Gavin, Winkler, Tony, Drake, Drew, Norian and Thurlow. Jayd and Glinda were also there, for some inexplicable reason. I didn't speak to them. Glinda looked sad. I wasn't in any mood to attempt a fix for that. I'd been past that for a while, I think. All of my mates had come, including Nefrigar, plus Corolan, Astralan and Kevis. Ry looked angry. Actually, they all did. Teeg was grimly determined, somehow.

"Sit down, baby," Teeg said. I sat between him and Nefrigar this time. Nefrigar had altered his height so he'd fit the furniture. A blue hand held mine tightly as he leaned down to kiss me.

"The baby is fine," he murmured, kissing my forehead next.

"Here we go," Lendill said and used the remote to turn on the vid-screen. A special report was announced and Hild Marolla, an older and much respected investigative journalist, appeared on screen.

"Good evening to all in the Alliance," he said, using his normal greeting. "Tonight we bring a special report that I have been putting together for weeks now. I hope that it will disprove many current and popular rumors that have circulated recently. All these rumors began because this woman," a large photograph of Ceerah Kade was shown in an inset on the screen, "desecrated the delicate patient-physician privilege, in addition to blatantly violating the patient's rights laws that exist in both Alliances. We have done our homework on Ms. Kade and have investigated her background thoroughly," Hild Marolla added.

"You see, she has not always been Ceerah Kade. When she began her medical career on Tulgalan nearly half a century ago, she was known as Cedrah Dane. Although the charges there have been dropped against her since so much time has passed, she was charged with theft of controlled drugs, which she distributed for non-identifying Alliance credits. When the authorities came close to an arrest on Tulgalan, she escaped to Pridded, using the name Bynda Wark. There, she was accused and convicted of smuggling drakus seed, using her medical career as a front for distribution of the dangerous drug. Once again, when the authorities came too close, she escaped, using yet another alias."

Hild Marolla hesitated for a moment before continuing. "For years, Ceerah Kade has done this, hopping from one world to the next, paying shady members known for their criminal activities for false identities but always using her medical background as a front for her crimes. Until she arrived on Refizan, that is. There she took the name Ceerah Kade and began working at Sea Winds, a well-known psychiatric clinic. From the beginning, when she wasn't passing off fake drugs to unsuspecting recipients and selling the actual drugs to waiting dealers on the outside, she and her accomplice, Jalan Wolk, would break into the sensitive, private vid recordings of patient sessions and watch them as a source of amusement." Hild Marolla paused for a moment before continuing.

"If you are outraged at this information," he went on, "be assured that I and my investigative team are just as outraged. The ASD has taken Ms. Kade into custody, because there is no time limitations placed upon drakus seed distribution." Another inset was shown of Ceerah in cuffs, being led away by special agents. Hild Marolla continued his broadcast.

"The proof has been collected and at least sixteen deaths have been associated with her dealing of that dangerous drug. The other charges against her are nothing in comparison to this, but that still brings us back to her current victim, the one known as Reah Nilvas." A photograph of me was displayed in an inset.

"At first, I imagined that Ms. Nilvas was an unfortunate victim in Ms. Kade's scheme, and I was not wrong," Hild Marolla continued. "What I discovered after researching Ms. Nilvas' background, which was graciously opened to me, and after interviewing those who are familiar with her work, I can only say that I am astounded at the complexities of this woman. In order to illustrate what disservice both Alliances are doing her, and she is a member in good standing of both Alliances, I might add, I would like to take you through a journey tonight to show you just who—and what—Reah Nilvas is."

The scene changed and now we were shown a beautiful study filled with books and artifacts, all of it tastefully decorated, of course. Ildevar Wyyld, founding member of the Reth Alliance, sat behind a carved, wood desk.

"Hello," he said, "I am Ildevar Wyyld. I'm sure all of you recognize that name, if you aren't familiar with my face," he smiled gently. "I agreed to this interview because a member of the Reth Alliance has been treated unjustly. If you will come with me, I will show you just a little of what Reah Desh Nilvas Silver has done for the Reth Alliance."

Hild Marolla was there, a camera right behind him as he followed Ildevar Wyyld out of his office, down an ornately designed hallway that I recognized from a trip with Lendill, and into Lendill's office. "Here," Ildevar pointed to the wall that held all my awards and certificates, "is a sampling of what Reah has accomplished for me and the ASD. She is currently working special assignments for us. Can you focus on this one?" Ildevar pointed out one of the awards that lined the wall.

"As you can see, hopefully, it says for service provided to the Alliance in bringing down the drakus seed trade," he said. "You see her name, here?" He tapped the certificate. "This one," he pointed to another and the camera focused on it, "This says that Reah was solely responsible for taking down Arvil San Gerxon and at least a hundred other criminals who were providing drugs to the Alliance and convicted of assassinations, smuggling and other crimes against our worlds. And this one," Ildevar added, "is for taking down one of the worst threats to both Alliances. I'm sure few of you have heard the name Zellar before tonight, but I assure you, for those who know, he was the worst of the worst. He it was, using the power he had, who tapped into the cores of many planets. He killed Cloudsong, Thiskil and numerous others. Many of those worlds still lie dead, as you know. You've all heard that somehow the core energy leaked away, but you have not been informed until now how that was accomplished. Reah tracked Zellar for a very long time until she found him and the ones he'd allied with, destroying all of them. And this award, which is neither the last nor the least, recognizes her for single-handedly removing the threat of the controllers." Ildevar sighed and bowed his head for a moment before looking at the camera again.

"Reah, at great risk to herself, suffered a personal attack and other indignities at the request of the ASD, in order to obtain valuable information for the Director and Vice-Director of the Alliance Security Detail. After that, when she found they intended to bring their own controlling brains online in order to dominate both

Alliances, she destroyed them, while saving nearly seventy women from being sold into slavery. You see, that's what was happening. These criminals intended to enslave all of you. Each and every one. Oh, they started by selling pretty girls they targeted at Stellar Winds, but it was scheduled to go beyond that. The blackout was their doing, my friends. Reah destroyed their comp-brain before it could go farther than that. And those women? They owe Reah their lives. Don't take my word for it, however. Mr. Marolla has interviewed some of them. I'll let them explain what they saw during that terrible time." Ildevar smiled and the location changed.

Four women sat in comfortable chairs inside Hild Marolla's studio. The "live" caption showed at the bottom of the screen. They were being recorded right then.

"I know how difficult this is for all of you," Mr. Marolla said. "But if you could, please tell me, in your own words, what happened."

"I was kidnapped from work," one of the girls said. "I'd gone to Stellar Winds about six moon-turns ago. I had no idea they'd marked me." The others were nodding; their experiences had been similar.

"I was kidnapped from my apartment," another said. "From a clothing store," the third said. The fourth and last one had been taken after visiting her parents.

"They transported us back to Stellar Winds, but we were taken in cages to a huge underground cave there," the first one said. "We were fed once a day and allowed to visit a restroom twice a day, in shifts. We were kept there for days, allowed a bath every fourth day and taunted and ridiculed."

"How large were your cages?" the journalist asked. I nodded when they said six blocks by six blocks. They weren't large and it was difficult to stretch out in one. "So, these were uncomfortable, to put it kindly," Hild Marolla said.

"There was nothing kind about the cages or our captors," one of the girls huffed. "We thought that was bad, but then the day of the full moon came. We four, along with several others, watched while they brought the white-haired woman in. We recognized her right away when they ran those awful videos. They were making fun of her, as if she didn't suffer, too. Her cage was loaded onto the ship, just as ours were. We weren't frightened at that moment, but we should have been. We thought they were just moving us. We were wrong. The ship landed us on the small moon nearby, inside a landing shield. There our cages were unlocked, men came in who turned into terrible monsters and we were assaulted and raped. Many of us required medical assistance afterward. The white-haired woman became very sick. I saw two doctors come to visit her cage afterward." The girl wiped tears away.

"And then what happened?" Hild Marolla asked gently. Another girl took up the story. "Two eight-days later, we were loaded into another ship. We were all frightened, this time. We remembered what had happened before. This trip took longer. Several clicks. I know now we landed on Cloudsong."

"One of the worlds where the core was drained by Zellar," Hild Marolla nodded. "What happened after that?"

"We found out that buyers had come. For us," another girl wiped her eyes. "They came and rattled our cages. Touched us in intimate places. We were all afraid. I could see, too, the huge, round things built in a corner of the castle. It looked like old photographs I've seen of castles, anyway. Several men were fussing over the round things, and several men and one woman, who seemed to be in charge, were talking excitedly about them. I was too far away to hear everything they said, but I did hear them say that it was coming online tonight."

"This was the night of the blackout," Hild Marolla explained for the audience's benefit. "Fortunately, we have obtained vid images of part of what happened in that throne room of Cloudsong's deserted castle. I'll show the images, and if you'll explain what we're seeing?" Hild asked. The girls nodded. A vid-screen lit up on an adjacent wall and I gasped. How had they gotten these images? How? I didn't know they existed. Teeg gripped my other hand, now. I was going to have to watch this, as painful as it might be.

The auction was about to start but prior to that, Dantel Schuul had made a big speech before flipping the switch to the brains, effectively taking over everything in both Alliances. And that's when I made my move. My decision had been made and I was committed.

The camera angle switched to one overhead, as I turned to my smaller Thifilatha, escaped my cage and began soaking up the sun's rays through a hole in the palace roof. You could see the transformation clearly as I made it. As soon as I'd gathered enough energy, making my scales glow brightly, I aimed my hands at the brains, exploding them one by one. Chaos then broke out inside the castle's great hall, and I was fired upon. I refused to run or remove myself from the doorway—I'd been protecting the girls inside.

Dantel and Nedrizif were now commanding an army of Greater Demons, who moved to attack. The only thing that stood between sixty-seven helpless women and slavery or death was me. That's when I changed to my larger Thifilatha. I could imagine the gasps around the Alliances as they watched a small, white-haired woman first become a six-foot Thifilatha, and then when things became desperate, become a fifteen-foot Thifilatha, golden and glowing.

I was pulling energy from Cloudsong's daystar as quickly as I could at that point, while Greater Demons fired all kinds of weapons at me. The more solar energy I pulled inside, the less effect any of them had. And then Dantel Schuul and Nedrizif were screaming at them to attack. All the Greater Demons turned into those foul creatures and rushed at me. They winked out when they hit my scales.

At that moment, I sent energy toward the last of the brains, blowing it to bits. Everyone ducked or was knocked to the ground by the explosion. I went to my knees, it was so powerful. Dantel Schuul screamed at the slaves there, ordering them to attack after the last of his Greater Demons had died. The images died too, when everything in the Alliances went into massive blackouts.

"The ASD arrived shortly after that, but if it hadn't been for that woman, we'd have been killed or sold. I don't think we would have lived long," the first girl said as the others sobbed. "So many died that night. If that poor woman needs therapy now, I can certainly understand. We've been in treatment since the ASD brought us home."

"I thank you all for your willingness to talk with me tonight," Hild

Marolla said. "And now, we go to another recorded interview." The images changed. I was shocked. Jayd walked through the Kifirini gishi fruit groves with Hild Marolla. "You're telling me that you're High Demon." Hild Marolla said.

"Yes. I am Jaydevik Rath, King of the High Demon world of Kifirin," he replied, smiling slightly.

"And you know Reah Desh Nilvas Silver."

"Yes. Females among our kind are extremely rare. Rarer, even, than female vampires. Their numbers are certainly greater at the moment. Reah has been instrumental in bringing Kifirin back from the brink of bankruptcy the past twenty-five turns. These groves she planted for the benefit of the Crown. As you can see, these are gishi fruit trees."

"But I heard Reah was an operative for the ASD," Hild Marolla remarked.

"She was, before her first set of twins were born. Now, three sets of twins later, all girls I might add, she works special projects for the ASD. All of those things she said to the doctor are quite true. Reah doesn't lie. I find that nurse's actions reprehensible, and I would be glad to extradite her to Kifirin, where she will be charged with crimes against a citizen," Jayd said. "Reah will never be able to work undercover for the ASD again, since that program revealed her identity. I find that unusual in the extreme. Have they explained why that happened? I'd prefer to bring charges against that network as well, if I could."

The image changed again, to Norian's office at Lissa's palace. Norian sat behind his desk, dressed in his ASD uniform.

"Director, thank you for taking the time to speak with me," Hild Marolla said.

"I feel it is the least I can do. Reah deserves much better than she's received, don't you think? Dantel Schuul, his daughter and the others who were determined to enslave both Alliances, brought down by my best operative, who is then ridiculed in exchange because she requires a bit of therapy? What would you do, sir, if you were violated and made ill, and then were forced to fight off hundreds in order to keep seventy women and both Alliances safe?

If she hadn't acted as she did, where do you think we'd be right now?"

"Is she truly married to Teeg San Gerxon? I ask you that because you are in a position to know."

"Of course Reah is Teeg's wife. Has been for more than twenty-five turns. Both Alliances recognize multiple mates. Reah's daughters are all High Demon, but as you heard in the vids released by that awful program, she is pregnant again. This child belongs to Teeg San Gerxon, and he is justifiably angry that his wife was treated in this manner. As are we. As King Jayd aptly stated, Reah's cover is now gone. Our best operative will no longer be able to work undercover for us. Both Alliances will suffer because of this, but you haven't seen everything yet, Mr. Marolla. I have vid images here that will greatly interest you. Reah, in that state you witnessed as she guarded women and protected the Alliances, can also do wondrous things. To our knowledge, she is the only creature besides the Larentii who can bring dying worlds back to life. This one I especially want to show to you. Watch." Norian flipped on the vid-screen behind his desk. I whimpered as I recognized where I'd been in that vid. Xordthe.

"Here are the records, and these are available through the Science Institute on Xordthe, of the dying core twenty-six turns ago. The ASD knew that Zellar had tapped into it, but that information wasn't shared since Xordthe wasn't a member of the Campiaan Alliance at the time. This predates the Campiaan Alliance by several moon-turns, actually. Now, watch this. You see Teeg San Gerxon there—he is tracking one of Zellar's trainees. Zellar taught several how to tap cores of planets in order to enhance their power. The other men are two of San Gerxon's bodyguards. And this," the camera moved, capturing me, sitting on the ground and glowing in full Thifilatha, "is Reah, who is repairing the core with her own power. I have readings, before and after, for every world where Reah has repaired the core. These include Tulgalan, Karathia, Bardelus, Mazareal, Campiaa, Cloudsong, Thiskil, Xordthe, Shillverr and Roorthi. All the information is provided on this comp-vid and is available on each of those worlds except Cloudsong and Thiskil, because Reah repaired those after the populations had ceased to exist. Those worlds lie as a warning to the others of what might have happened to them if Reah hadn't intervened. And just so everyone knows, Reah did those repairs on her own time. She was never compensated for any of it."

"Is it possible to speak with her?" Hild Marolla sounded breathless as he flipped through record after record on the comp-vid Norian had given him.

"I don't think she is willing at this point. We sold her out, did we not? I know where she is, but her mates are protecting her, as you might imagine. We thought she was safe when we placed her in Sea Winds. That turned out badly, as you well know. The Director has resigned, leaving the clinic under an interim Director."

"What will happen to Reah now?" Hild Marolla asked.

"I don't know," Norian sighed, looking away for a moment. "She has suffered trauma in this last assignment, and there are those who are attempting to help her overcome it. I do not know what the final outcome will be."

"Is she dangerous? To anyone?"

"If you are a danger to others, or to the Alliance, perhaps. You see that Ceerah Kade is still enjoying life, although Reah could have come after her at any time. Reah, as ASD, could use any resource to locate anyone. Ceerah should breathe a relieved sigh because Reah has such high principles and a respect for life."

"So, all those things she said were true," Hild Marolla said.

"Yes. Every one of them," Norian agreed.

"She really isn't insane."

"No. Troubled over the trauma and illness from her last assignment, but certainly not insane. If she were here before you now, you would see that she isn't dangerous or, as the other network put it, crazy."

The image shifted back to the present, with Hild Marolla sitting behind his desk. "Shall we believe one with multiple identities who has sold drugs time and again, or one whose story is backed by the founding member of the Reth Alliance, firsthand eyewitnesses and the Director of the ASD? Shall we ask that a devoted husband step down from his position with the Campiaan Alliance, when his wife has helped to form that Alliance and keep it safe? Or shall we listen to a handful of bureaucrats who only seek to protect or further their political careers? I know what my decision is. What will yours be? Good night and sleep well," Hild Marolla said.

"I won't ever be able to walk anywhere again, without being recognized," I sighed. Everyone had likely seen my image. If not tonight, they'd see it tomorrow or the day after. And what would happen to Teeg? I shook my head and rose from my seat.

"Reah, do you need something?" Kevis was suddenly there, reaching out a hand.

"I feel dizzy," I said.

"Baby, don't pass out on me," Teeg was right there with Kevis. I wobbled; Teeg lifted me in his arms. "Let's go to the kitchen and get something to drink," he said softly. I fainted on the way.

CHAPTER 10

Vampires lean over their mates when they sleep. That act provides protection for those they love. It is instinctual to cover their mate as much as possible, because vampires are vulnerable during the day. Gavril had explained it to me once, long ago. Aurelius did it. Teeg also. I knew that one of my vampires was in the bed with me when I woke. His body was huddled over mine, careful not to place any weight on it.

"Awake?" Teeg's voice.

"Mmm," I mumbled. Queasiness made its presence known. Teeg had me out of the bed and in the adjoining bathroom in a blink. He must have sent mindspeech; at least half a dozen people appeared, including Kevis, Lok, Aurelius and Edward.

"Breathe slowly, Reah," Kevis had my head as low as it would go. My face was washed when I stopped heaving and I was hauled straight to the kitchen and given something to drink.

"Better?" Aurelius held me on his lap, brushing hair away from my face as I drank the juice I'd been given. A bowl of hot cereal was placed in front of me next, with fruit and brown sugar mixed in.

"Here we go," Auri held my hand steady when it shook trying to get the spoon to my mouth.

"I'll get my people started on ice cream and be right back," Edward said. There wasn't any way I could do it, feeling as badly as I did. Teeg got a communication on his comp-vid, so he stepped out of the kitchen to take the call. Lendill showed up and accepted a cup of coffee while he watched me eat. All of them were watching me eat.

Plates of food appeared for them shortly after, and Edward came back, sitting down and eating with the rest. Edward's four supervisors also came in for a meeting. Keedan grinned at me while he had breakfast. Edward and his supervisors talked about spraying the groves after the harvest.

"Insects are afraid of High Demons in Thifilatha or Thifilathi, that's how I kept Kifirin's groves naturally insect free," I said after eating as much of my breakfast as I could. Aurelius was rubbing my belly absently while he listened to the others.

"Really?" Keedan gave me a smile.

"Are you teasing me or questioning my methods?" I asked.

"Both," he said. "Little girl, I'm living for the day when you show me what I saw last night on the vids."

"That didn't scare you?" I asked, my skepticism showing.

"Just turned out badly for the evil ones," he grinned. "I saw you standing in the doorway, keeping the rabble away from those girls. Have you seen the morning news?" He pushed a comp-vid toward me.

"I was busy heaving in the bathroom," I said. Aurelius, using a little power, pulled the comp-vid toward me. "He did that," I pointed to Auri. I still sat on his lap, after all. I tapped the comp-vid and found all sorts of responses to the news program the evening before. The best one, however, was from Xordthe. People were crowding outside Cynthin Gerg's Presidential palace, with vid signs. Some were downright nasty, calling her a bitch and other unkind names, but my favorite was the large sign held up by a group of people that said *Reah Nilvas saved the planet. What have you done for Xordthe, Cynthin?*

I laughed as the aud proclaimed that those people were scientists who'd seen the weakening core firsthand. They were puzzled when it magically healed itself. Except that it hadn't healed itself. I'd done it. Local media were interviewing some of those scientists, who did indeed have official numbers in hand and gladly showed anyone who wanted to see.

"Reah, I have a group of Council members assembled outside my palace, demanding to see you," Teeg walked back in with a sigh.

"What for?" I asked. Aurelius wrapped his arms around me when I shivered.

"They want to know that you're all right."

An hour later I was showered, dressed and transported to Teeg's palace on Campiaa. Teeg had shifted the Council members to one of the smaller ballrooms inside the San Gerxon Casino. Astralan, leaning down to give me a kiss, transported us over. Stellan, Celestan and Galaxsan were already there, providing security. I didn't know it would turn into a press conference. Someone had brought Hild Marolla in as well.

"Sit here, baby," Teeg settled me onto a seat at the center of a long table. The crowd inside the ballroom was growing.

Do not fear, my love, I have shields in place, Nefrigar sent to me. He was standing in shadow at the end of the table. I think he had himself shielded and was visible only to those he chose. And when I looked, I found four more Larentii standing in the corners of the room. They were protecting me, at Nefrigar's direction. I was also being recorded as Teeg sat next to me.

"Was that true, what I was shown?" Hild Marolla started the questioning. "Can you really heal cores?"

"I've done it several times," I nodded to him. "I've been back to Thiskil recently and there are a few weeds and plants growing, but it's still mostly dead. I wish there was something else I could do to hurry the process, but it's going to take time. The others, like Xordthe, had been tapped recently when I healed them, and Xordthe had only been tapped from one place. That made it easier to repair."

"Some planets were tapped in multiple places?" A scientist from a respected journal had come to ask questions.

"Yes. Tulgalan was one of those. The energy I poured into it was leaking out the other site, so it was more difficult to repair."

"This energy, where does it come from?" The scientist asked.

"From a renewable source that constantly puts out energy," I said. "It's stellar energy. I act as a conduit and siphon it to the damaged core before sealing it up. Isn't that where all the energy came from in the beginning? That power should be natural, and I've been assured it's the best way to heal the cores." Nefrigar had smiled when he'd told me that.

"On the original vid," someone else said, "shown on Temporary Insanity, the doctor asked about a suicide attempt. Would you care to explain that?"

"No," I said.

"But you did try it, according to the vid, by a volcano, is that correct?"

"I contemplated it. I didn't try it. Trying it implies that I went through with it, or attempted to do so. I was talked away from the edge." I squinted to see the one speaking. "Step forward, please," I said. The man walked toward the front. "Your name?" I asked. "And affiliation?"

"Seve Dibolus, from network ninety-one," he hung his head.

"And what do you intend to do with this information?" I asked. He was from the network that produced Temporary Insanity. The others in the room recognized that fact immediately and there was some grumbling.

"We just want to get to the truth of the matter," he said.

"Lie," I said. "Try again."

"We wanted to publish a retraction on the program," he said.

"Another lie. Why not tell the truth for a change?" I said.

"We want as much information as we can get to form our defense against the allegations that we broke the laws," he whined.

"Truth," I sighed. "Come here. Sit beside me," I patted the empty chair to my left. Teeg still sat on my right. "Now, what else do we have? I warn you that I was heaving this morning due to the pregnancy, so I don't think I can go on much longer today. Ask your questions now."

"How badly has this whole incident hurt you?" Hild Marolla asked. His question made me sigh.

"This is beyond awful," I said. "I have no hope of going out in public anonymously. Or taking my child out in public. While others might find that attractive, to me it is upsetting."

"Tell them the story about the rats." Kevis walked in and sat next to Teeg.

"Are you crazy?" I looked at him. The crowd found that funny.

"Come on. Tell them."

"I was chasing Thaddis Grund through the sewers on Ooklar," I said. "Are you familiar with him?" Most of the people in the crowd nodded. Thaddis was a crime kingpin from that portion of the Reth Alliance. He'd eluded the ASD for decades, until Lendill sent me after him. That's what I said. "The Vice-Director of the ASD sent me to Ooklar after Thaddis blew up a bank in the capital city. He had escape routes throughout the city, and all of those escape routes ran through the archaic sewer system. It has since been upgraded," I said.

"I thought I'd trapped him until he used a remote to open a hidden portal into the sewers. While the heavy steel cover would have foiled any humanoid, I turned Thifilatha and jerked it off to follow him. Once I turn, my clothing is destroyed. So rather than turn back and chase him naked as a humanoid, I remained Thifilatha."

Chuckles came at the thought of chasing a ruthless criminal through the sewers while nude. "Rodents and insects are frightened when they see or scent any High Demon in Thifilatha. The rats in the sewers, and there were many of those," I put heavy emphasis on the word many, "were running before me in an attempt to escape. Thaddis, still running ahead of me, was overtaken by thousands of rats, and in their attempt to flee what they considered a larger predator, they knocked Thaddis down and ran over his back, squeaking at the top of their little rat lungs. Thaddis was an easy capture, after that. I believe he might be the only criminal actually brought down by rodents."

The crowd was really laughing now. I smiled at them. Even Seve, sitting next to me, was snickering.

"What are you doing now?" someone else asked. "I see the doctor, there. Is he treating you?"

"As much as I can," Kevis commented dryly. "She lets me know when we're done for the day." That also brought laughter from the crowd.

"So, Doctor, in your professional opinion, is Ms. Nilvas dangerous?"

"If she were, I'd be a goner," he said. "I've pried into private matters so much and gotten her angry enough at me that I'd have been toast if she were dangerous. She still hasn't forgiven me for the nurse betrayal. Reah calls Ceerah nurse nasty, but that's the extent of her violence. Does that sound dangerous to you?"

"I called Ceerah Kade worse when I learned she was involved in the drakus seed trade," someone in the back stood. "My son died of drakus seed."

"Then I am sorry for your loss," I said. "I burned those fields on Birimera, when Arvil San Gerxon was growing that filth," I added.

"And yet you're married to his heir," the man nodded in Teeg's direction.

"A long story. Teeg was never involved in any of that. In fact, Teeg was Arvil's construction contractor. When Arvil's brother and cousins died, courtesy of the RAA, by the way, Arvil went looking for a replacement heir. Teeg was the only trustworthy person he could find. He ran the casinos here on Campiaa, and honestly, I might add, while Arvil was bent on destroying the Reth Alliance with drakus seed. Arvil was staying on Birimera while the fields grew. That's where we took him down. Teeg, as you know, decided that the Campiaan Alliance was a good idea and ran with it. You see that the Reth Alliance has allied with it, after all. They recognize the value of it and actually went over their constitution and rules before reaching out a hand."

"You were a building contractor?" someone asked Teeg.

Teeg almost blushed. Almost. "I have architecture and engineering degrees," he said. "I'm used to building things. The Campiaan Alliance was no exception."

"Do you still do construction?" Hild Marolla smiled.

"I know when they aren't installing my wife's new kitchen cabinets properly," he grinned.

"Did you buy new cabinets for me?" I blinked at Teeg in surprise.

"I did." His smile was directed at me, now.

"What do the countertops look like?"

"A honey-brown granite, with flecks of gold," he said.

"I love that color," I sighed. The crowd laughed.

Teeg shooed everybody away shortly after that, sending them to another room where they were served drinks and a complimentary meal. Hild Marolla was brought to San Gerxon Palace, though.

"I just wanted to meet you in person," he held out a hand. I took it.

"These are the new cabinets?" He glanced around the kitchen.

"I'm seeing them for the first time, too," I said. "Want to try them out?" Teeg offered Hild a seat at the wide, kitchen island, Astralan and his brothers sat down, too, and I made crepes for all of them.

"I don't lie about food, either," I said, when Hild Marolla said the crepes were the best he'd ever tasted. He sipped gourmet coffee with his meal and seemed satisfied. "And I do have a Master Cook's license on Tulgalan," I added.

"So, you really are related to the Desh family," he said.

"You did a piece on that, years ago," I told him. "You were looking for me after you did the exposé of Breszca Loffus. I'm her granddaughter, but I barely know her. She's married to my grandfather, now."

"Why couldn't I get into your records?" The journalist asked.

"The ASD had them locked up," I replied. "Want more coffee?"

Vid from my unplanned press conference spread like wildfire across both Alliances. People were calling for Cynthin's resignation, as well as that of the other two who'd backed her accusations and then demanded that Teeg step down. I didn't know how all of it would end, but for the moment, at least they weren't dragging my name through the muck.

Then the ice cream started selling. People stood in lines outside ice cream shops, waiting to pay thirty-five Alliance credits for a single scoop on a cone. Reporters went out to interview customers about the gishi fruit ice cream, all while money poured in. The recipe was protected by patent quickly and EastStar Groves wallowed in a tsunami of fame for creating the best and most expensive ice cream. I'd told Edward to leave my name out of it and keep the ice cream under the EastStar Groves label. It worked out very well and we got the new plant open quickly.

~

"Beg her to come look at the groves," Glinda said. "They're not thriving and the fruit is smaller than it should be." She sat in Jayd's private study, watching her High Demon husband closely.

"Are they watering properly? Is someone checking to make sure the sprinklers are all working? What the hell are those people we hired doing?" Jayd rose to pace. "And now that gishi fruit ice cream is selling everywhere and making a ton of money, we can't get our hands on the recipe."

"Because Reah patented it through the Campiaan Alliance," Tory skipped in looking dejected. Glinda had sent mindspeech to him earlier. He'd finally shown up to see what his aunt wanted.

"This is Reah's. I shouldn't be surprised," Jayd muttered.

"Edward Pendley, who owns EastStar Groves, has already asked her to marry him," Tory grumbled.

"You could ask her," Jayd pointed out.

"You think I haven't thought of that? If I ask now, she'll treat it with suspicion, and rightfully so. She has no reason to trust anything I say."

"Will she come look at the groves, at least? I'll pay," Jayd offered.

"I'll ask," Tory sighed, "but she'll likely throw it in my face." Tory skipped away.

~

"Torevik." I acknowledged his presence while monitoring ice-cream makers inside the new building. The facility was everything I wanted it to be. Our ice cream was selling before it was made and Edward was negotiating with the owner of SouthStar for blemished fruit. He was offering top credit for their less than perfect gishi fruit. Edward's employees inspected the fruit before it was purchased; he had a knack for choosing the right people for those things.

"Reah, the groves on Kifirin aren't doing very well. Jayd has offered to pay if you'll come to the Southern Continent and take a look."

"What's wrong with them?" Edward, who was there and watching me work, asked.

"We don't know. The Crown was never involved with the groves. They depended on Reah to do everything."

"And now they pay the price," Edward said. "Reah, let's go take a look," he sighed.

"Edward, you're not obligated," I pointed out.

"I know. But the trees are being mistreated. I feel it. Let's go look." Less than a click later, we were walking through the Kifirini groves that I knew so well with Jayd, Glinda, Lissa and Garde. I wanted to snarl at Garde but held it back. Astralan, alerted by Teeg no doubt, showed up as well.

"These sprinkler lines are broken, see?" I pointed out where the soil was saturated with water, keeping the roots too wet surrounding the break. "And these past that point aren't getting water at all. Aren't they walking the groves?" I asked. "What are they doing?"

"No idea," Jayd raked a hand through his hair. Glinda seemed very upset.

"Let's find out," there was a light in Lissa's eyes. We folded to my old cottage, which had been enlarged, I discovered. What we found inside it had Gardevik raging. I thought he would tear the house apart. The new grove manager was running a gambling establishment. I saw many of the disabled inside, playing for coveted items.

"I think you're under arrest," Lissa informed the manager pleasantly.

"Now what do we do?" Garde held his head in his hands later as we all sat inside Jayd's study.

"I have a suggestion," I said. "But Lissa might not like it."

"What will I not like?" She looked at me curiously.

"Bring Corent," I said. "At least two days a week. He's a gentle soul, but if you mistreat the trees, I think you might be surprised at the temper that will cause. And he can heal the ones that have been over or under watered."

"Corent?" Edward looked at me.

"Green Fae," I said. "He takes care of the apple trees and such on Le-Ath Veronis. He's the last of his family."

"I'll lend him out for two days each week," Lissa agreed. "But you'll pay him fairly," she poked Garde in the chest. He almost fell back. Lissa was vampire, after all, and she held the strength of a Queen.

"Right now, I'm willing to do almost anything to get the groves back on track," Jayd agreed.

"Good," I said. "I need to get back to making ice cream."

"You're making the gishi fruit ice cream?" Garde stared at me.

"Yes. I'm making the gishi fruit ice cream. Why?"

"Kifirin said I'd cut my own hand. He was right."

"Too late now," I said. "I was going to ask Jayd for funds to build a plant here when the debts were paid. That won't be happening, now. Edward is handing half his profits to me. He offered all of the profits, but that was too much. Would I still be walking barefoot through your groves, dressed in rags if things hadn't gone as they did?" I asked Garde. "You'd have kept me like that forever, wouldn't you? Was it all because I was only a quarter-blood? Is that what it was?" My emotions were welling up again. They were a major downside to being pregnant. "How much do you hate me, Gardevik Rath? How much?" I was weeping by that time.

"Reah, can't you see there is nothing left in him? I don't think he feels." Edward took my hand, nodded to all present and Astralan folded us to Avendor.

∿

"Garde, what happened to you?" Lissa demanded. "Surely you know better than this."

"He was first-born," Jayd sighed, dropping onto his desk chair inside his study. "He took the heat from Father for the rest of us. Father always blamed us and our mother for either not being daughters or not having daughters. He knew the race was dying even then, our father did. And he was angry because he couldn't do anything about it."

"So, you're really angry because Denevik went out and made a daughter with a humanoid, is that it? And then his daughter had a quarter-blood-daughter. Are you blaming Reah for all of this, Garde?" Lissa looked up at him.

"It was so easy for her," Garde turned away. "So easy to have daughters. I lashed out at her. Our parents are dead. Mother dropped into Baetrah because she couldn't handle the pressure any longer. Father, not realizing how much he actually depended upon our mother, followed closely behind her. I did wrong. Placed blame. Let my prejudices show. Lendevik was right to keep me from the Kingship. I was helpless to keep Kifirin from bankruptcy, and that little slip of a girl comes in and creates solvency out of nothing. I am supposed to be the one to do that. I should have found a way out of that mess. I didn't, so I did my best to persecute the one who did."

"This is so fucked up," Lissa tossed up a hand in resignation.

"Reah, you can't help that other people make mistakes. They may not always intend for the consequences to be so devastating. You have to take care of yourself, first." Edward and I swung lazily in the covered swing outside his suite. He'd dried my tears earlier. Astralan lounged on a chair nearby, watching me closely.

"I know," I said. Kevis came out and took a chair next to Astralan. The doctor was waiting with one of his sessions, no doubt. "I wish I could get drunk right now," I added.

"You'd be swigging straight from the wine bottle, wouldn't you?" Edward teased, grinning at me.

"I'm that desperate," I nodded.

"Most people get medication, Reah," Kevis said. "But you're pregnant and High Demon. The levels of the drugs you would require would be too hazardous to the child. We can't risk it," he added.

"I know," I agreed. Edward held me tighter against him. Kevis pulled me away after a while, herding Edward and Astralan away. I'd have stayed and napped on one shoulder or the other if he hadn't.

"Reah, what happened earlier?" Kevis asked as he settled onto the swing with me, comp-vid in hand.

"I don't know. It's easy to blame it on the pregnancy," I said, leaning back and staring at the underside of the canvas canopy.

"I believe that's part of it," he agreed. "Perhaps not all."

"You don't ever get to choose your family," I breathed deeply of the fresh air rising above the gishi fruit groves. "And like it or not, I'm connected to Glinda and Jayd and Garde. Glinda is my great-aunt, whether I want that or not. She's never deliberately mistreated me, but when Garde handed my girls to her, she never questioned. She just took what she wanted."

"Was she a bad parent?"

"No. Not in that sense, no."

"But they didn't see their real mother when they should have. Gardevik feels inadequate, I think, and he passed the anger he felt in your direction. He wanted to make you suffer, perhaps, for doing what he wasn't capable of doing alone. I think he was a loner for a very long time. Kept to himself for a very long time."

"I had nothing to do with that," I pointed out.

"I know. I'm just trying to sort out why he is the way he is."

"Good luck on that," I said.

"Reah, he has made you suffer. I want to get to the bottom of that. I'm hoping to put a stop to it."

"Then you're more of an optimist than I am."

"I think you've seen too much of the terrible side of life. You haven't had many of the good things. Why don't you come with me for a little while this afternoon? We can get into the pool at the villa. You can sleep there if you're tired. I know you are," he said. "I can feel it. How about a massage? I think Rik is available."

"Rik. He has such nice hands." I smiled at the memory of one other time when the tall Falchani had given me a massage.

"You've gotten one from him before?"

"Yeah. It was wonderful."

"Then we'll get another. We can set it up on a regular basis, if you want. It'll be good for you. He even has a special pillow so we won't squash Garwin Wyatt."

"We can't squash Wyatt," I agreed. "We love him."

"We do," Kevis grinned.

"Just relax," Rik told me later as I lay face down on a table. What little belly I had was encased in a special pillow, hollowed out to surround Garwin Wyatt. Rik's hands moved gently over my body. Kevis had undressed me using the power he inherited from his parents and he watched as Rik put his hands on me. When he finished with the back and turned me over, I felt like softened clay. Rik paid such special attention to the baby when he rubbed my belly, I fell asleep.

I'll take her. Kevis lifted Reah from Rik's arms. He'd carefully wrapped the sheet around Reah without waking her.

She's like a bird with hollow, fragile bones, Rik sighed. *She needs to eat more.*

I know. Kevis floated Reah onto the bed to keep from waking her. His and Rik's conversation had been mindspeech only. *I'm warming the air around her. I hope she doesn't wake up.*

Later, Kevis sat in the kitchen, having a cup of tea with Rik when his mother walked in.

"How are you, Gracie?" Rik gave her a smile.

"I'm good. How's Reah?" She looked at Kevis.

"Sleeping."

"Ren says she's exhausted but refuses to just sit down and rest most of the time."

"Kifirin," Kevis said. "She only had a few workers and half of those were disabled, so she pushed herself for years. I think she's afraid that if she stops completely, something terrible will happen."

"If she had stopped on Kifirin, they'd be bankrupt," Dragon wandered in with his twin brother, Crane. "Lissa says that they made the last payment on their loans a few days ago. They're in the clear unless they go into debt again. If they can manage those gishi fruit groves as well as Reah did, then they're on their way toward industrialization."

"They certainly need to get away from that feudal system they have," Crane agreed, setting about making tea for himself and his brother. "Falchan doesn't have much in the way of technology, but the people are allowed to own land and open their own shops and restaurants. On Kifirin, the Crown owns nearly everything."

"They certainly owned Reah," Kevis leaned his head into his arms. "I don't think they'll see this baby unless they come to her."

"What have Jayd and Glinda done for her? Anything?" Devin asked. She and Grace shared eleven mates, including Dragon, Crane and Karzac.

"I don't know that they've offered anything. Certainly not money," Kevis muttered. "But Lendill says that the ASD is very close to confiscating all the funds the pirates and their cronies put together. Reah will have half of that."

"How much is it?" Dragon asked, accepting a cup of tea from Crane.

"The last I heard, trillions," Kevis said. "Reah will never have to depend upon another male for money. Ever."

"Is Reah asleep?" Lok, Aurelius and Renegar folded in.

"Yes. Is anything wrong?"

"Someone is asking to see her," Aurelius said. Kiarra, Adam, Merrill and Pheligar folded in. Someone, likely Dragon, had sent mindspeech.

"Why are they asking to speak with Reah?" Kiarra was puzzled.

"I do not know," Renegar replied. "But they are requesting an audience with her. This is mystifying."

"Who is asking to see Reah?" Kevis rose from his seat at the island.

"The Copper Ra'Ak Prince," Renegar replied.

CHAPTER 11

"When?" Kevis was upset and he didn't normally react to anything that way. "Have the others been told? What do they want?"

"They want to talk peace," Nefrigar appeared, with two of his sons. "They want Reah to act as the broker for that peace. The Copper Ra'Ak that she took down not long ago were among the rogues that this Prince has been chasing. A few rogues are still out there, but these wish to ally with the Saa Thalarr and the Black Ra'Ak to hunt them down. These Copper Ra'Ak want things as they were in the beginning. They want their old world back."

"Has Kifirin been notified?" Kiarra asked, staring up at the Larentii Archivist.

"Messages have been sent," Connegar folded in. "We are waiting for a reply."

"He knows," Belen appeared, accompanied by Thurlow.

"We are here," Teeki and Neeki appeared. "But we have not good news. The rogue Ra'Ak that remain have allied with those two bad brothers of Lendill Schaff. They are all hunting Reah. The bad brothers want her dead. They blame her for Lendill becoming Prince-Heir. They seek her death. The rogue Ra'Ak want her dead, too, for killing those they sent after the Saa Thalarr. The bad elf brothers have promised these rogue Ra'Ak joint rule of Gaelar N'Seith and other worlds, if they help to kill Reah and the Saa Thalarr. Things do not look good," Teeki shook his head.

"I don't believe this," Kiarra rubbed her forehead.

"Were the elves the ones who shot her?" Lok asked.

"Yes. With an old weapon they should not have. One outlawed by the Alliance long ago. They still have that and others—they are collecting them. Now, they seek to harm the Lifegiver."

"Are you calling her that because she is pregnant?" Nefrigar asked calmly.

"No. Reah is the Lifegiver."

"What does that mean?" Grace asked.

"It means that Reah can heal more than cores," Kifirin folded in. "She can bring those dead and dying worlds back to what they were before they were drained. Much faster than you might believe. She has not yet discovered this particular talent, however."

"It will be similar to what we can do when we manipulate atoms," Pheligar nodded, "only Reah can do it with living things. She will be able to import the building blocks of life and accelerate the process. Several records on this prophecy are stored in our Archives," Pheligar smiled at Nefrigar.

"I had not realized you'd read them," Nefrigar nodded to Pheligar.

"It interested me early on," he said. "We might manipulate those things, but we do not have a specific talent for it."

"You were a curious child," Nefrigar smiled. "If our father were still alive, he would be very proud."

"I still can't believe you didn't tell me you had a brother," Kiarra stared at Pheligar and then at Nefrigar. "For centuries I believed my Larentii was an only child."

"Yes, we are brothers, although he is much younger. He comes when he will, and we talk. His nephews show him what is new in the Archives," Nefrigar offered Kiarra a smile.

"I can't believe Pheligar didn't just sprout from the ground," Merrill laughed.

"That would be quite difficult. Larentii have never accomplished that feat," Pheligar huffed, causing several snickers around the kitchen.

"Father, I love you," Renegar embraced Pheligar. Pheligar grinned and hugged his son.

~

"Reah, my love, we have a meeting." Nefrigar was using power to dress me. Was that strange? In the strangest of ways. Clothing slithered over my body and fastened itself swiftly, and my hair was braiding itself.

"Who are we meeting?" I asked as my Larentii lifted me off the bed.

"You will see. Do not fear; you will be in no danger. They hold no power over you, and even if they did, I would separate their particles. You look very nice. We will go."

~

Ra'Ak in humanoid shapes. Six of them waited upon a deserted world not far from Kifirin, as it turned out. This world was not dead like those Zellar and his trainees killed. This one held plant and animal life in abundance. *Trasindelim*, Nefrigar's voice whispered in my mind. *Their ancient world.*

"Reah Nilvas," one of them stepped forward and bowed. I nodded politely in return. Nefrigar stood at my back, as witness and protection, I think.

"I do not know your name," I said to the one who'd addressed me.

"I am Maldak, Copper Prince," he introduced himself. "And I requested this meeting with you. Except for the rogues still among the worlds, the Copper Race wishes to sue for peace. We want you to broker that peace. We have watched you, Ms. Nilvas. You are the candidate to act as liaison between us, the Saa Thalarr and our dark cousins, the Black Ra'Ak. We wish for things to go back as they were in the beginning, with a few exceptions. Then, we were subjected to the Black Ra'Ak and compelled to do their bidding. We wish to be a separate and equal people and recognized as such. We will police our own, as our dark cousins do. We will gladly accept help from them and the Saa Thalarr to hunt down any rogues or criminals among us. In the meantime, we will follow the rules that the Black Ra'Ak set for themselves. We will draft a treaty with representatives from the others, and if there are disagreements, we will work through those to the benefit of all."

He wasn't lying. Maldak was completely truthful in everything he said. "Very well," I told him. "I will carry this back to the others and a date will be set. Meanwhile, do you have information on the whereabouts of the remaining rogues?"

"We do not. They have been hiding from us for quite some time, willing only to send their youngest children out to create havoc among the worlds. I find this repugnant—they transformed humanoids without thought to their character, and then forced them out to be killed by the Saa Thalarr or some other faction capable of doing so. You do not send your children out to be destroyed in such a way. They must be carefully taught so they will know not to kill."

"You are not from this time, are you?" I said, watching him carefully.

"No. I brought these forward from long ago, to escape those who thought to destroy everything. I looked for an appropriate time to re-establish ourselves. A time when the threat against us would be in measures we could handle. Now, all we need is the proper candidate to bring us together with our lost cousins and those created to hunt the rogues of our kind. If we may meet here in three days, that will suit us very well."

"I'll do what I can," I replied, nodding to Maldak. He smiled.

"He said they came from the past, to get away from the rogue faction that was taking over," I said. We were all inside Lissa's library on Le-Ath Veronis. "They want to inhabit Trasindelim again," I said. "And I have a suggestion."

"I'm agreeable," Lissa said. The suggestion I'd made was to allow the Ra'Ak, Black and Copper, to feed twice a turn from Evensun. I knew that every prisoner was sterilized before they went, so there were no children. The youngest would be sixteen or older, I knew that, and all certified as adults. Only the worst of criminals were sent to Evensun. "And limit the take to one day for each hunt," I said.

"Where will they get their new children?" Kiarra asked.

"Shall we ask Ildevar?" I suggested. Lissa sent a message to Norian, who contacted his patron. Ildevar appeared, walked straight to me and hugged me warmly.

"Little Reah, are you well?" he smiled at me.

"As well as can be expected," I said, asking him to sit with us. We were in a circle in Lissa's library. "Do you know why we're here?" I asked.

"Willem informed me that this would come. It is a glad day," he replied. "And I think that we will form a committee. Worthy citizens' names from across the Alliances might be suggested, and we will choose from that list when they are dying. The Ra'Ak will limit their numbers, as they always have, replacing what is lost only, once the full complement of our kind is reached. Then they will look to replace what is lost when the time comes. The committee will decide and then take suggestions to the Ra'Ak, who must also agree. The King of the Black Ra'Ak and the Prince of the Copper race will make final decisions from the list submitted. And then the ones suggested make the final choice. It is only fair."

"I agree with that," I said. "Some may not want that sort of life. The final choice should be theirs."

"And I want Reah on that committee," Ildevar smiled at me.

"If you'll do it with me," I said.

"I would be honored," he nodded.

"Jerigar and I will also be on that list," Willem and Jerigar, the only white-haired Larentii I'd ever seen, appeared. Jerigar came over and lifted me up, placing a hand over the baby.

"He is quite fine, but his mother needs to gain weight," he said.

"We need one more member," Willem announced. "Edward Pendley should take that spot."

"Edward Pendley will do it, as long as Reah is there," Edward was folded in by Aurelius.

"Good enough," I sighed. "And the first person I want to put on that list is Flyer from Falchan."

"Yes!" Lok stood and shouted his approval, something so unlike him. Dragon and Crane were pounding Lok on the back. I just shook my head in amazement.

"Flyer is ill," Jerigar whispered in my ear. "They should take him soon."

"There is a vacancy with the Black Ra'Ak now," Youon appeared. Someone had likely called him.

"Lok, do you, Dragon and Crane want to go to Flyer?" I asked. "To see if this is what he wants?"

"Wait," Belen appeared. "We owe a debt to Reah. Several, actually. Reah, we will hand Flyer's life to you. We will make him like Lok and Aurelius, immortal with a bit of power, with an invitation to join the Spawn Hunters. He will not become Ra'Ak. Is that what you want?"

I didn't even have to think about it. "Yes," I said. Flyer had been more of a father to me than most other men in my life.

"We will go," Belen said, and every Falchani in the room disappeared with the Nameless One.

"Now I'm back to looking," Youon sighed.

"Then go see Plovel on Bardelus," I said. "He was a good policeman and investigator. I hear he's retired, now."

"Good choice," Jerigar smiled at me.

"I will go with Youon," Ildevar Wyyld said. "And with Willem." Those three disappeared.

"I like it when I get instant results," I sighed.

"Reah, I have it on good Larentii authority that you should eat more and rest more," Kevis was ordering me to bed as soon as I finished dinner.

"And which Larentii would that be?" I asked, dressing in pajamas.

"Renegar. Remember, you said you loved him."

"I do," I said.

"Do you love me, too?" Ry appeared in the bedroom.

"I do. I was wondering what happened to my warlock King." I wrapped my arms around Ry's neck as he lifted me off the floor. I waved for Kevis to go away as Ry started kissing me. And when he loved me, it was gentle and perfect. I went to sleep in his arms afterward.

"I think Ry just made it around all the bases," Teeg sighed and swallowed his bourbon. Kevis had joined Teeg, Tory, Aurelius, Lok and Lendill for a drink at Edward's kitchen island. Edward had taken the reptanoids out to the groves to look for whatever was chewing on gishi fruit trees in the eastern grove. Teeg stared when they brought the dead predagator back. The reptile was nearly twelve feet long and not native to Avendor. An omnivore, it loved small mammals and fruit trees, chewing the bark off the lower portion of the tree and killing it that way. They also built dams similar to beavers.

"I can't imagine where it was planning to live," Edward said, examining the creature with the others. "These things require ponds, lakes or rivers. The nearest river is fifty clicks away."

"Planted?" Teeg asked.

"Undoubtedly. I grow tired of these pranks by my neighbors," Edward sighed in frustration.

"Buy them out," Lendill suggested.

"Do you think there are more of these out there?" Tory asked.

"Possibly. I've lost nearly fifty trees in the past six days."

"Then I'll go out. They won't stay anywhere near a High Demon. Reah would do it for you, if she were awake. Since she's not," Tory finished his drink and made ready to hunt predagators.

"Which one of you did this?" Teeg grinned at Farzi and Nenzi after examining the dead predagator.

"I do this," Nenzi was quite proud.

"Nenzi, you are definitely the man," Teeg slapped him on the back. "Come on, let's all go looking for predagators."

No less than sixty were rounded up and set on the neighboring gishi fruit groves. Terrified of Tory's Thifilathi, they couldn't get away fast enough.

"You think that might drive down the price?" Teeg laughed as they watched the reptiles rush away.

"Can't hurt to check," Edward nodded.

"Lord Kifirin?" Farzi stared at Kifirin, who stood inside the bedroom he and Nenzi shared at Edward's manor. Nenzi, who gaped at the god, wondered why Kifirin had come to them.

"I wish to give you—and Reah—a gift," Kifirin said. "It will not hurt in the least. I know it was painful when you experienced it in the beginning. This will be a return of what is rightfully yours." Light formed around Kifirin.

"Ry, you get more handsome every time I see you," I pulled his head down to kiss him. He'd wakened me with a smile.

"Just what I wanted to hear from my future Queen," he said and kissed me again. We were late getting to breakfast. I was weeping in no time when a very young-looking Flyer was sitting at the table, having his first meal as an immortal. He was up from the table immediately, hugging me.

"How is my daughter?" He held my face in his hands and kissed my forehead.

"I am better, seeing you," I wiped tears away. "I missed you so much."

"I missed you. My customers missed your cooking," he grinned. "It took years to bring them around again."

"That's not true," I said, hugging him. "Come on, finish your breakfast."

~

"You told me those things would stay in EastStar's groves," Crorver Ride cursed at Erbrin Dondl. Their groves bordered EastStar's on the western side only. Mountains bordered EastStar on the eastern side and SouthStar bordered all of them to the south and west, stretching toward the jungles protected by law. Those jungles contained rainforests that helped sustain Avendor. Crorver and Dondl's groves were surrounded by SouthStar and EastStar, and they didn't like it. They had no trouble expressing their displeasure with the owner of EastStar in ever-creative ways, but they were terrified of SouthStar's owner and his grove manager.

"They usually don't travel far if they find a food source," Erbrin whined about the reptiles they'd loosed on EastStar. The predagators had found their way back to their groves, somehow. "It's egg laying season, too," he went on. "I found a wallow and an egg cache right next to a broken sprinkler line this morning. We'll have to hunt the creatures down."

"Those things are difficult to find and harder than that to kill," Crorver snapped. "This was your idea. I suggest you get your employees to my property and hunt them now."

"My staff is committed to protecting my own trees," Erbrin argued. "Hunt them yourself." Crorver cursed louder.

"A letter—for each of you," Crorver's assistant appeared with two expensive paper messages.

"What's this?" Crorver opened his first. "He wants to buy me out?" Crorver cursed again.

"And me as well," Erbrin sighed. "You know, I'm almost willing to hear what he's offering."

"Shall we go together, and then throw his offer back in his face?" Crorver grinned.

"Yes. That sounds like the perfect way to spend an afternoon; ridiculing your neighbor and rival."

"Want to invest in gishi fruit, my love?" Merrill smiled down at Kiarra. They'd spent most of the morning in bed. "I hear Edward Pendley is looking to buy out his two neighbors. According to Avendoran law, he can't hold the title to all three groves in his name only. I figure he'll put Reah on, but if she marries him, that's just shy of breaking the law."

"You think Adam would like to invest in that?"

"He says yes," Merrill pulled the sheet down, uncovering a breast. He didn't talk for a few minutes. "I can't tell you how long I dreamed about this," he said.

"After four hundred years, you still dream about it?" Kiarra smiled at him.

"All the time. And we have Glendes Grey willing to invest, with Dragon, Crane and Lissa."

"You like making a deal almost as much as you like sex," Kiarra kissed him.

"Sex with you," Merrill grinned.

"Wow," I said, repeating one of Teeg's favorite phrases. Edward's patio was crowded with people, and his staff was moving among them, serving drinks and finger food. Even Farzi and Nenzi were there, with Teeg and Ry. Dragon and Crane had come, with Kiarra, Merrill and Adam. Glendes Grey of Grey House was also present, along with Lissa and her Grey House mate, Shadow Grey. I seldom saw him, so that was a surprise. Crorver Ride and Erbrin Dondl walked in with Edward. I think the crowd shocked them as well.

"We want to make an offer on your groves," Merrill was brokering this deal, looked like, with Adam Chessman right behind him.

"You don't have enough money," Erbrin snapped.

"Hear us out, first, and then decide whether we have enough," Merrill smiled. "Now, I know your family is fighting among themselves already, positioning for a better portion of what you'll leave behind when you die," he said to Crorver, who was aging. "While you have everything sorted out in a will, I can guarantee that your heirs will fight over the money anyway and ignore the groves, letting them go to waste while they destroy one another. Is that what you've built these groves up for? To let them die while your heirs fight over the proceeds? Be honest, do they care about the trees?"

I watched Merrill, blinking in amazement. This man was a shark when it came to business. He turned to Erbrin Dondl next. "Your trees need better care than they're getting. You can't seem to hire the employees you need at the price you want to pay. They let the sprinklers go untouched for days, while some trees drown in leaking lines and the rest dry up. Your shipments have dwindled for three turns running; I checked those figures myself. Perhaps if you'd turn your attention to working your fields instead of destroying your neighbor's trees with imported reptiles, your profits would rise again."

"That was not me!" Erbrin insisted.

"No? I have records here, showing that you paid a ship to make the delivery. The Campiaan Security Detail is looking into illegal animal smuggling against the ship's captain now. Predagators are not allowed in any portion of either Alliance where they are not native already. That smuggling trail will lead right to you and the fine is five hundred thousand credits per predagator, plus months of prison time. I understand one hundred of those creatures were shipped, according to the logs. How much does that come to in time and credits?" The corner of Merrill's mouth twitched. If I were ever in a business deal again, I wanted him with me.

"Now," Adam began, standing with Merrill, "Our offer is more than generous. One trillion each, plus fifty carats of uncut Tiralian crystal. Credits are much easier to distribute to the family than gishi fruit groves, are they not?" Adam smiled at Crorver. "With the pending debt and probable jail time, during which your groves might be overrun by jungle, I'd say this is the best of all possible solutions. We will return the predagators to their original habitat and all will be well. If the CSD cannot find the reptiles, they cannot bring charges. Is that not so?"

Crorver cursed while Erbrin just looked frightened. Merrill was correct; smuggling illegal animals carried a sentence up to a full turn per animal. Erbrin might not live long enough to serve out his sentence. Crorver was pushing two hundred; Erbrin had to be at least one hundred fifty. Their life expectancy was at best two hundred fifteen or so.

"And what if we file coercion charges?" Crorver growled.

"Go ahead. I just pointed out facts to you. There is no coercion. Go back to your groves. Go ahead. The CSD is already on its way, though. Did you both invest in these creatures, or only one of you?"

Crorver gave Erbrin an evil look. "Get rid of the creatures and we'll talk," he said and stalked away.

"Unbelievable," I said. Nearly a hundred predagators were snapping and hissing at one another inside an enclosure only clicks later. Crorver and Erbrin were back to survey the animals. "Two were killed by snakes," Merrill said. "The bodies are inside the barn if you wish to see them," he added.

"How did you capture them so quickly?" Erbrin whispered.

"You need to ask?" Astralan and Stellan lifted their arms and predagators rose in the air.

"Warlocks," Crorver nodded. "I should have known. The amount is generous. I spoke with my solicitors, they say the property is worth close to that amount, and fifty carats of uncut Tiralian crystal is worth the land by itself. We'll have the records prepared and we'll sign tomorrow if you want. The family wants this as well," Crorver added.

"My solicitors say to do the deal and leave Avendor," Erbrin grumbled. "While I still can."

"Sounds good," Merrill said. "We'll meet you here tomorrow."

"They're almost cute," I watched as predagators sunned themselves. Someone had installed a sprinkler inside their pen and they seemed happy.

"And dangerous," Edward put an arm around me. "I have to tell you, those two over there managed to do the impossible, I think," he smiled down at me. He meant Merrill and Adam. I agreed completely.

"Wow." The field we met the Copper Ra'Ak in looked like a carnival. Beautifully colored tents littered the wide expanse of grass. Maldak came and bowed over my hand. While a kiss might adversely affect someone else, it wouldn't do harm to a High Demon. Nevertheless, he did not place his mouth on me. Nefrigar and Pheligar flanked me, with Youon and Kyler, Lissa's niece, walking beside Pheligar. On Nefrigar's other side strode Kiarra, Adam, Merrill and Belen. Maldak had others of his people beneath the open tent, as did we. Many of the Saa Thalarr had come, as had Lissa and most of her mates. Ildevar was still unwilling to reveal himself or the twenty members of the Grand Alliance Council, preferring to err on the side of caution. I didn't blame him a bit. The three that surprised me by coming were Jayd, Garde and Glinda. I had High Demon backup if I needed it.

"Bright One," Maldak bowed to Belen next. And last of all, in a rush of wind, Kifirin appeared.

"High Lord," Maldak also bowed to him. Maldak had two others with him at the table as we looked over treaties, argued over this point or that and by the end of the day had a tentative peace agreement hammered out and signed.

One of the agreements we had was that Black and Copper Ra'Ak would pursue the last of the rogues and their spawn, and request help from the Saa Thalarr if needed. I didn't know how many rogues were out there and they weren't sure, either. They did promise to let Kyler know, who would then contact the Saa Thalarr if help were needed. I thought it a very good system. Belen folded all of us to Adam's ancestral home, and I had no idea of the celebrating that would occur once we arrived.

I was kissed and hugged by dozens of people as they laughed and uncorked champagne. I got a huge kiss from Franklin, Shane and Tomas, plus Celestan and Galaxsan, who were with their new mates as often as possible. I'd never seen them smile so much. Things had changed so much for them—from when they were doing Arvil's bidding to now. Teeg had changed things enough for them that the Saa Thalarr considered them fit mates.

Teeg brought Edward and the others, with enough gishi fruit ice cream for everybody. "Reah, we sign the papers on those other groves tomorrow, but we need experienced supervision," Merrill and Adam came to me. "Some of ours have volunteered to come but we want you to teach them what they need to know. Since we now have a reduced workload, they'll be available to do the work."

"Frank looks so much like you," I smiled at Merrill.

"He was the son of my heart before he was reborn. Now he is truly my son," Merrill smiled back.

"If I ever find myself in need of a business negotiator, I will pay for your services," I said. "That may have been the most impressive thing I've ever seen when you took on Crorver and Erbrin."

"That was nothing," Merrill blew the whole thing off. "Come, dance with us." I went a careful round with Merrill first, who smiled and twirled me gently before handing me off to Adam. Then Edward cut in.

"Reah, I want to take you home and sit in the pool with you, since we can't do the hot tub," he grinned.

"Can we get away?" I asked.

"I think so, as long as we tell a few people." A few people were notified and Nefrigar folded us to EastStar.

"No suits," Edward whispered, undressing me in a secluded spot near the pool. Fruit and tropical trees were everywhere around the pool and a small portion of it was very private, with a waterfall making soothing sounds as it emptied nearby. How had I missed Edward being naked before? He was a beautiful man and he didn't hide his desire. "We won't unless you want it," he sighed against my mouth.

"Just take it slow, all right?" I asked, leaning my head into the hollow between his neck and shoulder.

"I would take forever if I could love you at the end of it," he murmured against my mouth. "I love you. Since the moment you walked into my life, I knew. Someone told me long ago that the woman I would love would come to me in the most unusual of circumstances, and that I would recognize her immediately. That's how it was, Reah. I looked at you and I knew. Like lightning striking or something. Now, let's talk about these breasts. And how perfect they are." He lowered his head and showed me what he thought of them. The rest followed naturally and I wanted him as much as he wanted me at the end of it. I think I was tugging on his hair and begging him to move faster at the last. He smiled, kissed me and obliged nicely.

"Now, all of you know that Reah is more than capable of taking care of herself," Belen announced as the party was winding down. "But it is time we all stepped forward and announced how much we care for her. The day will come very soon when she will need protection. I want to ask all who are willing to show up. I wish to show any enemies, present and future, just what it is they will deal with should they come against her. Ever. You will know the time. Until then," Belen nodded to all and disappeared.

"This goes against everything that is in us," Reldill complained. Naldill didn't care. The loss of his power, which was something he sorely missed, would not be taken without revenge of some sort. "Surely you can do as those fool warlocks, and gain power from it," Naldill hissed. "Do it! Tap the core. See what happens."

"Cynthin, did you think your little grab for power would go unanswered?" Her Council stood as she walked into the meeting. Her second-in-command had called the meeting, with a majority backing him up. She'd been forced to appear. "You have embarrassed Xordthe and made us into the laughingstock you thought to make of that girl and Teeg San Gerxon. Did you think to put yourself in his place, or at least higher than you are now? We here all agree that you couldn't form a quorum in the Council, let alone keep the Campiaan Alliance together. You know that if we have a unanimous vote of all three hundred members of this Council, you may be removed from office. Here is the vote, Cynthin." He handed the comp-vid to the president of Xordthe. "These numbers have been forwarded to all media outlets. They will report this on the late news. I imagine you might be bombarded with the usual requests for interviews. Get your tissues ready or get out of the city, Cynthin. Your pretty face will not get you far with the people now." Cynthin stared at the unanimous vote to remove her from the presidency. A general election would be held within the next moon-turn, to elect a president to complete her current term. Cynthin flung the comp-vid at her former second-in-command and stalked from the Council chamber.

"The only reason you are still enjoying your position is that you are my only son and I have no other choice, Andelis," his father the King, shot Andelis of Roorthi a severe look. "While your part is not great in this, it has opened the royal house to ridicule. We are being hounded by the media and our own subjects because we followed Cynthin of Xordthe blindly. Or you did, since I leave the dealings with the Campiaan Alliance to you. From today, that will no longer be true. I am sending my trusted First Advisor to those gatherings instead. For a period of five turns, you will smile and nod and take hands at factory openings and the like. You will rebuild this image you have tarnished. Do you understand?"

"Yes, Father." Andelis bowed low to the King.

"Good. Leave me. I am quite angry."

"Yes, Father." Andelis walked backward a respectful distance before turning on his heel and scurrying away.

"I feel like the biggest fool." Tevan of Shillverr rubbed his forehead, attempting to relieve the headache. Three scientists sat in his private office. All of them had come, presenting him with the evidence that the core had indeed been tapped more than twenty years earlier, then also presented the most damning evidence of all; recorded satellite images, showing the golden creature seating herself on the grass in a remote location before beginning to glow. The recordings from the satellite were quite clear, once they'd known what to look for. The numbers after that date showed the core energy levels nearly normal and rising. The ASD Director had not fabricated any of his story.

"We did not know to look for this; we thought nature had reset itself somehow. We now know that help was provided, unasked for and unappreciated. I think we should rectify that now."

"But how?" Tevan asked, turning troubled eyes to his scientists.

"Under the Campiaan Alliance, we are allowed to operate without fear of the criminal element. Before, we were tortured by those who ruled here if we did not cooperate with them in their scheming to overcome this one or that. We are a free people, now. You have not harmed us. In fact, we appreciate the funding you helped to pass. This will enable Shillverr to create new technology that will place us among the best of both Alliances. This area in the photograph is still empty. We suggest a memorial to the one who saved Shillverr and her citizens."

"How long will this take?" Tevan played the recorded vid from more than twenty-five turns earlier.

"If we use bronze and employ laser sculptors, not long," the scientist smiled.

"Good. Get on this right away. We will invite the media and offer our thanks."

"Sir, I hate to interrupt, but Cynthin of Xordthe is calling," Tevan's assistant walked into Tevan's office.

"I will no longer accept her calls," Tevan stood and nodded to the three scientists. "We have other, more pressing matters that require our attention."

CHAPTER 12

Crorver's entire family came to the signing, dressed for celebration, it seemed. I felt sorry for Crorver, who'd given his life to his groves. He'd allowed Erbrin to draw him into petty rivalries with Edward, however, who saw no need for such trivialities. In his opinion, there was more than enough room for competition. He'd grown gishi fruit before his rivals, and was foresighted enough to buy the land that made up EastStar Groves. He had no time or desire to involve himself in petty rivalries.

Erbrin and two employees had shown up as well. The local magistrate was there to witness the signings, as had everyone's solicitors.

Edward had a small interest in both groves, but the majority was owned by the others, who'd put up nearly all the funding. I had no idea how they'd gotten their hands on fifty carats of Tiralian crystal—that was worth a fortune by itself. "We will have all our belongings out by this afternoon," Crorver and Erbrin acknowledged to the magistrate, who had them sign agreements to that effect, along with the promise to not damage any of the property or fines would be levied. I think Dragon and Crane were going with them to make sure nothing was amiss. I wouldn't want to cross either of those strong Falchani.

"If I donate a portion of my gishi fruit allotment, will I get ice cream out of it?" Glendes leaned down to whisper.

"Of course," I laughed. "As much as you want."

"We will invite you to Grey House very soon, to a family dinner. As our guest," he added.

"That sounds nice," I replied.

"Some updating needed," Adam inspected the Crorver estate with a practiced and critical eye. The house needed enlarging as well, especially the kitchen and baths. I think Adam was planning a larger pool area, too, when all was said and done. With the power the Saa Thalarr held, it would probably be done within an eight-day.

"Reah, you and Edward need to tell us what the groves require," Merrill stood at my elbow, a drink in his hand. "This one is yours, mine will contain alcohol when it comes," he grinned and handed the fruit juice over.

"Let's go look now," I said. "And we'll have to interview employees. I have a feeling we'll be forced to send a few packing."

We did. Almost half from both groves. Adam and Merrill, both former vampires, laid compulsion on the exiting employees, telling them there would be no retaliation of any kind. They nodded, gathered their things and loaded onto buses bound for Adrixx.

"We'll be hiring more employees, and both groves will be combined," Merrill said as we examined sprinkler systems, talked with supervisors about harvests, pruning, fertilizing and insect control. Edward offered very good advice, in addition to the services of one or more of his supervisors, just to make sure the transitions went smoothly. Lissa went with us, as did Shadow Grey, who pulled her against him as they walked through the spaces between trees.

"You'll make your money back in three years," Edward predicted. "We've gotten rid of the fruit thieves and the incompetent workers.

The next harvest will come in four moon-turns. There is much to do within that time. We'll need at least six more supervisors. We'll either hire or train."

"In four months, Reah will be out to here," Drake and Drew appeared. Drew, the scoundrel, made that observation, holding arms far out from his stomach. I swatted at him. He answered by lifting me for a careful hug. "That's our great-nephew, you know," he laughed and rubbed my belly. "We'll be happy to teach him bladework."

"Hah. In less than a year, your own will be driving you crazy," I snapped before thinking. And then blinked at Drake and Drew in embarrassment. "Uh, Lissa," I said, "where's Karzac right now?"

"I don't know. Do you need him?" she smiled at me.

"I don't. Except to check on something for me."

Karzac and Kevis were there in seconds. "What is it, Reah?" Kevis came right to me, his green-gold eyes displaying concern.

"It's not me. I think Lissa's pregnant. With Drake and Drew's babies. Don't ask me how I know. I can't answer that."

Karzac put his hands on Lissa's belly while she stood there, staring at her healer-mate. "It's true," Karzac grinned. "Young Falchani, I hope you are ready for fatherhood. Both of you." Drake whooped and slapped his palm against Drew's.

"I don't know what to do with twins," Lissa grumbled. "Tory and Ry were bad enough together."

"Come on, baby. We have plans to make," Drake and Drew now flanked Lissa, who was vainly attempting to fend both of them off.

"I'll laugh if it's girls," Kevis whispered in my ear. I snickered.

During the next moon-turn, I had more than enough to keep me busy. Kevis took up my mornings, at least two or three clicks, followed by lunch, a click or so in the ice-cream plant, mostly to make sure things were going smoothly and the employees were doing what they should, and then it was off to the newly-acquired groves. Many new names were kicked around, but eventually it was decided to call them

NorthStar Groves. They were slightly to the north and west of EastStar, after all.

"Come on, Reah needs baby things. We'll need baby things," Drake and Drew were coaxing Lissa away to go shopping. The entourage that went with us was enormous. I saw people staring, openmouthed when the stores were invaded. Dragon and Devin, about to be grandparents, were there, as were Crane, Grace, Kiarra and half the Saa Thalarr, I think. All of my mates had come, including Nefrigar, who'd shortened himself but retained his blue skin. Teeg held me against him as we looked at cribs.

"Reah, money is no object," Lendill handed over a comp-vid. I stared at the information on the screen. It showed funds. In my name. In the trillions. I almost dropped to the floor. Teeg held me up. "This is what Ildevar and the others said should come to you, breah-mul. Half of what was hidden in accounts for the pirates. The rest went to pay restitution to the victims and provide new equipment to the ASD. This is yours, Reah. All of it. You shouldn't have to worry about money for a while."

"Yeah," I whispered hoarsely.

Furniture was purchased. A crib each for Teeg's palace, the reptanoids' plantation and EastStar's manor. Garwin Wyatt would have a bed no matter where he slept. Lissa was having a friendly debate with Drake and Drew over what to buy for their children. I think Karzac already knew the sex, he just wasn't telling. And Lissa, hands on hips, was telling her twin Falchani they were getting ahead of themselves since she was only three months pregnant. I snickered, thinking about how it was that she was pregnant by both at the same time.

"What are you laughing at?" Lissa stared at me.

"Nothing," I burst out laughing. I couldn't help it. Teeg had to hold me up; I laughed so hard tears came. And these were going to be his half-brothers. I wiped more tears away.

"Are you all right?" Kevis asked, his concerned face in front of mine.

"I am," I said. "Teeg's going to be a brother."

"True," Kevis agreed. "Come along, I think we're done for the evening."

"Hey, honey," I said to Astralan, who'd appeared inside the kitchen while I drank a protein fruit jumble that Kevis shoved at me.

"Reah, my love, are you well?" He looked worried.

"I am."

"What was that laughing fit about?" Kevis was almost tapping a foot.

"Well, since they're not here," I snickered. "I was just thinking about how it was that Lissa is pregnant by both her Falchani at the same time."

"Ah," Kevis gave an exaggerated nod. Astralan laughed, sat next to me and laughed again.

"See, even you're smiling now," I poked at Kevis. His smile widened. "How about some ice cream?" I asked both of them. We ended up sharing a small tub of gishi fruit ice cream. I even fed Astralan and Kevis the last few bites. Astralan leaned in to kiss me afterward.

"Come to bed with me," he kissed me again. "I want to hold you against me. Fuck you until you see only me for a little while. And someday, this bump will be mine." He rubbed my belly.

"Are we possessive?" I asked.

"More than you know," he said.

"I like it," I wrinkled my nose at him.

"Good," he said and folded me to his bed.

"My brother will treat her like a queen," Stellan put a hand on Teeg's shoulder. "Reah's all he's seen for a very long time."

"Here," Edward handed over a generous dish of ice cream. He

pushed another in Ry's direction, and soon Tory, Lendill, Farzi, Nenzi, Lok and Aurelius were having gishi fruit ice cream.

"This is amazing," Aurelius sighed.

"We're on our way to being wealthy, just from the ice cream. My distributor is offering even more money if he can get his hands on more of it."

"We'll be making NorthStar Groves more efficient and profitable, with your and Reah's help," Merrill appeared with Adam and Kiarra. "We've got half the updates done on the house." He grinned and accepted a bowl of ice cream. Edward handed one to Merrill and Kiarra as well.

"Reah is a genius," Kiarra sighed, dipping into her ice cream. "This recipe is perfect."

"It's a shame none of her girls showed an aptitude in the kitchen," Adam agreed. "I don't think any of them know how to approach her, now. To offer apologies or anything else."

"They don't see her," Teeg mumbled. "Garde and Jayd and Glinda. They don't see how beautiful she is. On the inside as well as the outside. They wanted what she had. What she could give them. Was it selfishness? Jealousy? I don't know," he shrugged. "But she gave it to them. Her girls. Her time, her talents, her dignity. And they stripped her bare. Never gave a damn thing back. I realize I don't have much room to talk, but I never want to see her standing on the edge of that fucking volcano again."

"Here, boss." Stellan handed Teeg a glass of bourbon.

"Let's take a little trip," Kevis suggested. "To Cloudsong."

"Something happened here, I'm sure of it," Kevis said, as they looked around the cold and empty stone shell that had once housed the audience chamber of the royal palace. "Those cages were in this anteroom," he walked to the western edge of the vast room. Black marks where blasts had been leveled at Reah littered the stone floor. Some of the cages, with metal bars melted and misshapen, were still scattered about the smaller room. If Reah hadn't protected the prisoners, they'd have died in the firefight after she turned Thifilatha.

"They were all trying to kill her," Adam pointed out. "How many blasts did she take? If Kiarra had been pregnant and in that situation, I might have taken the entire planet apart."

"But nobody came for her," Kevis sighed. "Not until she'd already taken most of them down. The ASD showed up in time to take Dantel Schuul, his daughter and some of their cronies into custody. That's all that was left. They'd sent everything else they had against Reah, and she was forced to kill them all while they blasted her with lasers and anything else they had."

"It was the same thing she'd faced for twenty-five years, don't you think?" Aurelius sighed. "Nobody came. She was forced to do it by herself. With no help."

"Any other High Demon female in this situation would have had half the population of males enraged and tearing the place apart," Tory admitted. "We've cast her out, haven't we?"

"I gave the King and Queen what they desired as I promised," Kifirin appeared. "At great cost."

"You did this for Jayd and Glinda?" Merrill studied Kifirin disapprovingly.

"Yes. It was a promise to them. It almost cost us something far greater. I promised Jayd that the race would thrive. Reah was the path to that promise. I robbed her of her children. I did not remove the mute from them. They will provide the High Demon race with other daughters. All their children will be female. I know not how to make this up to Reah."

"I don't think you can," Kiarra stood before Kifirin. "Everything you attempt to hand her from now on will be tainted. You failed in your creativity, dark god."

"Those girls will never belong to their mother. As they should." Aurelius observed. "You did that to her? And you call yourself a god?"

"I cannot take it back now," Kifirin sighed. "It frightened me when she almost died with the last set of twins. I'd overstepped my bounds. I knew it then. My father's way of telling me I'd erred. If she'd not been so fragile, I'd have forced other pregnancies upon her. I would have. She wouldn't have stepped back from the edge of Baetrah, then. I allowed Gardevik's prejudices to go unchecked, just to keep Reah where she was. Keep her under the Crown's thumb until things were brought back to where they should be. I slept while my planet almost died. I promised Jayd it would thrive again."

"I hope they know how to stand on their own feet, now. Reah's done it for them up to this point," Lendill said. "She won't willingly go back there. Ever. That was supposed to be her homeworld. She's High Demon. Only Garde doesn't think much of her ancestry, does he? Do pointed ears matter that much?" Lendill knew that bitterness. He was half-Elven. That had burned when his older brothers had tortured him with it.

"Part of your mistake is not calling your King and the others to task for not giving aid to Reah. For not working alongside her. If they had, they would not be facing the troubles now, in their groves." Nefrigar appeared. "We do not interfere. Not with mortals or immortals alike, unless they threaten us or our mates with death. And the Wise Ones came and said not to interfere with this," he gestured around the audience chamber. "They said that something would come of this that we could not stop or alter, else I would have come and none of these would have survived. Their particles would have been separated quickly. But you, dark god; has not your parent called you to task? The Wise Ones said that this would come to be."

"He has called a meeting. I have been putting it off," Kifirin admitted.

"I will not pity you, whatever happens," Nefrigar snapped angrily. "I know what happened here. Every Larentii does," Nefrigar turned to Kevis. "Had anyone come, it might have been avoided and Reah would not now be torturing herself over it. It was something that could not be helped or averted, given the circumstances. I hope you get to the bottom of it, soon. I grow tired of waiting." Nefrigar disappeared.

"Wow. I've never seen a Larentii that angry," Kiarra blinked in astonishment.

"I wish we had all the images from this," Kevis said, examining the floor beneath him. Black soot was everywhere.

"The Larentii gave as much as they were willing to recreate for us," Lendill pointed out. "If it weren't for them, we'd have had nothing. There were no working cameras here."

~

"Reah, you were moaning in your sleep, my love." Astralan stroked hair back from my forehead gently.

"Honey, I'm sorry I woke you up," I mumbled, my eyes refusing to open completely.

"No," he whispered, pulling me close. "It sounded as if you were in pain. I was afraid it was the baby or something."

"No, honey. I think the baby is fine."

"You're not feeling ill, are you?" His fingers stroked my belly.

"No, honey. Maybe a little hungry, but that's it. What time is it?"

"Nearly dawn. Lie here with me a while longer, and then we'll find breakfast for you and Master Garwin Wyatt." I ran my hand down Astralan's ribs. He drew in a breath and then followed up on my overture.

~

"Reah?" Teeg crowded against me as I put sauce together at the stove for eggs. Astralan and I wanted eggs and shaved ham on toasted bread with sauce. The cook and her helper were waiting for breakfast just as Astralan was—all of them seated at the island.

"Teeg?" I leaned back my head to look at him while I stirred. He kissed me, and then kissed me again before going to sit with the others.

"I wish my sauce would turn out like this," the cook sighed. She was in her fifties, just as I was, and in her prime. I liked her. Very much. Edward had a knack for hiring the right people.

"It will." I smiled at her from my seat between Teeg and Astralan.

"What? Where's ours?" Lok looked upset at what we were eating. Flyer, who'd been off with some of the Saa Thalarr Falchani, learning some tricks, as Lok put it, was right behind Lok.

"I'll get you some breakfast, stop fretting," I flipped his braid before going back to the stove. I'd made enough sauce for everybody; I only had to do the eggs.

"Reah, this is very good," Flyer complimented me.

"I'll let you make noodles later," I smiled at him.

"Be happy to," he agreed.

"Reah, can I get something quick before going off to fight the war for justice?" Lendill walked in dressed in his ASD uniform.

"I've got another egg right here, keep your clothes on," I muttered, putting a plate down in front of him. He gave me a brilliant smile as he began to eat.

"Oh, good, breakfast," Ry came in with Erland and Corolan. Three more plates of food were set down. Lendill rushed off as soon as he finished, giving me an egg-flavored kiss first.

"Brush your teeth!" I yelled as he folded away. That caused a bit of snickering around the table.

Farzi, Nenzi and Edward walked in, followed closely by Kevis. The cook and her helper were clearing dishes away by that time. I gave them a conspiratorial grin as they worked beside me.

"Reah, can I get a kiss?" Cory asked as I leaned against him to put a plate of food down for Edward.

"Cory, you can have whatever you want," I threaded my fingers through his dark-blond hair.

"Good," I was on his lap in seconds. "Now, want a bite of this?" he offered some of his food to me.

"I'll take toast."

"Here." He put a bit of jam on it before handing the piece to me. "Want some milk with that?" A glass was poured using power and it floated to me. His fingers stroked my ribs while I ate. "Too thin," he kissed my shoulder. I still wore my stretchy pajama top and cotton bottoms.

"She is," Ry agreed. "Let's take her to Desh's tonight. I'll see if we can get in." Ry has a slight dimple, but it doesn't show itself often. The dimple was present now.

"Good. I want to check on Dee's while we're there," I said. "Since I have money now, I'd like to see if anything needs upgrading."

"We can go today, if you want. I'll take you," Kevis offered. "Feel like visiting your relatives at Desh's to make the reservations?"

"We could. I wouldn't mind seeing Fes." Lok and Aurelius escorted Kevis and me to Tulgalan. Fes broke into a huge smile when we walked into his kitchen.

"Uncle Fes," I hugged him back when he wrapped me in his arms.

"Reah, I was so scared for you," he said while his kitchen staff served us coffee and tea inside his private office. "I saw those vids, and mother and I were shouting at the screen. We knew better, we just couldn't convince anyone else. When Hild Marolla did his exposé, it was such a relief."

"How is your mom?" I asked. Farla was nearing one hundred fifty.

"She's fine. Comes in and helps on Six and Seven-days."

"Have you been to Dee's lately?" I asked.

"Things are great since we got rid of those two," he snorted at my question. He'd meant Ilvan and Radolf. Ilvan was his brother, so I was surprised. "Reah, they stole from you. You know how I feel about that. That's not just theft, it's theft from family. Baby girl, you could have asked us for money anytime. Mother and I would have gladly helped."

"I know. But you have your own business to run and the family to support," I said. "It wasn't your responsibility."

"It was ours, and we failed that test, too," Aurelius growled.

"It's behind us," I said. "Fes, does Dee's need any upgrades or remodels? I can do that now, if it's needed."

"The three banquet rooms need to be redecorated, and some of the kitchen equipment needs upgrading. I can see to it," he offered.

"I'll get somebody on it, but if you wouldn't mind checking on the progress now and then," I said. "You have my comp-code. Just keep me informed."

"Do we have an inside source on getting gishi fruit ice cream?" Fes gave me a shrewdly disarming smile.

"I think we might be able to supply it to Dee's and Desh's, as an exclusive item. And I'll show you how to put that expensive dessert together that they were serving on Stellar Winds."

"That thousand-credit dessert?" Fes was excited, now. The price had jumped and then jumped again as it gained popularity and became more scarce during my illness after moonrush.

"Yeah. That's mine. They called it sex by dessert, but I think we should rename it, don't you?"

"Probably." Fes laughed.

"Reah, I'd like to speak with Fes in private," Kevis said. "Why don't you go check on Dee's and see what they need. We'll order everything and find a work crew afterward."

I blinked at Kevis. They wanted to discuss me, I knew. "All right," I stood and nodded. Aurelius put an arm around my shoulders.

"I'll send mindspeech," Kevis said. Aurelius folded Lok and me away.

"She seems to like you very much," Kevis looked Fes in the eye.

"She does. Mother and I love her. More than she knows or suspects. Reah kept the business from going under after Father died. He kept his best recipes away from all of us. In spite of all that, Reah managed to recreate all of them, and even improved some of them. When mother sent her a note after Father died, telling her what would likely happen with the business, we got a reply from Reah immediately, and that reply included every recipe that Desh's needed to stay open. Mother and I have discussed this over the years. We knew Marzi was an evil, we just never did anything about it. She intimidated everyone, including mother and me. Unfortunately, we didn't know about the abuse Reah suffered when Father sent her off to Edan when she was eight. I'd like to believe we'd have turned Edan in over that if we'd known."

"Do you think your father knew or suspected?"

"I don't know. He may have, but back then, Edan was the golden boy. Desh's number two raked in all the top awards. Of course, we now know that Reah was responsible for those awards, and she wasn't even an adult. Was Edan jealous? Very likely. He hated me because I was first son and Father kept me here at Desh's number one. He, as number two son, was sent to Desh's number two. Edan never got over that, I think. Yes, I know he isn't the same person, now. He and Ilvan both tried to explain that to me. And I should have punched Ilvan in the face as soon as I found out what he was doing."

"I want to have a talk with Edan soon," Kevis said. "To see what he remembers from those days. Recently, I was transported to a time during Reah's youth, where I witnessed a beating he gave her when she was ten. She almost died in that attack. Edan bribed the hospital officials so they'd record the beating as an accident."

"Someone you know can manipulate time." Fes shook his head in wonder. "I wish I had that talent. So many things might be different, now."

"But that's why we don't have that talent ourselves," Kevis pointed out gently. "Any changes in the timeline can result in disaster. We have to leave things alone most of the time, as horrible as that might sound."

"Are you going to be able to help her?" Fes asked. "Sometimes I wish I could bring her to the house and let mother look after her, but she won't come."

"I'm trying to sort this out. She doesn't know it yet, but Ceerah Kade's hearing is tomorrow and the magistrates on Refizan have politely requested her presence. Jalan Wolk has worked out a plea, since this was her first offense. The charges against Ceerah are much more serious."

"I learned so many things about Reah from that program," Fes sighed. "She never talks about those things. Ever."

"The ASD usually prevents their agents from discussing anything they've done. The information is generally too sensitive. Ceerah and that stupid program ruined Reah's cover. Why they thought not to hide her face is beyond belief. Ildevar Wyyld gave permission to release the information on Reah, to clear her name and her record.

Those awards are generally kept by the ASD and never shown to the public."

"Did she really take down the drakus seed trade?"

"In ways you can't begin to imagine. Reah is very special, even among High Demons. None of the others can do what she does."

"She's not full High Demon, though. Is she? I'd like to say it's her Desh family genetics, too, but that probably isn't true. Go ahead, dash my hopes that my children might be special if I have any."

"I can't say whose children might be special and whose won't," Kevis smiled. "But in my opinion, aren't all children special? At least to loving parents?"

"Mother seems to think that about me. I try not to disappoint her."

"And there's your answer, right there," Kevis laughed.

"Get estimates," I told the head cook, who nodded and smiled at everything I said. Aurelius was also smiling and sending mindspeech, telling me the poor man was star struck. Lok, who was also grinning, told me he'd *Looked*. The man had watched the Hild Marolla special at least six times. I breathed a troubled sigh and went back to explaining what we needed done to Dee's. Head cook Jorden told me he'd get on it right away. We went over the books while I was there, too. Jorden seemed an honest man; Fes had done well when he'd hired him for me.

When I walked onto the floor of the restaurant, there were stares. And then whispers. I thought to duck back inside the kitchen, but Aurelius and Lok had firm grips on my hand and shoulder, so we went through the place. Jorden spoke to some of the lunch crowd, who seemed to be enjoying their food.

"Excuse me," a mother who was there with three children and an older woman, held a hand toward me when I was about to walk past.

"Can I help you with something?" I stopped at her table.

"You're that woman, aren't you? The one from that program." I wanted to sigh or skip away. Other diners were watching, so I could do neither. All I could do was extricate myself as quickly as possible.

"Yes, I am that woman," I nodded and smiled as pleasantly as I could.

"I saw that conference, too, where they asked you questions."

"Yes, that is certainly me," I agreed amiably. "I own this restaurant, and have for many years. I'll understand if you don't wish to bring your little ones here any longer, although I can assure you that your children would be very safe here. I seldom come. I'm only here today to see what upgrades are needed."

"But you're a hero," the woman sighed. "I stopped watching that stupid reality program after I saw what they did to you. I couldn't help thinking that some of those other people might have suffered at their hands as well. I find that attitude demeaning and revolting."

"As do I. I've never been able to watch those programs. We make fools enough of ourselves as it is. There isn't any real need to publicize it."

"I totally agree," she smiled. She was a pretty woman, with pale-blonde hair and hazel eyes. Her children—three girls, must have ranged in age from six to eleven or so. They were all staring at me while I spoke to their mother.

"Auri," I turned to Aurelius, "will you get some ice cream for our guests, here?" I winked at him when I looked him in the eye.

"Right away." Aurelius walked through the kitchen door and disappeared, coming back with two kitchen helpers, a load of bowls and an armload of gishi fruit ice-cream containers. He'd had to fold to Avendor to get it, but he'd accomplished it swiftly.

"We'll be providing free dessert today," I announced. Jorden placed bowls around the tables while the kitchen helpers dipped out generous portions of ice cream for each guest. The screams and excited shrieks began immediately. "This is the ice cream it's impossible to get," the woman was smiling after she tasted it.

"Yes, it is," I agreed. "We'll carry it here as well as Desh's. Here's my comp-code, if you need anything," I handed a small card with the code to her. "It was a pleasure speaking with you."

"Kevis is ready," Lok said when we finally escaped into the kitchen.

"I'll bring in contractors right away," Jorden's eyes were shining. "When will we have the ice cream?"

"Tomorrow," I said. "But I've been working on a special dessert for Dee's, using the ice cream. We'll unveil that next week, perhaps."

"Thank you," Jorden sighed.

"Call me when the estimates come in," I said as Lok, Auri and I walked out the employee entrance.

"You don't need another mate," Lok laughed. I thought about elbowing him in the ribs. Aurelius folded us back to Desh's.

"I've got one of the banquet rooms reserved for tonight," Kevis said when we appeared. "And an offer for a free meal, if the King of Karathia and the founding member of the Campiaan Alliance will agree to pose with Fes, here."

"What, you're passing on the Prince-Heir of the Elves?" I laughed at Fes.

"Funny, baby girl. Give me a hug before you go," Fes said. I gave him a hard hug and Aurelius took us away.

"Lunch and then a nap," Kevis ordered.

"Do people always do what you say?" I wrinkled my nose at him.

"If they know what's good for them," he replied. "Come along. I think lunch is ready."

It was. A nice soup with crispy finger sandwiches. The soup was wonderful. Farzi and Nenzi, who'd been out with Edward, came in and sat on either side, eating with me. "We lie down for nap," Nenzi announced when I was pointed to my bedroom.

"Sounds good," I said. I brushed my teeth first, as did my reptanoids. They helped me into lounging pajamas and crawled into bed with me.

"Kiss me?" Nenzi said hopefully.

"Sweet man," I brushed his mouth with mine.

"Your sweet man here for you, Reah-love." Nenzi deepened the kiss, placing hands on my face. His kisses became more demanding. As if he wanted something he'd never gotten before. I blinked at him when he pulled away for a moment. "We give Reah what we always want to give," he said, and came right out of his clothing. When I saw what he wanted and what he now had to get it, at first I was shocked. And then I smiled at him.

CHAPTER 13

"Dee and Aurelius talk to us," Farzi was smiling, his nose rubbing mine. Had I ever known that lion snake shapeshifters had a few extra vertebrae? It makes them very limber. I was exhausted and now knew exactly how Lissa had ended up pregnant by her Falchani twins. My reptanoids, given back what was taken from them at an early age, had gotten a quick lesson in sex education from two very old vampires. Farzi and Nenzi appeared to be fast learners.

"You sleep now. We want to do this again soon," Nenzi said. "That amazing. We always wonder what fuss all about."

"Fuss?" I turned to Nenzi and gave him a kiss. "That wasn't fuss. That was fun. Amazing."

"Yes. Reah amazing. We do this again. Often."

"Did Kifirin say whether you might father children?" I asked, hugging Nenzi.

"He not say. We not ask. He just say we get back what we lost. And Aurelius say that this not hurt baby. We skeptical at first."

"He's safe, unless somebody means harm," I said.

"We not ever mean harm. We know what happened at awful place. We never do anything like that."

"Honey, I love you. And my Honey Snake, too. I know you wouldn't do that." I rubbed the back of his neck with my fingers. He seemed to like that. He leaned in to kiss me. "You sleep. Tired. Kevis say not to wear you out."

"He knew about this?" I lifted an eyebrow at Nenzi, who smiled.

"He did. He examine us afterward," Farzi turned me to him. His brown eyes held a bit of laughter. "We not know what to think when this happen," he placed my hand on a newly formed erection.

"Honey, you may have to take care of that yourself," I yawned, covering it up as well as I could.

"He say that, too," Farzi grinned. "He say that what showers for."

"Honey Snake, you're going to make me laugh," I said, settling on his shoulder to sleep.

"Just relax. Let the water support you," Kevis said later. We were having a session in the pool.

"I don't think I can relax when you're asking me personal questions," I said.

"Sure you can. My hands are beneath you. Do you think I'd let you sink?" he asked.

"Hmmph." I glared up at him, his face was over mine and he seemed grimly determined about something. I guess it was a good thing that we'd gotten a swimsuit that would cover Garwin Wyatt when we'd been out shopping for baby things.

"Reah, close your eyes. I wish you'd learn to trust me."

I crossed my arms over my chest, almost turning over in the water.

"Now, what did I say? Wasn't it relax?"

"That's just a word."

"And it means something. Relax. Just let yourself go limp. Nothing will happen when you do. I'll hold you up."

I tried. Really. It wasn't going to be easy. "Now," Kevis said when I'd gotten halfway there, "why are you so angry with Tory for not marrying you?" I almost turned over in the water again. "Reah, you're not trying. Meet me halfway, here."

"All right," I stared up at the clouds floating overhead, instead of at Kevis' face. I still wanted to cross my arms over my chest. "He never made any promises to me. Like he did Darletta. The marriage vows are standard across the Reth Alliance. Both parties promise to love, honor and support one another. Tory never said that to me. He did say it to someone he barely knew. How was that supposed to make me feel? He'd made me pregnant—twice—by that time, and there I was, carrying his twins, and he walks away because Wylend lied. Well, lied is the wrong word. Withheld part of the truth, I guess. And he didn't even come to me to ask me about it. He just got all pissy and went off to make promises to Darletta, because she was pretty and crooked her finger at him. I figure that's what I can expect from him always, if we stayed together. He'd get angry over something and find a way to retaliate. I can't live with that."

"Reah, he's one of your last ties to the High Demon race. Are you attempting to isolate yourself?"

"Kevis," I attempted to stand up, discovering that my feet wouldn't touch the bottom of the pool. He was holding me up. My choice was either grip his arms or swim away, and he had a firm grip on my waist. I looked at him, frowning deeply. "As Garde so eloquently put it, I'm only a quarter-blood. I don't belong to that race, in his eyes. They've made that clear. They took what they wanted and cut me loose. And then Tory can't help but mention his bitch ex-wife while we're in bed together. Maybe he didn't see what I saw on Cloudsong or Stellar Winds, but she was in just as deep as her daddy and any of the others. She didn't care that those girls were raped or sold. She didn't care that both Alliances were about to be enslaved. She didn't care that she'd controlled her husband all those years. She wanted to play with people. That's what they were to her—playthings that she could toss aside when she tired of them. I don't care if Tory did mean what he said as a compliment. I don't want to hear her name or her daddy's name or Nedrizif's name or any of the rest of them." I skipped to the side of the pool, lifted a towel and wrapped myself in it before stalking angrily away.

~

"You asked. Is that what you wanted to hear?" Kevis turned to a corner of the pool, where Nefrigar and Tory appeared. Nefrigar had shielded Tory from sight while he listened to Kevis' questions and Reah's answers.

"I'm never going to get her back," Tory sighed and skipped away.

~

"Son, what are you doing?" Garde walked into the palace kitchen in Veshtul. Tory had one empty bottle and another half-empty bottle of bourbon sitting in front of him.

"Drinking."

"What happened?"

"I never made promises to Reah, but I did to Darletta. When we got married, I said those vows, whether I meant them or not. Reah won't ever forget that. Then I made the mistake of mentioning Darletta's name when we were in bed together not long ago. It was a stupid mistake. I'll never get her back. She's walking away from the High Demon race as a whole. I heard what Kifirin said a few days ago on Cloudsong. He said he made a promise to Jayd that Kifirin would thrive and the race would recover. He used Reah to make good on that promise. He released the mute in her mates, but he didn't release it in our daughters. They think of Jayd and Glinda as their parents, just as Reah says. Kifirin did that to her. And he said he'd have made her pregnant again if she hadn't almost died when Dara and Sara were born. He said that it was a sign that his parent was angry with him over what he did."

"There's a mute in place with those girls?"

"I don't think Kifirin will ever release it," Tory swallowed more bourbon. "They'll never go to their mother. Never recognize what she did for them. And I fucked them around too, didn't I, Dad? I guess the good news in all this is that all my daughters' children will be female. Kifirin said that. Go get Uncle Jayd and do a little dance on top of the palace. Reah won't come back, but you don't give a shit, do you?" Tory lifted the bottle of bourbon and skipped away.

❧

Reah, wake up my darling, my love.

"Reah? What's wrong, sweetheart?" I'd jerked awake when I thought I heard Edward's voice. It turned out to be nothing and Teeg was trying to soothe me as I breathed ragged, uneven breaths. "It's all right," he pulled me against him. "We'll get up in a moment." We'd made love the night before—for the first time since he'd gotten me pregnant. He'd followed me to bed after the dinner at Desh's in Targis. Fes had sat with Farla, his mother, and they'd shared a very good meal with us. Now, Teeg was placing my arms around his neck and pulling me against him.

"Reah, I've loved you since I was twelve," he murmured.

"That makes me sound like a cradle robber."

"I'm older than you, now," the corner of his mouth twitched into half a smile. "If you count the number of years I've lived, I'm nearly a hundred. Almost twice as old as you." He tapped my nose gently with a finger.

"And you're so mature," I grumped.

"I can be. I usually don't laugh behind the Council's backs or throw spitballs at the ones I don't like."

"An admirable trait in the Founder of the Campiaan Alliance."

"It's part of my job description."

"That you wrote."

"I did, didn't I?" He kissed me, his mouth warm and comforting. "Come on, let's get a shower and get dressed. We have an errand to run this morning."

"What errand?"

"I'll tell you after breakfast. Come on, sweetheart. We have to get up."

I groaned as I slid off the bed. Teeg steadied me and kept an arm around my shoulders as I walked toward the bathroom.

"This looks good." Teeg picked my outfit. A deep-green top, gathered a little to cover Garwin Wyatt with a sprinkling of tiny beads across the yoke, coupled with off-white slacks and light-brown, low-heeled shoes. The outfit had been expensive and he'd paid for it. "Just a little jewelry," he helped put the emerald earrings in my ears. My hair was partially clipped back, with most of it hanging loose. "Now, breakfast," he said. He'd dressed in a very expensive suit and looked to be the founding member of the Campiaan Alliance. I found all my other mates, including Edward, Astralan and Corolan in the dining room, having breakfast when Teeg and I walked in. Kevis was there as well. I was still a little miffed at him, I think.

"Where are we going?" I asked again after I'd brushed my teeth following breakfast.

"To Refizan," Teeg said. It looked as if everybody else was going, too. When we arrived, I knew exactly what was happening and I tried to back out of the hearing chamber. Ceerah Kade sat at a table, cuffs on her wrists and her legal counsel sitting next to her.

"Reah, stay with us," Lendill said behind me. "You and Kevis may have to testify."

"I don't want to," I whispered. Nobody was listening. I was led to a witness box off to the side and sat there with Kevis, Norian and Lendill. The rest of my entourage sat in the seats reserved for the public. They took up nearly half the space. Many other spectators had come to this trial, too. I blew out a breath.

The Citizen's Panel filed in and sat down first, and then the magistrate walked in with his clerk. Everyone in the room stood for that. The trial would be held on Refizan, since that was the location of Ceerah's last crime, but the magistrate was likely a High Magistrate from another world, and he would decide on all pending charges, since Alliance laws concerning drug trafficking were universal.

The clerk went through all the charges against Ceerah, including the aliases she used. "Now, Ms. Kade, how do you answer these charges," the magistrate asked.

"I am not guilty," she said. "I was insane at the time and not in proper control of my faculties."

"But you are not insane now?"

"Yes. I am still insane."

"Has a mental evaluation been performed?" the magistrate asked. A clerk brought a comp-vid forward and offered it to him. The magistrate scrolled through the information for a short time.

"It says here that you are competent, Ms. Kade. Now, are you still insane? Remember, the truthfulness of your statements here will be considered when you answer questions later. Bear in mind that you took—and passed—a mental evaluation when you began working for Doctor Halivar. He would not have hired you otherwise, and those records have been provided to this court." He held up the comp-vid.

Ceerah conferred with her counsel for a moment and then said, "I was only insane after I began working at the clinic."

"And those are the least of the charges I see against you," the magistrate observed. "Very well, we will proceed with this hearing."

Ceerah's defense was very weak. All she could do was deny that the fingerprints were hers and insist that the vid-images had been altered—most on unalterable chips recorded by the constabulary or certified businesses. She'd once sold drakus seed to an undercover constable, who identified her from photographs. She'd managed to escape, however, when he attempted to arrest her.

After lunch, several people were brought in, all of whom testified that they'd purchased various prescription medications from Ceerah while she'd worked for Kevis. Many patients in the facility had gotten placebos or sugar pills instead of the proper medication as a result. Kevis was seething beside me at the magnitude of her duplicity. A midafternoon break was allowed, then the magistrate went after it again. I was hoping I could stay awake. Hearings often went far into the night, with a short sleep break before continuing the next day. Some could go on for weeks. I was hoping that wasn't going to happen with Ceerah. I just wanted her to go away. For a very long time.

"How are you feeling?" Kevis asked as we walked out of the Courts and Hearings building into a muggy, Refizani night. We were in the capital city of Ordinandis, which was near a river and the ocean.

"Tired," I said.

"I know," Aurelius said sympathetically, taking my hand and kissing it. "We have a suite of rooms nearby. Edward and some of the others have to go back, but Lok, Lendill, Kevis and I will be here with you throughout."

"Let's get something to eat," Kevis suggested. "I know a good restaurant not far away." We were led to a circular booth in a quiet area, comp-menus were handed out and I looked it over.

"What are you having?" Kevis leaned over to look at my menu.

"I don't know. Steak or prime rib sounds good, but I don't know how they cook it here."

"Go ahead and get it, we'll send it back if it isn't good."

"We shouldn't have to send anything back," I pointed out.

"Come on, you're tired. We'll get food and then put you to bed."

The prime rib was decent. I ate half of it; Lok helped himself to what was left. Bed was next, and Aurelius slept with me. "Reah," he said, pulling me close, "we'll take some time, very soon. Just us, all right? We'll find a place where we won't be bothered and we'll do whatever we want."

"That sounds nice, Auri." I snuggled into his embrace and closed my eyes.

The hearing resumed the following morning, and Ceerah was preparing to answer questions when something happened. Later we learned that it was a planned event from two factions on Tulgalan, Ceerah's homeworld. Yes, she and I had that in common. Little else as it turned out, but then Tulgalan was home to around four-hundred-million or so. It was a large planet. These two factions had worked just to the legal side of the law since drakus seed had found its way there a quarter of a century earlier. They saw Ceerah as the worst kind of traitor.

Both groups were prepared to not only kill her, but destroy that section of the Courts and Hearing building as well, in addition to anyone inside that chamber. We were knocked around from the explosion that came; Aurelius and Lok managed to protect the ones in the public seating. The roof caved in and fire whooshed through. It happened so quickly to those watching from outside, so slowly for those inside. Instinct took over for me.

Turning to my larger Thifilatha, I gathered everyone in the hearing area, wrapped them in my arms and shielded them with my wings. I'm afraid I may have squashed some, but they were alive when I walked through the fire and out to the street. No fire will ever harm a High Demon; it's the way Kifirin made us. Setting the people down I'd rescued, I watched calmly as Ceerah was held back by the two bailiffs I'd saved.

The magistrate stared up at me, as did Kevis. Lendill had protected Norian with whatever power he held as the Elvish Prince-Heir. Both of them proceeded to herd people toward the perimeter surrounding us. Aurelius and Lok brought out the ones from the public section of the hearing chamber, which was being sprayed by robo-hoses. All of them were drenched but still alive.

"The hearing will resume tomorrow in an undisclosed location," the journalist reported as I watched the news later at our hotel. "Both antidrug factions from Tulgalan have claimed responsibility, although they seem disappointed that Ceerah Kade did not die in the attack."

"They didn't care that others might have died," Lendill tossed the vid-remote onto the bed and paced angrily. The images of me, carrying an armload of people out of the building and setting them down was getting more airtime than anything else, though. The sun was shining through my wings, making them glow.

"Reah, you look as if you're protecting children," Norian sighed as we watched yet another vid-version of my larger Thifilatha.

"I was afraid they'd get hurt," I said, shaking my head at the images that splayed across the screen. "Humanoids aren't fire resistant."

"The Governor of the Realm has invited you to his palace after the trial," Kevis walked in and handed over an expensive, paper invitation.

"I guess there's no way to gracefully refuse that, is there?" I flopped back on the bed.

"No, breah-mul, but Norian and I will come with you. You don't have to talk much if you don't want to." Lendill sat beside me and gently rubbed Garwin Wyatt. "And we've had to provide extra security for Ceerah Kade and her legal counsel, in addition to sending agents out to track the ones who did this."

"My Lendill's work is never done," I said, rubbing his back.

"I'm your Lendill?" He settled beside me and smiled before kissing me.

"Your father married us. I don't know how to get out of that."

"If the Elf King marries you, there isn't any way to get out of it," Lendill grinned before kissing me again.

"Says who?"

"Says the Elf Prince-Heir."

"Convenient," I muttered.

"Decidedly so," Lendill gave me a better kiss this time. The others faded from the room.

"So, this is your parents' fault," the magistrate stared at Ceerah. She'd cried when she was asked why she'd done terrible things. The evidence against her was overwhelming at this point, so she was trying a different tack.

"They were too strict. I was never allowed to go anywhere or do anything. The drugs I began taking in school helped me deal with their tyranny." Ceerah wiped tears with a tissue.

"Did they beat you or lock you inside a closet?" Norian was

allowed to ask questions and he was doing so. "Were you ever hospitalized due to injuries? How cruel were your parents? I've looked into your background, I believe you were rushed to a physician when you were six because you had a bruised ankle, is that correct?" Norian consulted a comp-vid in his hand.

"I fell off a swing," Ceerah muttered.

"Your parents didn't cause this injury?"

"No."

"I see no records of hospitalizations, and you seldom missed school."

"But they wouldn't let me go out with my friends, or date until I was sixteen."

"Is that all?" Norian flung up a hand. "I have nothing further."

Immature, even now, Kevis' voice floated into my mind. *Probable sadistic personality disorder.*

Lovely, I sent back. *And all that from parents who wouldn't let her run with drug addicts.*

Add sociopathic tendencies to the previous diagnosis, Kevis' voice sounded amused in my head.

You hired her, I reminded him.

And I will regret that for the rest of my life.

I thought you were immortal.

I am. You see what I'm facing.

Poor thing.

Yes, someone needs to take pity on me.

I'll make cookies for you later, and if you're good, you can play outside, I told him. Kevis had to hide the snicker.

"Director, if you and Ms. Kade's counsel will approach," the magistrate beckoned to both. Norian rose and walked to the magistrate's high seat. Ceerah's legal counsel did the same. The conversation was whispered, but Aurelius, former vampire, heard it clearly and gave the information to Lendill, Kevis and me.

He's asking what a fair sentence would be in this case, Aurelius sent. *Norian is arguing for Evensun. Legal Counsel is arguing for house arrest.*

For drakus seed charges? Lendill was shocked. *That's Evensun, for sure.*

Norian and the counsel returned to their seats. The magistrate tapped information into his comp-vid. "We will now turn this case over to the Citizen's Panel for a determination," the magistrate said. "I ask that the incident with the bomb and subsequent fire be put out of your mind, as it should have no bearing on a fair verdict. You must decide whether Ms. Kade is guilty of any or all of the charges against her, and then set sentencing if she is found guilty. The ASD is asking for a life sentence upon the penal planet of Evensun, while Ms. Kade's counsel is requesting house arrest. All these things must be decided by you."

The seven members of the Citizen's Panel, all of whom I'd hauled out of the courtroom, wrapped in my arms and protected from the fire by my wings, were led from the courtroom by the bailiff.

"Let's get something for Garwin Wyatt to drink," Kevis suggested. Norian, Lendill and Kevis surrounded me as we walked into the marble hallway outside the makeshift hearing room. The basement held a restaurant for visitors and employees, so we took the stairs to the small eatery and sat down. Quite a bit of whispering and pointing occurred while I drank a cup of decaffeinated tea and nibbled on a scone.

"Feel all right?" Norian reached over and pushed a lock of stray hair off my face. We'd come a long way, Norian and I.

"Yes. I just wish this were over with. I want to go home."

"Where is home?" Kevis asked.

"The groves on Avendor," I sighed. "I like looking out the windows of my bedroom and seeing gishi fruit trees as far as I can look," I said. "And there are mountains off to the east, if I walk outside. All I hear is birds calling if I sit out on the swing."

"The verdict's in," Norian's comp-vid buzzed. I had to leave my tea on the table; Kevis paid hastily and we walked back to the hearing room.

The magistrate thanked the Citizen's Panel for their service, then accepted the comp-vid that they'd handed to the bailiff. "Ceerah Kade, also known as Cedrah Dane and Bynda Wark, among other aliases, please rise to hear the verdict," the magistrate said. Ceerah and her legal counsel rose.

"The People of the Reth Alliance find you guilty of all charges, the most serious of which is selling drakus seed," the magistrate announced. "And they have placed a sentence of life upon the penal planet of Evensun. You will be transported immediately. Do you have anything to say?"

"I'll kill you," Ceerah turned and shouted at me. "I'll kill you, bitch. Just wait. You'll die, and in the worst way possible."

"Shut her up," Norian snarled. The bailiff and two constables hauled Ceerah away, still shouting vengeance.

"Reah, don't let that upset you," Kevis said gently. "Let's go see the Governor, and then we'll go home."

The magistrate was having a drink with Refizan's Governor of the Realm when we were led inside his office. The Governor's hair was silver; his face lined a bit with wrinkles. He looked as if he'd seen much of life. He bowed over my hand. "I received a message from the founding member of the Reth Alliance yesterday, after lives were saved in the magistrate's hearing chamber," Governor Odrillus smiled at me. "He said that there is a certificate among the many awarded to you, which says you will bow to none in the Reth Alliance, including him. He also says that no other citizen has ever received that award. You appear to be quite special, young woman."

"I don't feel special most of the time," I said.

"If you weren't, I imagine we'd all be dead," the magistrate observed. "I owe you thanks, at the very least. That creature we sentenced earlier owes you for her life as well. In my opinion, I don't think she's ever thanked anyone for what they've done for her."

"I get that a lot," I said. "It doesn't matter. I've come to expect it." I received a framed certificate from Refizan's Governor, proclaiming me a hero. I didn't feel much like a hero. Mostly I'd been desperate to keep people from burning. I thanked the Governor, said good-bye to him and the magistrate and Norian led us out of the office.

"Here," I handed the certificate to Kevis when we landed inside Edward's huge kitchen. I wanted to see Edward. Make sure he wasn't something I'd dreamed up. He appeared moments later, a huge smile lighting his face when he saw me. I did something I never do. I ran to him and wrapped my arms around his waist.

"I missed you, sweetheart," he lifted me up and kissed me.

"I missed you, too," I wrapped my arms around his neck.

"Let's sit on the deck by the pool," he said. I let him take me.

"Why don't we ever get that?" Aurelius muttered.

"Are you ever that glad to see her?" Kevis asked.

"I am now. I guess that hasn't been the case for the past twenty-five years, though."

"Want to take a little trip with me?" Kevis looked at Aurelius and Lok.

"I suppose. How painful is it going to be?"

"No idea. I want to talk to Edan Desh."

"Let's go," Lok sighed in resignation.

"What can I do for you?" Edan Desh, now Doctor Edan Desh, sat behind his desk at a small clinic on the southern half of Ooklar. He treated the children in a particularly poor section of that world. He was also campaigning for better education for them. Things were looking up at the moment; a very generous sum had recently been donated.

"Tell me what you remember about Reah. When she was small," Kevis said, sitting in the chair Edan offered. Lok and Aurelius also sat.

"Those memories are hazy, like they're from a vid that I watched when I was young," Edan sighed. "I know they're borrowed from that other lifetime. I try not to call them up if I can help it."

"What can you tell me of the motivation that other Edan had, then, when he hurt her?"

"I only sense anger," Doctor Desh replied. "Extreme anger. I can't explain it any better than that. He was striking out at something, to assuage that anger. Only it never seemed to work."

"You shouldn't waste your time here," Kifirin appeared. "This one cannot help you, and it will only upset him to attempt to remember things for you. He is not to blame. Come, I will take you to the one who is."

Kevis didn't have time to protest, Kifirin had folded him, Lok and Aurelius away. "So, the real Edan Desh." Kevis walked around Edan, who lounged on a small cot inside a prison cell.

"Go away," Edan growled.

"No, I think I'll stay," Kevis said quietly. "Aurelius, will you place compulsion, please, for him to tell the truth?" Kevis wasn't going to ask Kifirin for anything. The god had a way of making someone pay for anything asked of him.

Aurelius had Edan's face in his hand in less than a blink, staring into his eyes and telling him that he would only speak the truth. Edan, frightened out of his wits, could only nod.

"Now, tell me about Reah," Kevis said pleasantly.

"I hated her. Hated Ilvan, hated Wald, hated my mother and hated my father. But mostly I hated Fes. I should have been firstborn."

"What did you think, when your father sent Reah to you when she was eight?"

"He saddled me with a kid. His kid. Or so I thought. I was skimming money from the business that he didn't know about. I had to worry about keeping her in clothes and school supplies."

"Yet you never spent much on her. Did you? You took the money your father sent for her upkeep."

"He sent four hundred a month. I was able to keep three hundred fifty of that."

"When did you put her to work in the kitchen?"

"Right away. Wasn't about to spend a single credit on childcare. She could do dishes. That's what she did."

"But she started cooking quickly."

"She watched the others and picked it up. I ignored her."

"Unless you wanted to beat her for something."

"I liked listening to her scream. And beating her got rid of my frustrations with Father." Edan was clenching and unclenching his fists.

"You will not be violent now," Aurelius commanded. Edan's fists stilled.

"Tell me about Raedah, Reah's mother."

"Small. Weak. Mother was jealous of the time Father spent with her. He might have loved her. He never loved the rest of us."

"Why did you conspire with your mother to kill her?"

"She didn't belong. Didn't fit in. Fes was even older than she was. We didn't know Father was seeing someone else until he brought her home with a ring on her finger."

"You felt usurped."

"Yes!" Edan cursed. "And so did mother. She approved of all the other wives. She never saw Raedah until after Father married her."

"Did you try to kill Reah when she was a baby?"

"Yes. Mother and I fed her poison. Only she didn't die. Then Farla became curious and started checking on Reah. Since we were afraid of getting caught, we backed off. I thought I'd killed her when she was ten. But she came back after that, too. Then she began cooking, and the awards started coming in. She was the prize. If Father had found out about her, he'd have taken her back to Targis, so I kept beating her and told her to keep her mouth shut. She did. Until that fucking conscription notice came."

"Would it interest you to know that your father manipulated that?" Kevis asked.

"What the fuck did Father have to do with that?"

"Ilvan's name was the one selected. Your father went to the state recruitment office and paid the officer there to change the name to Reah. She was hauled away, while Ilvan remained in your kitchen.

Your father thought he was protecting the business, because he saw Reah as worthless."

"Number two never got another top award after that," Edan grumbled. "We tried. Used the recipes Reah left with us, to the letter. And then varied them, attempting to duplicate the results. It was never the same."

"Reah was very intelligent. She knew not to give you everything."

"She got her revenge."

"I don't think of withholding a few recipe ingredients as revenge for broken bones and the hate you spewed in her direction," Kevis said.

"But she led the ASD to us. You see where I am, now."

"For crimes you committed against her mother. Do you not see murder as a crime?"

"Not against Raedah. We hated her. She took Father's affection."

"I think I'm done, here," Kevis sighed. "The one I need to speak with is dead. Too bad one of his own sons killed Addah Desh."

Ceerah stared at the empty field before her. The guards had removed her cuffs and shoved her away. Now, they watched as she walked into tall grass.

"This is like a park," she turned and sneered at her guards. "Someone will come for me. They promised."

"Nobody gets on or off this world without permission," one of the guards said softly. Ceerah snorted at him.

"You don't know of whom I speak," she said, laughing. "He's the son of the Elf King. He has power. Just wait, he'll get me away from here."

"Young woman, I am Gavin Montegue. Teeg San Gerxon is my son. His mother is the Queen of Le-Ath Veronis, and holds more power than that fool Reldill Schaff will ever realize. When I say that none gets on or off this world without permission, I mean it. Now, if I were you, I would run. Maldak is coming. You might live past the next few moments if you hide."

"How do you know of Reldill?"

"Reah is married to the Elf King's Prince-Heir, who is Reldill's brother. Of course, Naldill is calling Reldill's tune, although he no longer holds power. His father, the Elf King, removed it for a reason. What did they promise you, to distract Reah and the Director and Vice-Director? Do you think they are stupid, or without resources? Too bad, you might be able to warn them. If you had mindspeech."

"Is this my meal?" A dark-haired man appeared at Ceerah's side. She almost shrieked at his sudden appearance, and backed away immediately.

"Go ahead and run, you won't get far," Maldak smiled. "I will not hesitate to take you. You brought harm to the Lifegiver." Ceerah turned and ran. Maldak folded after her, appearing before her as the Copper Ra'Ak. Ceerah screamed before she was bitten in half and swallowed in two bites.

"Quick and effective," Tony sighed. Gavin nodded in agreement.

CHAPTER 14

"They're gathering allies. The rogue Copper Ra'Ak have already gotten on board," Pheligar held a three-dimensional image of Xordthe above the table. Most of the Saa Thalarr were there, listening. A careful plan was being laid out for them, in order to trap as many rats as possible in a single move.

Did Cynthin think her world wasn't being tapped a second time? She'd accepted the advances from Reldill and Naldill, after being ousted as president. "Others are being approached by the allied elf brothers and rogue Ra'Ak. We will see what their answer is." Pheligar was content to wait. The Wise Ones said only a short time would be needed. Pheligar smiled. As a Larentii, he'd always stood on the sidelines, never having gone into battle before. But now—the Head of the Larentii Council had listened to the Wise Ones and given permission. Pheligar and several others were looking forward to this.

"They have offered a way off the planet," Perdil hissed in Zendeval's ear. Zendeval lifted an eyebrow. He'd been King of Nrath for twenty-five thousand years. Yidrizin still worked as his Prime Minister;

Perdil acted as advisor. Sometimes Zen listened to the dwarf. Sometimes.

"And how do they propose to do this, and what do they expect from us in return?" Zendeval asked, looking the two over that had come to him. They didn't seem like much; light hair, pointed ears, green eyes. One held power; the other did not.

Yidrizin had taught Zen many things through the millennia. One of those things was how to recognize power. Like the High Demons, power held no sway against the Greater Demons. Once, Kings, rulers and despots had approached the Greater Demons, specifically for that talent. None could harm them with power if their Greater Demon guard stood by their side.

"We ask your help in bringing down a High Demon," the one without power announced. "And we will see that you are transported anywhere you choose to go afterward."

"High Demon?" Zen displayed mild interest. "I need more information than that. They are very powerful, these High Demons."

"But this is only a female. Weaker than the males, most likely," Naldill smiled.

"The name of this High Demon female?" Zen's eyebrow lifted.

"Reah," Naldill smiled.

"Kill them," Zendeval pointed at the elves and growled.

"As soon as we're finished killing Reah and our brother, we're coming back for that filth," Naldill attempted to wrap the slice on his arm. He wasn't having much luck with it, one-handed. Reldill had escaped with only a few bruises before he'd grabbed his brother and folded away. He'd known how far back to stand from the Greater Demons, in order to retain his power. It had taken everything he had anyway, to escape Nrath with his brother.

"At least that bitch Ceerah distracted our brother for a few days, so we could make preparations. She was going to plead guilty. It wasn't easy, either, placing glamour on that fool she had for legal counsel.

Too bad she didn't know we can't get to Evensun. She'll just have to rot there," Naldill muttered.

"Father should never have treated us this way," Reldill snapped. "You should have been named heir. It was your right. That was how it should have been."

"We'll be stronger after this, brother. These Ra'Ak were just waiting for someone to lead them from the shadows. We'll take over. See how Father likes it when he's facing a hungry Ra'Ak."

"You think they'll get past the barrier surrounding Gaelar N'Seith?"

"What's to keep them out? Father won't bother, and Lendill is a half-blood. He doesn't have the strength," Naldill huffed. "We'll get through and then we'll watch the others flee before us."

"Is that what we want?"

"Reldill, you have strength but you lack vision," Naldill slapped his brother on the back. "Stay with me. We'll get my power back and I'll rule as was intended. Meanwhile, Xordthe waits. We'll begin our reign there."

"Just lie back, Dad's going to check on the baby. This is nearly six months, you know."

"He's fine, stop bothering him. And me." Yes, I was grumpy. The baby was growing, but he wasn't moving around as much as I'd like. I was worried, but too afraid to say anything about it. Kevis had my jeans pulled off my belly, my shirt up to my armpits and Karzac was wiping his hands after washing them in my bathroom sink.

"Reah, it won't take long and we won't hurt either of you," Karzac soothed. My right hand shook as I covered my eyes with it. Teeg walked into the room; I could tell by the footsteps. Karzac put his hands on my belly. They were cool against my skin.

"Not much room to move around," Karzac muttered. What did that mean? Kevis took my hands and held them over my head. What was he doing? "Reah, the baby is growing fast now, and he needs more room to move around. I've called Renegar and Lenigar; they're going to help with this."

"What are they going to do?" Karzac was scaring me. What did he mean, the baby didn't have enough room to move?

"Reah, look at me," Kevis' face hovered over mine. "Your body is small, and Gavril is a big man. The baby is growing really fast now. The Larentii can give him more room to move and grow."

"But I never had trouble with the twins," I said, shivering.

"I know. But that was twenty years ago, and your body didn't react so well when the last ones were born. The infection after the bite here didn't help." He touched my shoulder where Zendeval Rjjn had bitten me. "There is uterine scarring left from your last pregnancy, Reah. We're going to fix this. Just stay calm and trust us, all right?" Ren and another Larentii showed up, as did Nefrigar. I heard Karzac say words like adhesions and infection. I was terrified.

"Reah," Ren's face replaced Kevis'. "Teeki and Neeki did what they could for you when you were bitten, but they only protected the baby inside the sac. Your womb didn't react well to the infection, and it has lost some of its elasticity. We're going to fix that. Keeping you in a healing sleep has been difficult, lately, if you wanted to break out of it. I'm telling you now that we'll make this as painless as possible, and Garwin Wyatt will not be harmed. Now, you said you loved me, remember? You need to trust me, too. We'll try to make this as easy as possible, but there may be some discomfort if you break away from the sleep. Understand? Just lie still if you do wake, all right? Do this for me and for Nefrigar." I nodded as tears threatened.

Nefrigar knelt next to my head and began trilling—the song the Larentii sing for the mothers. Usually it puts me right to sleep. I was too terrified this time. Large blue fingers settled against my forehead and Nefrigar placed the healing sleep.

~

"She's out. Move." Karzac snapped. Lenigar, who had several hundred thousand years of experience with mothers and babies, put two long blue fingers inside Reah's vagina, after removing her clothing with power. Ren, who was perhaps the most talented Larentii healer, placed both hands on Reah's abdomen, placing the child in stasis. It would take both of them working, with Reah lying still and calm, to successfully bring the womb back to normal.

"Don't freak," Kevis said to Gavril as he gripped the edge of Reah's dresser. Nefrigar had both of Reah's hands enclosed in his, in case she moved. The others were waiting outside in the hallway. Kevis had noticed the lack of movement from the baby for the past three weeks. He'd hoped it was a normal cycle. It wasn't, so he'd called his father.

"What's he doing?" Gavril was shaking.

"Regenerating the womb cells. She wasn't treated properly after she was bitten, and the infection, combined with the scar tissue from her last pregnancy caused damage. The womb doesn't have sufficient elasticity, now. Lenigar is taking care of that."

"Are they going to be all right?"

"I think so, but Reah should take it easy for the rest of this pregnancy. We'll see how things turn out with this birth, and we'll know then if more repairs are necessary."

"She's moving," Gavril reached out a hand as Reah moaned.

"Reah, hush, darling. It's all right," Kevis said softly, touching Reah's forehead. "Go back to sleep, love. We'll take care of you." Karzac blinked at his son but never said a word. Nefrigar began to trill again while Kevis placed as much of a healing sleep as he could.

More than a click later, Lenigar removed his hand and cleaned a bit of blood away with power. Renegar took his hands away, removing the stasis he'd placed on the baby. Garwin Wyatt moved immediately—they all saw Reah's belly bulge and then relax before bulging again.

"Look at that," Gavril went to his knees.

"No sex for four weeks," Karzac said. "And no strenuous movement. Exercise in the pool only."

"Is the water warm enough?" Those were the words I woke to. I felt sore. My lower half was aching. I moaned.

"We'll take care of that, just give us a minute," Teeg's chin was the main thing in my line of vision. I closed my eyes and when I opened them again, we were in the pool. The water was warmer than usual. "Baby, do you have pain? Do you need Kevis to come? Or one of the others?"

"I ache," I tried to get away from him.

"No, no, baby. Stay with me," he murmured softly. "Kevis is coming. He'll take care of that."

"What's all this about?" I was still trying to get away from Teeg. Mostly I was trying to escape the worsening pain, when Kevis showed up.

"You're just achy because things are stretching that weren't before," Kevis soothed, putting his hands on me. I was naked—didn't anybody ever think to put me in clothes?

"Yeah? Next time you have the baby. We'll talk then," I snapped.

"Reah, just relax, all right? I'm taking it away," Kevis' hands moved carefully over my belly and then slipped between my legs. I jumped. "Reah, stay still," Kevis' voice was calm and even. "Close your eyes. Feel how warm the water is? We did that for you. Let us take care of you. We will. We won't let you go. We're right here." Why had he said that? The minute he said they wouldn't let me go, I was sobbing in Teeg's arms.

"What's wrong? Reah, tell me. You can tell me," Kevis was stroking my hair. I just clung tighter to Teeg.

"Reah? What's the matter with my little sweetheart?" Edward had come. I heard other voices behind him—Lendill, Ry, Farzi, Nenzi, Lok, Aurelius, Astralan, Cory, where had they come from? What were they doing here?

"You're wrong," I struggled to get out of Teeg's grasp, now. "The minute Kifirin crooks his finger, you'll all let me go." I skipped away amid shouting.

⁓

"I want to punch you, god or no god," Edward hissed at Kifirin.

"Just hold off on that," Belen appeared beside Kifirin. "Granted he deserves it, but we won't condone violence just yet."

"Where's Reah?" Gavril demanded. "She's terrified that he'll fuck her around again," he jerked his head at Kifirin. "Make all of us forget her again. And he could, and we're powerless to do anything about it. I warn you," he waved a finger at Kifirin, "you don't get to give this baby away to someone else."

"That will not be possible," Kifirin's parent appeared. Even Belen bowed respectfully.

"Father," he said.

"Kifirin, you will come. We will talk. Now." Kifirin and his parent disappeared.

"Reah is being watched over," Belen informed Gavril. "She will be returned to you in a little while."

"You will still have some command over the Dark Realm," Kifirin's parent pointed out. "Only your actions will be supervised."

Kifirin's breath was cloudy as he glared at the one who'd come with his parent. Dark-haired and dark-eyed, one of the Koh'Ahmari gazed placidly back, his arms crossed casually over his chest. Kifirin knew better than to argue with this one—he outranked his parent by several levels.

"He calls himself Li'Neruh Rath," Kifirin's parent said before Kifirin could voice the question himself.

"You take the name of the Royal House on Kifirin?" Kifirin's breath turned black with anger.

"It is a legitimate word in your High Demon language. Do you intend to quarantine all words, should they be used as a name? What will you call a star after this, if the need arise?"

"Darkest Star?" Kifirin knew he was being disrespectful in his interpretation of the Koh'Ahmari's chosen name.

"I choose the names I will allow others to employ. You will call me this. I will allow disrespect this time only. Do it again and I will remove your power." Kifirin blinked in astonishment as a curl of smoke drifted from Li'Neruh Rath's nostrils.

~

Lissa's Journal

Kifirin stood before me, as did Gardevik Rath. This wasn't going to be easy, and I wasn't looking forward to it. My pregnancy was making its presence known, too—I felt queasy and this made it worse. Garde hung his head—he likely knew what was coming. Kifirin blew smoke but knew better than to approach.

Belen had already come—I'd asked him, as Chief of the Nameless Ones, for advice before proceeding with this. He'd listened sympathetically and offered comfort as he'd agreed with my plan. He'd also offered to stay with me while I did this. He remained silent at my side, glowing softly while I studied two of my mates.

"I hoped your overseer would come with you, but I see that isn't the case," I spoke to Kifirin first. "I think I'd like to speak with him, but Belen tells me that he is of those who outrank the Nameless Ones, so his presence I cannot request or command." I was making this as formal as I could.

Darker clouds of smoke poured from Kifirin's nostrils as black eyes blinked at me. "Kifirin, you could have asked for help," I pointed out. "You could have explained things better. But you, thinking that the mighty god of the Dark Realm was above all that, refused. Instead, you chose to exert your power and will over the rest of us. Yes, I know you still outrank me—I am only a mid-level Nameless One, after all, while you are ranked in the highest echelon. It doesn't matter—I no longer consider you my mate. Perhaps in a century or two, I will reconsider, if you wish to keep your claiming marks on my neck. I loved you. A part of me still does, but you have done so much damage."

My last words were whispered as I wiped away tears. I still couldn't understand—and might never understand—his reasoning in this matter. So many had suffered as a result, but none more so than Reah. That pain would follow her forever, and she was the mother of my grandchildren.

"Avilepha, do not do this, I beg you," Kifirin held out a hand. "I have already received chastisement from my parent and the one who now rules the Dark Realm above me."

"You're getting it from me, then, too." I was hoping my lower lip wouldn't tremble and betray how much this was costing me, but it did anyway.

"Avilepha, I will return to you, and keep returning, until you take me back." Kifirin looked ready to weep but unlike me, he held back the tears.

"Then leave now," my voice trembled. "I'm not ready to take you back." Kifirin disappeared.

"Lissa, no," Garde dropped to his knees. He didn't attempt to hide his grief, as Kifirin had.

"Gardevik Rath, your Thifilathi is wiser than you. As old as you are, you should have known better. Get out and don't come back until Kifirin is welcome again on Le-Ath Veronis." I was done with him for now, and likely would be for a very long time. When he disappeared, Belen had to hold me up, I was weeping so hard.

"Reah, you are cold." I knew who he was—Connegar, one of Lissa's Larentii mates. He moved his hands and clothed me in a soft, white woolen caftan. The robe was long and covered my feet as I sat upon a boulder on Thiskil's southern beaches.

"I know you recognize me," the corners of his eyes crinkled a little as he smiled at me. "And you know my mother. You met her not long ago—Conner? Remember? Most Larentii are named after their mothers."

"Is that how it works?" I wiped wetness from my cheeks and stared up at him. He was tall, even for a Larentii.

"Yes. Renegar is Kiarra's son, but her name before she joined the Saa Thalarr was Renée. He actually is named after his mother."

"That's a nice name," I said. "And it suits him, to be named after that."

"It suits him well and he likes it. We choose our names, shortly after we are born," Connegar informed me.

"Then you can't get angry with your parents for giving you an awful name."

"Very true. We have no one to blame but ourselves if we dislike it after a while. Reah, I have met many during my life who deserved so much more than they received. Mother and I are prepared to give you a gift. She is the Guardian, you know. At times, she can stand at the line that separates the here and now from the ones who are not here and now. That is permitted if she commands it. We will be taking you to this side of that line, so you may speak to some. Come, we will pay a visit." Connegar took my arm and transported me elsewhere.

"This is where some arrive to cross over," Connegar walked beside me in a beautiful field filled with flowers. The flowers were so tall they came to my waist and I could smell the sweet scent of them as I walked through. Barefoot as I was, nothing harmed my feet as I walked. The grass was like the softest carpet beneath my soles.

"Nothing will harm you here. This is a protected area. There are other places to cross over. Some are dangerous. Those are reserved for the ones who have done evil during their lives."

"You do this? Bring people here when they can't find their way?" I don't know how I knew that, but I did.

"Yes. As does my mother. See, she is waiting for us." I looked ahead, and Conner was waiting for us, next to a shimmery curtain that reflected the field we walked through.

"Reah," Conner smiled at me and beckoned me forward. "I have arranged for you to see these. Remember, none can bring physical harm to you, now. There is no need to fear."

Connegar stood at my back, hands on my shoulders when the first one walked through the shimmer. I don't think he was allowed to walk farther than he did, and I was glad. Even so, I backed against

Connegar as far as I could. Edan Desh, the one I'd known growing up, stood before me.

"Reah." He dropped to his knees and bowed his head to the ground. I had no idea what he was doing.

"Now you recognize?" Conner's voice was hard and her eyes were bright as stars.

"I am not worthy to apologize," Edan mumbled.

"Will you not explain to her?" Conner asked.

"It is too terrible. I was wrong. I have to try harder next time."

"He is punishing himself," Connegar said quietly behind me.

"How is he punishing himself?" I looked up at the tall Larentii.

"He is planning his next lifetimes. He will suffer during those lifetimes. The Edan that Kifirin brought back has already suffered and his misdeeds are wiped away."

"You are not obligated to forgive me," Edan still hadn't looked at me.

"Stand up," I said. Edan stood, his head still bowed.

"Look at me." He lifted his eyes. Terrible sorrow clouded their depths. "I wanted you to love me," I said. "I didn't know why you wouldn't. I worked hard in the kitchen, thinking you would notice and give a kind word or something."

"I know that, now. Children are so vulnerable. They are born needing love. I robbed you of that. Twice. I was selfish and thought of myself and what I wanted." I looked into Edan's hazel eyes. He was being honest for a change. When I was growing up in the kitchens of Desh's number two, he'd seldom been honest—with anyone, including, most likely, himself. All had suffered at his hands who worked under him, but I was the one whose bones were broken.

"If I could take it all back now, I would," he said. "And not just because it would make my future lives easier. My path did not lie through this meadow," he sighed. "It lay through a dark land filled with sharp rocks that I walked through with no shoes. I was forced to walk through it with no help, daughter."

"Then I am sorry for you," I said. "I know what pain is, and it gives me pain to see another suffer, even if they are not kind."

"I know." Edan hung his head again. "I am so sorry. I see many things, now. And the ones who teach me, sit and show me things. Point out others still struggling through their lives. Ask me what path they should take. I am learning."

"Do they love you?" I asked.

"Yes. And I am not deserving in this stage of my existence."

"We all learn things," I said. "Or we should. I wish it were a good thing to see you, Edan, but I have terrible memories."

"I know. And I understand that. I wish I could offer comfort, but I am not allowed to touch."

"And I cannot trust, because you did what you did, and then others that came after you did the same. And I wish I could trust, Edan. That was a gift that was stripped away at a very early age."

"If I could give you a gift, what would you have of me?" Edan asked.

"Something you can't give," I said. "I will never have a father's love. Not as it should be. A father loves and protects his child, don't you think? Do you know what it was that I did in the life before this one, to deserve what happened to me? Do you know?" I was wiping tears away.

"I am not allowed to give information," he said. "Seeing you is like a flower drinking in rain after a drought. I wish I'd lived my life better, so I would see my grandson."

"I suppose you will see him in a way," I said. "You in another life will see him, but we don't talk much because he wears your face and the memories are too difficult to bear. We will never be close, I think."

"Yes. They said that to me."

"It is time. Is there anything else you wish to say to Reah before you go back?" Conner asked.

"I wish I could have loved," he said. "I could have done so much for you. Good-bye, Reah. I wish you well." I watched him turn and disappear in the shimmer, trying not to sob.

The next one to walk through was almost as bad. Addah Desh stood before me, and he wept. "I take it back, I take it back," he sobbed. "Tell all of them I'm sorry and I take it back."

"Take what back?" My tears were dripping onto the flowers, and they bloomed even brighter around me. Addah's tears sizzled on the ground.

"The jealousy. The mistrust. The hate. I take it back."

"I think they only wanted your love, Addah," I lifted the sleeve of my caftan and wiped tears. My cheeks and fingers were soaked.

"I know. And I let Marzi tell me what to do with you. She said to send you to Shirves and to Edan. I think she goaded him to beat you. It didn't take much, as it turned out."

"No, I think he took pleasure in it," I agreed. "My childhood was far from happy."

"Yes. It was a terrible time. I should have paid more attention. I only had one use for women. In my next life I will be female, Reah. And I will suffer. Will you take pleasure in that?"

"What do you think, Addah? You think I take pleasure in another's pain?"

He blinked at me. "No." His eyes dropped. "I see that you don't. Do any of them have love for me? Do they?"

"I don't know, Addah. They seldom speak of you."

"Are they poor now? The ones who teach me refuse to let me see them, since I treated them so badly."

"No. What you withheld, I gave back to them. All your recipes I recreated and the restaurants are thriving, now. Uncle Fes refuses to marry, I think. I believe he worries that he will mistreat a wife or wives as you did."

"You recreated all of it? You gave it back, for nothing?" Addah was trying to understand that.

"Stop looking at things from that perspective," a shining being stepped through the shimmer and took Addah's hand. "Come, we will discuss this." The being nodded to Conner and then to Connegar and me before leading Addah back inside.

"Marzi has not learned enough to come through," Conner sighed. "It will take a while for her. The next one is a gift, before she goes into the world again." My mother stepped through the curtain.

"Reah, you are so beautiful," she said and I wept again. She looked so much like Glinda, only she had green eyes, as I do. "I am sorry I wasn't there to protect you. I know you missed that when you were little."

"You couldn't help it," I sobbed.

"Reah, don't cry. Things will come to you. I promise."

"But they left me nothing," I wept. "Not even a photograph. Like you didn't exist. And now my daughters have forgotten me, too. Like I don't exist. What terrible cruelty is this?" I dropped to my knees and shook with grief.

"Little one," someone knelt next to me. Placed a hand on my shoulder.

"Who are you?" I looked into his face, my eyes swimming with tears.

"I am Lendevik Lith," he said.

~

"Thank goodness," Edward jumped to his feet when Connegar and Nefrigar appeared in his kitchen. He'd waited up, hoping Reah would return. Reah slept in Nefrigar's arms.

"This has been a very trying day for my love," Nefrigar kissed Reah's forehead. "Take her to bed with you. Let her wake in your arms. The baby is restless," Nefrigar smiled about that. "I believe he is making up for lost time."

"No doubt," Edward smiled. Nefrigar handed Reah over.

~

"Reah, open your eyes. The sun is shining on the gishi fruit trees." Edward kissed my forehead.

"Honey?" I stared up at him. He was holding me, wrapped in blankets on the deck outside our connected suites. He set my feet on the smooth wood boards of the deck, kept his arms around me and leaned his chin on my head as we watched the sunlight move over the trees below us. "You were a genius to put the house here," I said.

"I built it for you," he kissed the top of my head. "My Elemaiyan grandfather is a foreseer. He described you to me. The funny thing is, I was attracted to a girl when I was young that had nearly-white hair. He told me that she wasn't you. He didn't give me a name; he said that would be a surprise. But he said you'd be pregnant when I found you. When Keedan set you down at my table, he had no idea what you'd be to me. I sent him a case of wine afterward, plus a nice bonus."

"You're so good," I sighed.

"Reah, I can say the same thing to you. You are everything I dreamed of, only better. I was scared to death yesterday, when they had to fix you. I'm begging you not to let something like that happen again. I don't think my heart can stand it."

"I wasn't thrilled about it, either," I half-turned in his arms and tapped his nose with a finger.

"I know," he leaned down to kiss me. "They say no sex for four weeks. I think we'll go crazy in that time."

"And I'll be seven months pregnant and big as a house," I said.

"My erection might be almost as big by that time," he laughed.

"Farzi and Nenzi tell me that showers will fix that." Edward laughed harder. I was seated in the swing and breakfast was brought to the deck when the rest of them showed up. Chairs appeared everywhere, as did folding tables. Everybody was laughing, talking and eating.

"Here," Edward fed me a bite of ham. It was very good. Teeg knelt in front of me and put his hands on my belly. Garwin Wyatt was moving about as if he were happy about that.

"Honey, that's your daddy," I was rubbing my belly, too.

"Reah, are you feeling better today?" Teeg asked.

"I'm still a little sore. And I need to talk to Glinda."

"I can see if she'll come," he nodded.

"No, I need to go there," I said.

"Holy cow," Edward stared up at the life-size sculptures of High

Demons in full Thifilathi that lined the hall inside the palace in Veshtul. The palace was amazing, until you saw what Lissa had. But then the same vampire had designed both. He'd saved the very best for Le-Ath Veronis, and I couldn't blame him.

"You wanted to see us?" Glinda asked as we were led into Jayd's private office.

"Yes," I nodded to her. "I have a message for you."

❧

"We'll have to keep Reah away. She is in no shape to come," Renegar said. "It is fate that they're moving this quickly, but we will stand against them."

"We will stand against them," Kiarra smiled up at her son. "All of us. I've had visions of this, over the years. A last battle, with all of us charging the enemy. We'll do this. Win or lose, it'll all be out there."

"Yes, mother. It will. My son, the Wise One, and my grandson the Wise One say that we Larentii should hold back until the last. We will do so, although it may be difficult."

"Then that's what you should do," Kiarra said, rubbing his back affectionately.

❧

"Before I deliver the message," I said, "I have to give you something." Glinda looked at me expectantly, but she wasn't expecting where I went. I walked to a corner of Jayd's study, where rows of tightly fitted stones butted against one another to form a right angle. Windows lined both walls on either side of those stones. One of the stones gave way when I pushed against it, revealing a small space inside. I pulled a velvet bag from that space while Glinda and Jayd watched. I handed the bag to Glinda, who stared at me, openmouthed. He said she'd know who sent the message when Glinda received the bag. She did. I could see the shock in her eyes.

"How did you?" She couldn't finish the question.

"He told me," I said, shrugging.

"What is this?" Jayd demanded. Glinda opened the bag and poured the contents onto Jayd's desk.

"He said Tarevik hunted high and low for these, after he took the throne by force. Without these, Tarevik would never have ruled. And Rorevik, after him, didn't find them. These belong to the ruling King. Given by Kifirin, long ago, to Glinda's father, Lendevik Lith. I saw him yesterday and he told me where to find them."

"But what are they?" Jayd asked, staring at the thumb-sized blue crystals.

"Kifirin's tears," I said.

CHAPTER 15

"My father said that Kifirin came to him, from the future," Glinda's voice was hushed. "He said that Kifirin gave him a secret that couldn't be repeated. My father let me hold these stones; he said that Kifirin cried these and they fell to the stone floor like this."

"But what was the secret?" Jayd asked.

"I wasn't told," I said. "All I know is that we'll all know, soon enough. Lendevik did ask me to give Glinda a message. He said to tell you that he still loves you." I watched as Glinda wiped a tear away. "And he also told me to say this: That Denevik should have given my middle name, and if he'd pulled his head out of his ass, he would have known it."

"Known what? And that's exactly how my father talked," Glinda wiped another tear away.

"That my middle name should have been Belarok. I'm ready to go, now." I walked out of Jayd's study, Teeg and Edward running to catch up to me.

~

"Jayd, we have to get her back," Glinda ran out the door. Their guests had already gone, though. Likely, Teeg had folded them away.

"You're saying that this is your mother, reborn?"

"My father said that," Glinda was weeping again. "This is awful." She picked up the blue crystals and placed them in the bag again. "Reah won't ever return to us, and nobody could find these. Nobody."

The swing rocked gently as I sat on the deck outside my suite, staring across the groves of gishi fruit trees. The harvest was in and we were processing the last of the ice cream. It would take two months before another harvest of fruit would be ready. Orders were already placed for the ice cream we estimated would come from that harvest.

Adam, Merrill and the other new owners of NorthStar Groves had already agreed to provide us with their blemished fruit. Kevis came out to sit beside me, holding a cup of coffee. He didn't say anything, he merely sighed and sipped. My comp-vid vibrated in my pocket. I pulled it out to read the message. Shocked could only describe a little of what I felt, when I read the message and then saw who'd sent it.

"Would you like to come with me?" I looked at Kevis.

"I'll come, too." Edward appeared from nowhere.

"Good," I said, and skipped both of them away.

"Where are we?" Kevis craned his neck, looking around. A palace stood before us and tall, shapely buildings lined the street leading to it. The street was built of carefully placed stones, so closely matched and fitted that not even a blade of grass grew between them. The buildings and the palace were fashioned of gray stone that glittered in the early afternoon sunlight.

"This is Nrath," I said. "The Greater Demons' world." I walked purposely toward the palace. Edward and Kevis, exchanging troubled looks over my head, followed closely, unsure what to expect.

"Lady," guards bowed low as they opened the heavy, carved doors to the palace. "The master waits inside," they added, straightening up.

Zendeval Rjjn had his back turned to me when I walked in, his head bowed as if in thought. "Reah, I beg you not to be cruel," he whispered as I came to a stop ten feet away.

"How far into the past did Kifirin take you?" I asked.

"Twenty-five thousand years," he sighed. "I was fortunate that a few Greater Demons survived at that time. We have struggled to build with what we had, and it has taken that long to fashion the roughest comp-vid you could imagine. But the Alliance satellites function very well, and boosted the weak signal we were able to produce. I wanted to warn you," he turned. He was weeping.

"I thank you for that," I said. "I knew they were out there, but I didn't know how badly they wanted me dead." I held up my own comp-vid.

"I tried to kill them when they came here. The moment those evil ones said your name, I ordered my guards to attack. We couldn't move swiftly enough and they escaped with minor injuries. I did what I could to protect you, Reah, as little as that turned out to be."

"At least your mind is your own, now," I glared at Perdil. "I wasn't aware that Liffelithi dwarves lived so long."

"We are nearly immortal, but the ways of our race usually ensure that our lives are cut short—in some disagreement or other," he nodded to me. "I've learned a few things, Lady Demon. And Zen has pounded respect into my head, I think."

"Reah, please sit with me. Share tea or something. I wish to speak with you," Zendeval begged.

"Fine," I huffed a sigh.

"Reah, this is the one who attacked you," Kevis hissed.

"I know. We'll hear what he has to say."

Yidrizin, Zendeval's Prime Minister, sat with us at a beautiful table inside a small sitting room. Perdil had been sent away, grumbling.

"Reah, we don't go through moonrush any longer. There's a wine we make that prevents it," Zendeval began as soon as tea had been brought by a servant. The servant bowed respectfully and disappeared from the room.

"Too bad you didn't know about that sooner," I said.

"Yes. You were harmed. If I'd been in my right mind, it wouldn't have happened. Not like that. Every day for the past twenty-five thousand years has been torture for me, because I loved you every tick of every day, and there was nothing I could do about it." His face was filled with pain and worry. He was dressed well for all that, his hair neatly trimmed and combed back, his hands fine, the nails cared for.

"And what would you do, now that I'm here?" I asked.

"Get on my knees and beg you to be my Queen," he brushed another tear away. "I know what your answer will be, but I will hate myself more if I do not try." And right there, in front of his Prime Minister, Kevis and Edward, he knelt down, bowed his head to the floor and asked me to marry him.

"You know I have many mates already," I said. Zendeval was still huddled on the floor.

"I do not care. I am begging, Reah. I will never make you ill again. Or harm you. I will guard your life with mine. Always. That is as it should be. As it should have been before," he lifted his head, his dark eyes pleading—begging me not to reject him.

"Edward?" I turned to Edward, who sighed.

"Reah, he means it," Edward said. I nodded. I knew the truth in Zendeval's words as well.

"After this child is born, the King of Karathia expects me to marry him in a formal ceremony," I said. "And I will offer that privilege to any of my mates who have not yet taken that step. If you desire to be there and take the vows, I will not prevent it," I said, standing up. "Someone will come for you, if you do not change your mind. Here," I handed my comp-vid over. "Use this, if you wish to communicate with me between now and then. I have another comp-vid at home."

Zendeval's smile was blinding as he stood. "Reah," his hand shook as he reached out to touch my face. I worried my lip nervously as I gazed at him. "Do not be frightened of me, my love. Ever."

"Leave Perdil behind," I said, skipping Edward and Kevis away with me.

~

"She will never forgive me," Perdil moaned.

"But she will marry me," Zen slapped the dwarf on the back. "Who knows what will come after that?"

~

"What are those creatures?" Cynthin stared at several Copper Ra'Ak wandering through the clearing.

"You don't need to know," Naldill snapped.

"But they're on Xordthan soil. I demand to know what they are. Where is Reldill?"

"He's gone off to find sustenance for them," Naldill jerked his head at the Copper Ra'Ak. "It's nothing to worry about. We'll clear away from here as soon as the core is drained sufficiently again."

"What did you just say?" Cynthin had stalked away from Naldill, but now she was back. They'd carried her to this piece of worthless wilderness and somehow they'd managed to shield their growing army from Xordthe's authorities. "All I agreed to," Cynthin hissed, poking Naldill in the chest, "was helping you take down that bitch. You've tapped the core to do it? You piece of excrement, I'll kill you."

"You won't," Naldill slapped her hand away. "Not after you see what my brother is bringing." Cynthin stared as Reldill appeared, at least fifty poorly dressed humanoids with him. Cynthin began to scream as the Ra'Ak fed.

~

"They have violated the last of the Elvish code," Kaldill sighed. "Every Elf is obligated to hunt them, now."

"They've broken trust with every living thing?" Lendill rubbed his temple, attempting to prevent the headache.

"All living things," Kaldill agreed. "They kill innocents. Plant, animal and world. We are obligated to destroy them."

"And I intend to see that it happens," Lendill said. "Father," he nodded respectfully to Kaldill Schaff and folded away.

"The time is tomorrow. They plan their attack for the day after." Thurlow tapped a spot on the Xordthan map. "They're hoping that Reah will come, once they lower the shield and let everyone know the core has been tapped again."

"We will place a barrier around them, that they cannot cross," Pheligar said.

"Good enough," Kiarra nodded. She represented the Saa Thalarr, Pheligar represented the Larentii who would come: Renegar, Lenigar, Teligar and Jerigar. Nefrigar was only coming to observe, saying his presence as a warrior was not required.

"I and my father will come, as will Faldill, my brother, and one hundred elf warriors," Lendill appeared. "We will take custody of my brothers."

"Maldak and I will be there with our forces," Youon agreed. "I wish to take as many of the rogues as possible. Please allow us this concession. We will only ask for help if it is necessary," he bowed to Kiarra.

"Fine with me," Kiarra shrugged. Youon smiled at her.

"Lady, you shine," he smiled. "It reminds me of my youth."

"We ask that you keep her here," Aurelius said. "Edward, she's in no shape to go. We've got everybody else, I think. Rylend is coming and bringing warlocks. The Saa Thalarr are coming, with several Larentii. The Black and Copper Ra'Ak are coming, and they want first crack at the rogues. Lendill will come with elves his father chose. I don't know who else those foul elves are bringing, but we're preparing for the worst."

"Don't ever forget that Ra'Ak can travel the timeline, just as the Saa Thalarr and Larentii can," Edward pointed out. "And I will keep our pregnant High Demon with me. I'll keep her happy, one way or another."

~

Lissa's Journal

"Cara Mia, you cannot go. You are pregnant," Gavin pointed out.

"Tell me something I don't know," I muttered. I'd woke that morning feeling queasy, and Connegar and Reemagar had both shown up before I could make it to the bathroom. They cleaned up the resulting mess, too.

"But you and Winkler and Drake and Drew are going," I grumped, rubbing my belly. Drake and Drew were with me more often than not, and while they normally were the most easy-going of my mates, fatherhood had turned them into almost-tyrants.

"As are several others," Gavin agreed. "All the vampires who can stand in daylight are going. Our son holds most of the talents you had before you became a Nameless One. He will act in your stead."

"It just isn't fair," I huffed. "Reah and I can't go, for the same damn reason."

"Lissa, are you belittling your unborn children?"

"No. Hell no," I turned away, rubbing my forehead. "But the timing sucks. Even you have to admit that."

"I will not deny it," he sighed. "Although a part of me is glad that you won't be placed in danger."

"Gavin, everybody on that field will be in danger. Admit it. We both know the God Wars are coming—what if this is the beginning?"

"Lissa, we do not know that. Let us hope that this is what it appears on the surface—an act of revenge only."

"Then I hope that's all it is."

~

"They had errands to run," Edward woke me with a kiss and answered my question of where the rest of my crowd were when I asked. "But we're going to check the expansion on the ice-cream plant, I'm taking you to Adrixx to eat and shop and then we'll come back here and nap or swim."

"That sounds amazing," I sighed. "Is there a place to buy kitchen supplies and pans?"

"Do you feel the need to buy some of that?" Edward rubbed his nose against mine.

"Maybe."

"I'll send a message to my office in Adrixx. They'll have an answer for us when we get there."

"That's wonderful."

~

"Ship it to this address," Edward gave the address of his office in Adrixx later, after I'd purchased a load of pans, knives and gadgets from a specialty store. The clerk, smiling at both of us, agreed quickly. Edward's employees would send it to the groves.

"Now," he had an arm around me as we climbed into the back of a hover-limo after leaving the shop, "we'll go to the jewelry store."

"But," I said.

"No, we need a ring, love. You're not going to turn me down on this."

"Oh."

"Yes, oh," he smiled down at me. The hover-limo drove us to an exclusive shop, making me glad I'd dressed nicely for the day.

"Master Pendley," a doorman opened the heavy door for us. Edward had a hand at my back as I walked inside. Everything was decorated richly, from the Serendaan hand-woven carpets on the floor to the dark, polished wood paneling behind the displays. I knew the gray-haired man behind the counter recognized me, but as any good, discreet salesman should, he never made a comment.

"Now that we've cut the stones, you have to choose which you like and then select the setting," the man said, smiling. A black velvet tray was brought out, with cut Tiralian crystal lying on it. The stones glittered brightly against the dark fabric. A cut round stone was presented, along with a square stone and an oval.

"What do you like?" I looked up at Edward.

"The round one is my favorite, and we can put it in the center, with small, square cut crystal surrounding it," Edward said. "Show her the setting we looked at last time." The clerk nodded and pulled a comp-vid from his pocket. He had the ring image displayed in no time.

"This ring is done in diamonds," the clerk said, showing me a beautiful ring. "The Tiralian crystal will be even more stunning."

"Edward, I like this," I said.

"Is that what you want?" I watched his mouth as he smiled at me. He was a beautiful man.

"Yes," I nodded, mesmerized by Edward Pendley. I looked into his eyes and there were stars there. I didn't know anything else for quite a while.

"We're shielded," Kiarra announced to the huge crowd. She looked out at the Saa Thalarr, who'd changed to their fighting forms. The Spawn Hunters were prepared if they didn't have another form. Four Dragons stood together—Red, Gold, Silver and Black. The Lace Feathered Eagle, Refizani Skycatcher, Silver Eagle, Golden Eagle, Wyroc and Driskilhin Night Hawk represented the giant birds. Kiarra stood between the Black Gryphon and the Snow Leopard, prepared to turn to the giant Unicorn. A Gold Wyvern and a giant, Black Wolf were nearby. An array of Panthers, Wildcats, Leopards, Black Lions, a Hellcat plus a Bengal and Black Tiger represented the big cats, and then there were more giant Wolves. Several members of the Saa

Thalarr had once been werewolf; they'd kept that shape when asked to join.

Norian had come and he led Farzi, Nenzi and all six of their brothers as lion snake shapeshifters. Lendill came, backed by Kaldill, Faldill and one hundred Elvish warriors. Five Larentii had come initially, but that was before Shanalar, the first female Larentii born in a very long time, arrived with six of her twelve daughters. Pheligar didn't say a word about her appearance, he merely communicated battle positions to the new arrivals.

The Copper Ra'Ak had come, under Prince Maldak, six thousand strong. The Black Ra'Ak, five thousand of them under King Youon, also appeared. And then the High Demons came, led by Jaydevik Rath. Jayd had brought one hundred of his High Demon guards and soldiers. Glinda wanted to come, and she and Jayd had fought about it. Glinda stayed home. Gavin, in charge of Le-Ath Veronis' forces, had brought as many vampires as could stand in daylight: Tony, Roff, Aryn, Rigo and Cheedas. Of those, only Roff was a Winged Vampire. Rylend appeared with his father, Erland, and fifty warlocks at his back. Grey House had sent a handful of wizards.

"You know, this makes me think of the battle in *The Lord of the Rings*," Gavril slapped his oldest brother on the back.

"Yeah. Except the Rohirrim aren't on their way to save us at the last minute," Ry sighed. "And since we don't know what's waiting for us, we have to make do with what we have."

Be ready; we will drop the shields, Pheligar's mental voice filtered through to the gathered forces. Everyone tensed. The shields came down.

Cynthin Gerg was terrified. Had she expected her homeworld might become the battlefield for the apocalypse? Realization dawned that she'd had a hand in it. Shuddering, she huddled inside the tiny tent she and Naldill had put up. Some of the creatures outside she recognized

—from tales and mythology. They weren't real. Couldn't be real. Except they were.

Naldill informed her that they'd been destroyed long ago by the giant, coppery snake-like creatures that ate humanoids in a single gulp. Now, some of those creatures were allied with their destroyers, and Cynthin had unwittingly allied with them. Had she ever thought herself safe? She would never sleep peacefully again, provided she lived through the day. Hydras and Minotaurs stomped past her tent, making the ground shake. Harpies flew overhead, screeching out filth as they flapped past. Giants with only a single eye centered on their foreheads wielded clubs, growling and fighting amongst themselves. Naldill had pulled Cynthin away from the Satyrs earlier, they'd leered at her and she'd begun to undress in front of them. Naldill's comments hadn't been kind, either, when he jerked her away.

"You think you're going to survive with that crowd out there?" Cynthin hugged herself tightly.

"I will be in charge of them," Naldill preened. "I'll have my power back and we'll do what we please after that." Cynthin poked her head out of the tent briefly before fearfully jerking it back inside.

"There are Chimeras out there," she hissed. "And Manticores, Trolls and Kobolds."

"Nice, isn't it, when the Ra'Ak can transcend the timeline? They gathered these from the Dark Realm in the past. Too bad that fool of a god who created it promised not to interfere. We offered them life again, and these were the ones who agreed. The rest promised to fight us with their last breath, but that won't be long in coming," Naldill laughed.

"If I were you, I'd sleep with one eye open from now on," Cynthin muttered.

"You, Ms. Gerg, may be the last surviving member of your planet after this," Naldill smiled nastily. "None of those out there know how to repair the core after Reldill tapped it. It didn't help him much at all; somehow the elves can't use that power efficiently. Looks like only the warlocks can do that. We were supposed to be good, you know. My father is probably pitching a fit right now, if he knows what we've done."

Cynthin didn't say anything. Her parents lived, still. Now, they'd likely die at the hands of creatures they thought didn't exist.

"The shields are coming down!" Someone shouted outside.

"Showtime," Naldill laughed.

"Farzi! Take your brothers through there!" Gavril shouted. There was a path between roaring Ra'Ak, leading past the vanguard to the creatures standing behind them. Some of those might be vulnerable to lion snake poison, and the lion snakes might be difficult to see crawling through the grass. Farzi nodded and Norian, standing with him, joined the others.

Kiarra's Unicorn, leading the charge of the Saa Thalarr with Dragons and giant birds flying overhead, ran at the forefront with large cats, a Gryphon and Werewolves racing on either side. The Falchani Spawn Hunters, Turtle and Lok, were joined by Flyer, blades flying as they waded into the huge army of spawn set against them. The werewolf Spawn Hunters joined that battle, while Rylend's warlocks destroyed the ground beneath the charging feet of Minotaurs, Kobolds, Satyrs and Cyclops.

Wizards from Grey House joined their warlock brothers, throwing trees, boulders and anything else available at the advancing army. Ry, without much time to think, still wondered at the hundreds of thousands of creatures set against them. The Ra'Ak had emptied planets to bring these enemies. The Larentii, stationed around the perimeter of the battlefield, were keeping any from escaping, but that might mean nothing in the end. At the moment, they were keeping the population of Xordthe safe and little else.

Lendill and his elvish forces were setting traps for unsuspecting foes, removing deep pockets of earth and disguising them for creatures to tumble into. Once that happened, earth slammed down on their heads, cutting off the air supply. Kaldill knew that all of them required air to breath, and few besides the Ra'Ak had folding ability. Lendill looked for Reldill among the melee, but there was no sign of him.

The giant birds and the dragons dropped downward toward the center of the oncoming army, the birds clipping off heads with deadly talons, the Dragons coming to earth with a thump and a mighty roar. Dragon was the first to breathe fire, and all backed away from him, except the hidden army of rogue High Demons. Gavril, seeing this, went to work. Enemy High Demon heads began to explode with regularity.

The great cats crashed into a line of enemy Copper Ra'Ak and right behind them, Maldak's army came, clashing into their Copper cousins. Youon and his Black Ra'Ak came next, fighting viciously with the others. There was growling, hissing, screaming, and then dying.

"Ready?" Edward slapped Zendeval's thick armor. Zendeval nodded. Two thousand Greater Demons stood at his back, ready to go. Heavy pikes in hand, they thumped the iron shafts on the stone floor of Zendeval's courtyard.

"Good," Edward said. "We'll go." They disappeared.

"No!" Gavril shouted in anguish. Norian had sent mindspeech. He'd gathered five of the reptanoid brothers out of harm's way, but a Kobold had stamped down with a giant foot, crushing three. Gavril, doing as his mother could, wept and cursed silently as he became mist again and crowded inside unsuspecting heads before blowing his mist outward.

I've lost twenty! Lendill's voice came, then, and he was weeping. Faldill had been one of those, victim to a hundred charging rogue Ra'Ak. Glendes of Grey House had lost several wizards to rogue High

Demons before Gavril could reach them. Jayd's forces were taking on as many High Demons and giant Cyclops as they could.

The Unicorn was goring any enemy she came across, and they exploded as soon as she touched them, but the numbers didn't match up. The enemy's forces were overwhelming, and this was a battle to the death. The Larentii were prepared to step in when the flaming meteorite flew overhead, crashing into the center of the battlefield and lifting gouts of earth, rocks and enemy high into the air.

None escaped the raining debris that fell afterward and most ducked to keep from getting dust in their eyes. Then the strangest sight of all came. Taller—much taller than anything on the field, two creatures emerged from the burning ground where the meteorite fell. One unfurled golden wings—the other, feathered wings of solid black.

CHAPTER 16

I brushed myself off. Edward said we had to make a grand entrance, so we'd get the necessary attention. We'd gotten their attention, all right. Then, when our army of Gryphons, Dragons, Unicorns, Centaurs, Werewolves, Greater and Lesser Demons and Wyverns crawled out of the hole around us, and kept crawling out of the hole to line up with us, Edward and I both smiled. Now, things would come even, if th enemy still wanted to fight.

"Did you think you'd be the only ones to travel the timeline?" I glared at the Copper Ra'Ak in charge, who'd appeared before me, ready for my challenge. "And where's that coward, Naldill?"

I knew the Saa Thalarr were closing in at our backs, as were Ry's warlocks, the High Demons under Jayd's command, Lendill and his remaining elves, plus Glendes Grey and what remained of his wizards. In short, the allies we had. The Larentii, too, were making their presence known. The Wise Ones had asked them to wait until the last possible moment. They knew, as Edward and I did, that they did not need to violate their rules of noninterference.

"What are you?" The Copper Ra'Ak rogue asked disdainfully.

"Your death," I said. "Kifirin has a new supervisor and Renegar, Edward and I have joined the Nameless Ones," I added. "Kifirin no longer holds sway over any of you. He may have promised not to interfere, but the new Lord of the Dark Realm has made no such promise. He will come if the rest of us fall. Leave now, swear never to do this again and you will live. Fail to do so and your lives will be forfeit, one way or another."

"I find your threat amusing," the Copper Ra'Ak laughed. I held out a hand and forced him to the ground with power.

"Now, what was that you said?" I asked.

"I will never bow," he began, before I separated his particles. It was easy. I let them float away on the wind.

"Now, who among the rest of you, wish to deny my authority?" I asked. The ones that rushed me lifted into the afternoon air, their sparks as insubstantial as smoke.

"We've removed the Ra'Ak's ability to traverse time, from this point forward," I said, sitting cross-legged on the grass in the middle of the field. A brief skirmish occurred after I'd separated a lot of particles, but somehow, Zendeval had led the answering charge, accompanied by the Saa Thalarr. The battle was over quickly.

"I thought we asked you to keep Reah safe?" Teeg ventured to complain to Edward, who sat beside me, mostly looking like himself except for the black Eagle's wings he wore. Who knew that he'd been destined to become the War Eagle for the Elemaiya? Now, as a Nameless One, this is what he was. My Thifilatha was a Nameless One as well. When I was humanoid, I was High Demon. In Thifilatha, I was a god.

"She is safe. As am I, napping on Avendor, even as we speak," Edward smiled. "We came back in time to do this. It was our intention all along."

"But the reptanoids," Teeg brushed tears away.

"Bring them," I demanded. This was my fear, that those I loved might be lost. Teeg and Norian brought three crushed lion snakes to me.

"Oh, no," I wept, taking the bodies from them. Chazi, Perzi and Bekzi lay limp and lifeless in my hands. "Please, no," my tears fell on three mangled and lifeless lion snakes.

"Do not fear."

Those around me gasped as she appeared. The shining woman. She held out a hand and the power that came was staggering, before the white light surrounded us, leaving us momentarily blind.

~

Movement in my Thifilatha's hands woke me from my daze. The reptanoid lion snakes were stirring, when they'd been dead, before. Tears filled my eyes as all three woke and lifted their heads. I smiled at them, blinking back moisture. They crawled up my Thifilatha's torso, hiding in my hair and peeking out at the others. I laughed because it tickled.

"A part of our debt to Reah is repaid," Belen appeared and bowed to me.

"And it is most appreciated," I bowed in return. Farzi, Nenzi and the other three were crawling upward now, to join their brothers. I smiled at all of them. Nenzi, brave soul that he was, took himself to the top of my head and lifted up, looking about. That caused quite a few chuckles around us.

"My son is a Nameless One?" Pheligar appeared before us.

"Yes. And most deservedly so," Belen said. "As are Edward and Reah. Reah has moved to the Light and no longer belongs to the Dark Realm. Kifirin has taken a lesser spot—a new Lord of the Dark Realm has come. He now presides over the High Demon world." Belen gave Jayd a pointed look as he spoke. "You will bow to him when he makes his presence known, and those who fought beside Reah and Edward this day will live again on their own worlds. It is fitting." Belen disappeared.

"My love, are you ready?" Edward smiled at me.

"I think so," I agreed. "Farzi, Nenzi, Darzi, Chazi, Perzi, Yanzi, Bekzi and Hirzi, do you wish to travel with me or stay here?"

Nenzi slid down my Thifilatha's nose and plopped naked into my hand. "We go," he grinned.

~

"I don't believe this." Those were Teeg's words and they woke me from a sound sleep. My head was in Edward's lap, and he stroked hair away from my face. Kevis, who'd appeared with the others, was staring at me.

"What the hell is going on?" Ry demanded. Astralan didn't wait to ask questions; he came, knelt in front of me and kissed me. Very nicely, too.

"I said that those things weren't the only ones who could travel the timeline," I yawned, sitting up. "Edward stayed here with me, because I can't do anything like this," I patted Garwin Wyatt. "But a year from now? Different story."

"Unbelievable," Teeg shook his head. Farzi and Nenzi appeared from nothing. I knew their brothers were now safely on Campiaa. Both my reptanoids rushed toward me, and Edward had to move over so they could climb into the swing with me.

"We need to take a trip tomorrow," I said, "since I'm rested now."

"So, what does this mean? We'll be smited, or smitten or smote, if we don't do what you tell us to?" Tory appeared, arms crossed angrily over his chest.

"Tory, it doesn't mean any of those things. Neither Edward nor I will have any control over anything you do. It's only in our other shapes that we act as gods. While I look like this, I'm what I've always been and that's the one who will interact with my mates. Ry wants to marry me as soon as Garwin Wyatt is born. If anybody wants to be married to me, they can show up at that ceremony. If they don't, or if they want to dissolve what we already have, then stay away. It's as simple as that."

"Do I still have a hill to climb if I show up?"

"Tory, what do you think? Am I still hurt? Yes. I might understand things a little better now, but that doesn't eliminate all the pain. And

Kifirin has a very hard path to tread for his part in all this. The new Lord of the Dark Realm will watch him closely, and I pity him if he makes mistakes past this point. I want to go visit Lendill and Kaldill. Edward is coming with me. Lendill lost Faldill earlier, and he's about to lose his two remaining brothers. I want to be there to support him when those decisions are made."

"I'll come," Teeg stepped forward.

"As will we," Lok and Aurelius looked exhausted, but they were coming as well. Ry, Corolan, Astralan, Farzi, Nenzi and a latecomer, brought in by Nefrigar, also came. Zendeval Rjjn, smiling almost shyly, showed up.

"In or out, bro?" Ry looked at Tory.

"I'll come," Tory nodded.

Gaelar N'Seith held an atmosphere of mourning and Kaldill, when we walked into his beautiful palace, had been weeping.

"Reah," he placed his arms around me, holding me tightly.

"Kaldill," I kissed his cheek.

"My father told me once he saw tragedy surrounding my children. I didn't know what that meant until today," he said, his voice so thick with tears he almost couldn't speak.

"I know. But someone very wise once told me that things go in a circle. What we lose, we gain," I touched his cheek gently.

"But it hurts in the losing," he said.

"I know. That's exactly what I was thinking when you said it to me."

Lendill had already removed Reldill's power when we made our way to the two cells inside Kaldill's palace. Faldill's body lay in state before both cells. He'd brushed against a Ra'Ak while trying to take down one of the other creatures attacking Lendill and Kaldill. He'd died a hero's death, after he'd said he didn't have enough strength or courage to be King of the Elves. Reldill stared at his brother's body, hands on the bars of his cage. Naldill, the instigator, had his back turned. It was like him not to take responsibility.

"You, come," I put power in my voice and changed to my smaller Thifilatha so Naldill had to obey. I pulled him right through the bars of his cell. "You will bury your brother," I said. "You will watch," I crooked my finger at Reldill.

Kaldill chose a spot beneath an ancient, spreading oak. Oaks were special to the elves. I didn't question, I merely handed a spade to Naldill and told him to dig. Twice he tried to quit. I wouldn't allow it. Finally, weeping tears that he wiped away with filthy and blistered fingers, the hole was deep enough.

"Now, both of you will lower your brother's body. It is your doing that he lies dead," I told them. Reldill was shaking with sobs by that time. Faldill was laid in the grave by his two older brothers, while Kaldill and Lendill watched, wiping tears away. Nefrigar stood between both of them, trilling while they watched Faldill's burial.

"We will come for you tomorrow," Edward said to Naldill and Reldill afterward, stars filling his eyes. "You will be isolated on Cloudsong, and that world will not be approachable by any save the Powers That Be or those above them. You will remain there until your deaths. Since your power is now removed, you are mortal. Was your revenge worth that to you?" Edward turned and stalked away.

Lendill transported them back to their cells, and he offered towels and warm water for his brothers to wash.

"Did you want to stay with your father for a few days?" I asked Lendill.

"Yes," he nodded and held me briefly. "It could have been so much worse," he sighed against my hair.

"Yes, it could," I agreed.

"Where are we going?" Teeg asked the following morning.

"It's a surprise," I said. "But Kevis has to come."

"You wouldn't be able to leave me behind," he insisted. Therefore, the crowd went with me to Cloudsong.

"You wanted to know what bothered me, didn't you?" I took Kevis' hand as we walked through the audience chamber of the old palace. "Here," I pointed to a sooty spot on the floor. "This is what haunted me. Still does, somewhat."

"What?" Kevis turned his green-gold eyes on me.

"After Nedrizif sent his Greater Demons against me, I had no choice but to burn them to death against my scales," I sighed, staring at the ground. "But when the one who'd named himself the Greater Demon King saw that his Demons had no effect, he sent all that he controlled against me, including Zendeval," I nodded at Zen, who'd come with us.

"I saw him running toward me, so I held the fire back for only a blink to knock him away, then brought it to bear again. Another ran right into my left leg and burned to death in an instant. This is where my friend Bel died." I knelt on the stone floor and ran fingers through dark soot that had once been a trusted colleague. Aurelius drew in a breath. "I felt so much guilt. Blamed myself for so much. Was responsible for so much. I'd saved one of my captors and killed one of my friends." Kevis knelt beside me as I wiped tears away.

"But," I sniffled, "when Connegar came to get me, and took me to the place where this world connects to the next, I saw several people. My father was one of them. Addah Desh was another, and then I saw my mother and Lendevik Lith, Glinda's father. But last of all, and hardest of all—Bel came through. I could barely see him, I was crying so hard. He came and lifted me up.

'Do you think I blame you, Reah?' he asked. 'I do not. I had no mind left by that time, and my death was a mercy. Even if you had saved me, I would never have been whole in my mind. Now, I will come again, and soon. I will be born to you, Reah. This is promised to me. I will be your son and the heir to the King of Karathia.'" Ry drew in a breath when I made that announcement. "And we won't bother with middle names," I said, wiping more tears away. "Bel Erland

Morphis will be born in two years, and he and Garwin Wyatt will grow up together."

"Is this it, then?" Kevis came and pulled me against him. "Please tell me this is all. I have held back from touching you like I wanted for a long time."

"This is it," I said. "Except for the deep-seated anger I have against the Crown on Kifirin. Belen says to leave things as they are with my daughters, because to try to change things now will confuse and upset them. He says that Kifirin owes me a great debt, as do Jayd, Glinda and Garde. He says these debts may never be discharged, and I have to live with that. So, Kevis, you may have to listen to me for a while yet. But you can do it in bed if you want."

"I will be happy to listen to you, in bed or out," he smiled and gave me a warm kiss.

Pheligar can perform weddings. I didn't know that. He performed mine. I looked across a very crowded room and smiled at Renegar, who stood beside his mother and both his mates, Grace and Devin. Nefrigar was quite proud that his nephew was a Nameless One. I stood before Pheligar, who was smiling while every man who wanted to marry me stood in a semicircle around us. I was smiling, too. At all of them—Aurelius, Teeg, Lendill, Nefrigar, Rylend, Lok, Astralan, Corolan, Kevis, Zendeval, Tory, Edward, Farzi and Nenzi. Garwin Wyatt slept peacefully in Lissa's arms as Pheligar began the ceremony.

The End

www.ingramcontent.com/pod-product-compliance
Lightning Source LLC
Chambersburg PA
CBHW070517100726
47907CB00004B/877